"DON'T YOU HAVE FAITH IN US, ALICIA?"

Michael's words were uttered harshly. He drew near her, eyeing her with a naked hunger. Suddenly his arms were around her, cradling her, and his lips sought hers with a craving so intense she could feel herself melting against him with all the unspent passion of the last year.

But haunted by the image of his elegant companion, Elaine, and determined to resist him, Alicia jerked free. "Faith?" she cried. "When have you ever given me any reason for faith? Don't be a fool, Michael!"

With anger and pain clouding his eyes, he stormed, "Saving yourself for a guy with a bunch of promises? Well, you won't get that from me! You can take what I'm offering…and if that's not enough….."

"No, Michael, it's not… " she said sadly, turning and walking from the room, oblivious to the look of anguish on his face.

WELCOME TO...

SUPERROMANCES

A sensational series of modern love stories
from Worldwide Library.

Written by masters of the genre, these longer,
sensual and dramatic novels are truly in keeping
with today's changing life-styles. Full of intriguing
conflicts, the heartaches and delights of true love,
SUPERROMANCES are absorbing stories—
satisfying and sophisticated reading that lovers
of romance fiction have long been waiting for.

SUPERROMANCES
Contemporary love stories for the woman of today!

ANN MEREDITH WILLS

TEMPEST AND TENDERNESS

A SUPERROMANCE FROM

WORLDWIDE

TORONTO · NEW YORK · LOS ANGELES · LONDON

Published May 1983

First printing March 1983

ISBN 0-373-70062-8

Printed in Canada

CHAPTER ONE

"SHARK!"

The word streaked across the Catalina waters with the dazzling effect of lightning, searing into Alicia's brain. She stopped swimming and jerked upright, instantly forgetting the school of Spanish mackerel she'd been watching among the barnacle-encrusted rocks. With one hand she pulled the snorkel tube from her mouth and with the other she paddled hard, treading water, her eyes searching the swells for the dreaded gray fin. But she saw nothing, only frantic swimmers scrambling toward Catalina Island.

Then she heard it again, a woman's hysterical scream, "Shark!" Immediately Alicia sought refuge for she was too far out to make it all the way back. In this somewhat shallow area a few hundred yards from the island, rocks protruded here and there. Choosing one of the larger ones, she began to swim toward it, her heartbeat palpable in her throat. She reasoned that no shark would touch her if she could only get up out of the water. Above the waterline she was master; below, the shark ruled.

As she swam, she shoved the snorkel deeper into the straps of her face mask. Then, keeping her head down, she stroked with all the efficiency she could muster. Stroke, breathe, stroke, *let me reach that rock quickly,* she thought, stroke, breathe...*dear Lord, where is it?* She raised her head just enough to see the bottom edge of the rock and reassure herself she hadn't drifted off course. Then she resumed swimming, her heart pounding now from exertion as much as fear.

Moments later she began searching, one hand groping out ahead for the expected rock. Suddenly the palm of her left hand slammed against rough barnacles.

Wincing in pain, she dropped her legs and prepared to scramble out of the water. Her eyes focused on the rock and she drew in a startled breath.

In that instant she seemed to see a pair of feet already there. It must have been her mask, she thought, distorted by water, that brought her this apparition.

Her eyes traveled upward to...legs! Masculine. Dark and muscular. A yellow bathing suit, a sharp contrast against the darkly burnished skin. The man smiled down at her, amused.

She blinked and removed the mask from her face. Holding it, she gaped up at him, astonished by his presence on the rock. She was struck by the almost luminous quality of his dark eyes, lit from a source she couldn't see.

Unexpectedly he bent over her and lifted her up beside him in one deft movement, her weight apparently nothing to him. She felt his grip on her arms, firm and unhurried.

When he failed to release her immediately she became conscious of the warm wetness of his body and the strength of his hands. An aura of masculinity surrounded him and set her senses tingling. Even as these impressions flooded her mind she thought, *this is crazy, I don't even know this man.* Yet it was happening, her own inner rhythms thrown into a melee of disconnected thoughts and half-understood feelings. Then he let her go.

She backed away and looked up at him. He was tall, at least six-foot-one. He towered over her own five-four, overwhelming her. She noted his heavy dark brows and the dark brown hair that stuck wetly to his forehead. And his grin, friendly and teasing.

The grin became quizzical. "This is a large ocean," he said. "Couldn't you find your own rock?"

Alicia smiled back at him, "You own this rock? You have a deed to it?" She gestured expansively toward the ocean. "How odd that I happened to pick yours out of all the many available to me."

He watched her, amusement still on his face.

When he let the silence grow, she stared back

at him, increasingly aware of the smooth planes of his face—a broad face with prominent nose and chin. He was almost too good-looking, she decided, though his nose and chin gave him an air of authority and kept him from being a "pretty boy."

Suddenly Alicia shivered, remembering her purpose in being there. "I suppose you're here because of the shark," she said. "I didn't see him, actually, I just heard someone screaming. Do we *have* white sharks near Catalina?"

He shrugged. "I didn't stop to ask, if you want the truth. I thought this rock was the better part of valor." With a bronzed hand he pushed back his wet hair. "A shark is something I have a lot of respect for." He raised his dark eyebrows in feigned surprise. "Did I say 'respect'? There's a better word for it—'fear'!"

Alicia laughed. She found him disarming. Standing here with this man, the Pacific surging all around them, an island in the distance and suspected sharks in the water, she found herself thinking only of him. His physical presence made all other impressions dim. There was a vibrancy about him and an air of confidence she found compelling.

"Mind if I sit?" he asked, then dropped down beside her, keeping his feet on the sloping edge of granite. He twisted to look at her. "How did you get here? Were you on the Catalina boat?"

"Yesterday," she said. "I'm going back tomorrow."

"That explains why I didn't notice you on deck this morning. I usually notice redheads." Absently he brushed droplets of water off his legs. "Your hair must be a good color when it's dry."

"I've been told it is," she said, warming to his compliment. She sat down, wishing she could stay on this little perch with him indefinitely. But he was probably married, she thought. He looked at least eight years older than her twenty-one years, and he was obviously too good-looking not to have attracted women...lots of them. She glanced at his left hand but saw no wedding ring.

She realized she'd been obvious, for he held the hand up, laughing. "Look, ma, no ring. And you?"

She held her hand up, too. "No ring."

"Well," he said, "we've covered the important things. Now, what's your name?"

"Alicia. Alicia Barron."

"Michael MacNamee." He put out his hand. "Good to meet you, Alicia. I've just decided I'm glad I had this bit of real estate to share with you." He watched the ocean surge up over his feet. "You can seek me out here anytime. But you'll have to come in person—this is an unlisted address."

They sat companionably, and Alicia felt herself warmed. He had such a direct way of looking at her. It was suggestive and probing, too, as though he were digging into her mind. Something about him seemed overpowering—call it magnetism or strength, but it made her feel even younger than she was. What was it about him, she wondered half-angrily. She'd seen plenty of handsome men and dated enough of them, too, not to be feeling like a giddy young girl.

Perhaps it was the circumstances. One hardly expected to find an Adonis sitting on a rock in the middle of the Pacific.

Lost in her thoughts, she had to wrench her mind around when he said, "Tell me about yourself."

"What? Oh, well...do you want the long version or the short?"

He glanced at his watch. "Maybe you'd better make it the short."

Before she could begin, another swimmer paddled by, a young blond boy. Seeing them sitting there, feet drawn up, he said, "You don't have to stay there. It wasn't nothin'. Some lady got all excited when her old man saw a funny fin. It was only a blue shark."

The boy treaded water, looking them over, long wet hair falling over his nose. "Blue sharks don't hurt anybody, but I guess the lady didn't know."

"Well, that's good." Michael nodded, "Thanks." They watched the boy swim off.

"Let's see," said Alicia. "I'm a student at San Diego State in my last year. After this semester I have to take two more courses in summer school, then—well, I'm probably going to go on in oceanography. Meanwhile I'm boning up on scuba diving, taking an instructor's class. It's down in San Diego. It's one of the college's special programs. What about you?"

He looked at his watch again, then at her, his dark eyes full of regret. "Alicia," he said, "I'm sorry to leave just as we're getting acquainted, but I'm going to miss that boat if I don't get back on the dock." He held out a hand. "It's been a great half hour. Best moments I ever spent on a rock." He lowered himself into the water and looked at her, concerned. "Can you get back all right?"

"I'm a strong swimmer," she replied.

"Good." He reached up and patted her foot. "Bye, Alicia." She thought she saw a moment's uncertainty on his face, but she wasn't sure. He turned over and began to swim away. She watched his shoulders, rhythmic, smooth. How beautifully he swam, she thought. Then she sighed. He'd been... overpowering. That was the only word she could think of. His presence had made her feel heady and alive. She could have stayed here with him half the day, and in a strange way it was as if she could still feel him sitting beside her. Yet nothing had happened really. He hadn't found out her address, her phone number, anything.

Once more she sighed, looking down at her slender legs. What chance was there she'd ever see him again?

She watched him in the distance, the easy strokes carrying him farther away, his outline fading and blending with the ocean's patterns. What was he thinking, she wondered. Hadn't that spark of attraction gone both ways, as real for him as for her? Then why hadn't he done something so he could find her again?

She pushed back her damp hair in an unconscious gesture. So he wasn't married. But he hadn't said he wasn't committed to someone else. . . .

Well, she thought, smiling ruefully, *if he did like me, if he really does want to see me again, I don't know how it's going to happen—unless we rendezvous back on this rock!*

ALICIA WALKED ACROSS THE SAND to her scuba class feeling buoyant and carefree. A week had passed and she'd just finished a semester final, one class done and behind her. Day after tomorrow, two more finals and then a semester finished. And after that only two more courses in summer school.

But today she'd decided to forget school in favor of another underwater adventure. She never failed to experience a sense of rising excitement at the thought of dropping into a foreign land. Oh, yes, it was foreign—only fish down there—but not so disorganized as people thought. The fish formed communities, and the varied patterns of behavior of the different species amused and thrilled her.

In the distance she could see the class already gathered near the water, and she picked up the pace, knowing she was late. Her diving cylinder and regulator were down near the water waiting for her. Hurriedly she began to check them out, not looking to see who was in class today. One of the annoying things about being late, she thought, was the necessity to be inconspicuous, to blend.

She began attaching her regulator to the cylinder, her head bent over her task. She didn't notice that someone had come up behind her until she felt a hand on her shoulder. Startled, she turned around.

For an instant, staring up at the man who stood over her, she thought she must be imagining things, for the face, the smile, were Michael. Yet some things were different. Perhaps it was the dry hair, thick brown hair, no longer plastered to his head but falling in strands over his forehead. He looked handsomer than she'd remembered. And his eyes, dark wells of mystery so at odds with his easy smile. She'd never been near a man who so instantly affected her as he did, rousing both excitement and a sense of her own womanliness. Letting her hands fall away from the regulator, she simply sat back on her heels and stared.

He laughed at her. "Surprised?"

"Where did you come from?" she gasped. "How did you find me...I mean, find this class?"

He squatted beside her and she noticed he was wearing a yellow open-necked shirt and blue swimming trunks with the logo of a small diver sewn on the leg.

"You gave me just enough clues, so it wasn't impossible, just difficult. San Diego State—that was where I started. A few calls, trying to get the right person in the athletic department and knowing it was an instructor's class. They have several classes, you realize, but you said a few things that helped."

"You could have just asked for my phone number...." she protested lightly.

He smiled. "I thought of that—later! In fact I considered swimming back. But it was either your phone number or the boat—I had to choose." He grinned. "Sorry, Alicia, I had to choose the boat. Besides, I wasn't sure how long you'd stay on the rock. I looked back once and the way you were sitting you looked like a mermaid. I almost imagined a fishtail draped over the stone." He touched her arm. "Mythology never seemed particularly enticing until last week."

She heard what he'd said—"enticing"—and then she noticed over her shoulder that the class was preparing to enter the water. "Michael, can you go out with us?" she asked, feeling breathless having him here. It warmed her, knowing what he'd gone through to find her.

"I came prepared. I'm not an expert, but I do have equipment—old stuff. Still, it works. Your instructor already assigned me as your buddy." He grinned conspiratorially. "I told him we were old friends and I was a very experienced diver. That may be my quota of lies for the year."

Michael picked up his tank, regulator and mask, and together they walked to the water's edge. They stood for a moment listening to instructions from the teacher, a burly man with fat hairy legs. He told them they'd be practicing trying to free a student caught in the kelp and that teams would take turns in the rescue. Those teams not involved would simply free-swim for a prescribed time.

As the pairs of divers headed for the water Alicia noticed that Michael was making no move to put on his mask.

"You ready, Michael?" she asked.

"Just watching a minute," he said, squinting out to sea. "You ever been on one of these rescue missions?"

"Only once. Last week."

"How long are we out?"

She laughed. "That depends on how quickly we get our victim untangled. But since I've done it already, today I'm only going to watch. Shall we go, Michael?" She saw the others disappear into the waves as one by one they dropped in backward and were quickly swallowed up by foam. As the final man vanished she realized Michael had come close to her, and she stood still, feeling his nearness and magnetism. She was almost afraid to breathe as sensors in her mind, eyes and skin tingled expectantly. She wanted him to touch her; this man excited her as no other ever had. Then she looked up and saw him staring down at her. She felt warmed and beautiful in his gaze, as if she would easily float away in his dark eyes. Yet his eyes were probing, intent...hungry...expertly stripping her of all reserves of modesty and coolness. She drew in a quick surprised breath as his head came down over hers, his dark hair blotting out all else, his lips pressing insistently against her mouth.

In that instant she was aware of warm breath on her cheeks, his lips both firm and gentle. She wanted to reach for him but found herself immobile with surprise. Suddenly the moment was over. He straightened up again and, smiling, explained, "For luck."

Quickly he put on his mask, hiding his feelings behind glass.

She was glad she had a mask, too, for it made

her feel less vulnerable. Behind this screen she could smile to herself and not be seen.

As though he were no longer thinking about her, Michael ran out toward the waves, and Alicia followed.

For an instant as she plunged into the water, other sensations blotted out the magic of their special moment. She was on her own again, water rushing over her lens and the breath-stopping coldness of the Pacific covering her body. She had entered a world that swam in soft liquidity. Diffused light from above shimmered down lemon yellow. As always, she was overwhelmed by the beauty of the underwater seascape, objects seen as though through a photographer's silk screen, softened and gentled by water.

As she swam seaward, she found herself instinctively moving toward the kelp beds. The broad-leafed kelp wafted back and forth with the currents, some as high as a hundred feet. As she swam into it, she found the pockets where fish resided, different species in different areas, as though each species had rented its own "room."

She pushed the rubbery plants aside, thinking regretfully how much kelp had been lost to voracious sea urchins, propagating without restraint now that their natural predators, the sea otters, had been diminished by trappers. In time the sea urchins would have uprooted the last of the kelp, and then the kelp beds would have disappeared and so would these fish. But conservationists had intervened and prohibited the trapping of sea otters. Now the kelp beds were slowly returning. She sighed, thinking how dependent one life form was on another and how easily the chain could be broken.

As she made her way through the thick vegetation she was struck by how three-dimensional it was down in the depths of the ocean. The kelp filtered the light differently, so that in some places it was quite bright and in others almost black, creating illusionary tunnels and caverns.

Eventually she broke through the bed and caught sight of Michael's black fins far ahead of her. Kicking hard, she tried to catch him.

Abruptly her musing vanished and her mood altered. Seeing Michael ahead of her, she thought back to the moment before they entered the water, and she relived his kiss, her body stirred once more by the memory. It had been so unexpected. As she swam she thought about Michael's self-assuredness—he was at once bold and gentle. Her thoughts tripped off her heart rate, and feeling her respiration change she unconsciously held her breath. Then she told herself, *exhale, Alicia, breathe out as well as in,* and the mechanics of drawing life from a scuba tank momentarily absorbed her attention.

She swam blindly now, as rapture kept overtaking her, quickening breaths and the need for more air.

This was ridiculous, she thought. It was only a kiss. Why was she overreacting? It wasn't as if she hadn't been kissed before. But had she ever been stirred like this, she wondered. She thought of Michael in all his maturity and mystery. No, never like this. This man was different.

They swam on, catching up with the other divers who circled an area where one of their fellow students struggled frantically, ostensibly caught in kelp.

The scene absorbed Alicia, but her thoughts wouldn't stay focused. Instead she was conscious of a constant excited heartbeat, of breaths more frequent than normal. She left the scene and went deeper, looking for bottom fish to distract herself. Her thoughts shifted, drifted off, then focused again. Suddenly she was aware that time had passed and she was due to check her pressure gauge. She read it once, disbelieving, then read it again. Her air was almost gone!

To her chagrin she realized Michael had unwittingly sabotaged her. Here she was, forty feet down, her heart pumping madly, her lungs sucking up air like a vacuum cleaner! The pressure gauge was practically shaking its finger at her.

There was no question about it: she'd have to surface!

Quickly she found Michael, attracted his attention with her hand, pointed to the pressure gauge and began to swim upward, not caring if he followed. She could think only of reaching the surface.

As she ascended she thought how ridiculous this was—using up her tank of air at twice the normal rate. Wasn't she mature enough to control that inner pounding? But she knew she wasn't. And it had nothing to do with maturity, anyway. The fault was his, those eyes and that sensuous mouth. . . .

The light grew strong, then became blinding. She was up, swimming on top.

She looked around. Michael had surfaced not far away.

Now how do I explain this, she wondered, feeling silly all of a sudden. For the truth would tell him more than she wanted him to know.

But he saved her the trouble. He smiled. "If you hadn't signaled just then, Alicia, I was going to. I was almost out of air." He panted and the smile widened into a grin. "Remind me never to kiss you again just before we go down or I'll have to carry an extra tank every time we dive!"

Together they swam to shore and divested themselves of the heavy equipment. Michael picked up his towel and rubbed it briskly over his body. Alicia found herself following the towel's progress—back and forth over his broad shoulders, then to his waist, which was somewhat thick, she thought with amusement. Perhaps in a few years it would become bulky, but not now. His firm hips, his large thighs, his lower legs covered in hair. Consistent. Eyes and hair, all dark.

He caught her looking at him. "Well?" he asked suggestively, eyebrows raised.

"Well, it's okay," she smiled. *It's wonderful,* she thought.

In turn she felt him appraising her. She, too, had to take her time drying before putting on her rumpled clothes. She tried to turn away, embarrassed that his scrutiny was at least as detailed as hers. And she knew what he was seeing: perfect, delicate legs, of that she was confident. But the rest was not exactly Marilyn Monroe. She knew her hips were a bit on the flat side, her breasts too small. All her life she'd yearned to be taller, fuller, until this last year. Now, as a senior in college, she had decided she was better off the way she was, trading on intelligence and a well-developed sense of fun.

Michael took her wrists just as she was about to step into her slacks. "Time to go out for a cheeseburger?"

His grip was firm. She loved it.

She stopped to think. Two finals day after tomorrow. She hesitated. "Michael, I have to study."

He dropped her wrists. "So what did you plan to do for dinner?"

"Something canned." She shrugged. "I haven't thought about it."

"Then you have to eat anyway. This little place I know can whip up cheeseburgers about as fast as you can open a can." He tossed her shirt to her. "The result may not be much better, Alicia, but I suggest you not turn it down. I'll be out of town for two weeks."

Her heart did a small flip and disappointment shadowed her face. She hoped he hadn't noticed. Deliberately, lightly, she said, "You're right, I do have to eat."

He took her in his forest green Porsche—a surprise, since she somehow hadn't imagined him in this kind of car. He'd struck her as not the type, though what type actually drove Porsches she wasn't sure. But she knew they cost money, and she'd never seen him in any but the most casual clothes. Well, what did she know about him, anyway?

They settled into a small orange-colored padded booth in a place called Hamburger Heaven. There were four other booths but the place was almost empty now at 4 P.M. Behind a high counter where the orders were placed, a bored, curly-haired young man leaned on his elbows. He was perhaps nineteen, gangly—a youth. Compared to Michael, Alicia thought, he looked twelve.

As they waited for their cheeseburgers, Alicia asked, "How old are you, Michael?"

He gazed at her thoughtfully. "An old twenty-nine."

"Why do you say that?"

"Twenty-nine is old. If you've lived a lot."

"Have you lived a lot?"

"I think I have," he said quietly. "Part of my own choosing, part not. I've been married— once." The words implied, *never again.*

"Oh," she said, thinking of no better response. Then, curious, she asked, "What was she like, Michael?"

Lines in his chin hardened and changed him. The easygoing look was gone. His expression had changed imperceptibly, yet the difference was striking.

"You don't want to talk about her..." she ventured.

"She's not one of my favorite subjects."

"Where do you live?" she asked, feeling for easier ground.

"I have my own apartment." He slid down in his seat, his eyes resting on her face. "My father and stepmother live a few miles away—I think of that as my home actually, because I grew up there. The apartment is nothing. A bachelor place. Someday I'll build a house, but it's seemed pointless these last years. I'm out of town constantly."

Once again the conversation threatened to

lag. Alicia brightened suddenly. "You know, Michael, I have no idea what you *do*."

He gave her a tight smile. "I was wondering when you'd ask. Most women want to know that first. They see the Porsche, then they want to know, 'So, Buster, where do you get the money?'" It was as if she were hearing a different Michael speaking now, a cynical man. "And then the next thought, the one they don't say out loud...*how can I get in on it?*"

"Michael!" She tried to suppress her shock. "You're bitter."

"Not bitter. Just realistic. Women are practical, I've known that for a long time. 'What do you do, how much do you make, how is all this going to affect me?' Women want their little nests, want them all secure and feathered, then after they get them they want to go out and spend."

"Wow." She took in a sharp breath.

His eyes on her face were masked. She felt as if she were part of his contempt. The cheeseburgers came and they picked them up silently. In the midst of eating, it occurred to Alicia that he hadn't answered her question. It wasn't unreasonable to wonder what he did. It explained a man; in some ways it was what he *was*. And asking was natural—not warped, as he seemed to think.

Still she felt she must proceed with caution.

"You didn't answer my question," she said lightly.

"Which one?"

"What you do."

He stopped eating and looked at her, his dark eyes intent. "I was trained as an engineer, but that's not what I do. U.C.L.A....then I got into land development...and after that, resorts. I develop resorts. My own company now. I found I worked better for myself."

She nodded, thinking how strong-minded he was. Then her thoughts rolled forward with new questions. It seemed she was just beginning to know him. "What kind of resorts, Michael? Is anyone helping you? And where are you doing it?"

He answered with amusement. "If you mean, do I have a partner, no. And I'm doing it in Hawaii."

"Why are you smiling?"

"Because you're so inquisitive. Most women don't care that much. A couple of answers and they let it go. Shall I tell you more? I've been building high rises on one of the smaller Hawaiian islands. Seven and eight stories—transforming the place."

It was her turn to smile. "You really think high rises transform anything?"

"Sure I do. That island was mostly lava and sugarcane before, plus a few struggling farmers eking out a living. You bring in buildings and people, and things happen. All kinds of things."

"Are any of them good?" Her challenge was implicit.

Michael's eyebrows went up. "You've got theories on this?"

"Yes," she said. "I would think putting high rises on a nice spot might be the best way to ruin it."

"I see we're not going to agree on everything, Alicia. Tell me what's so bad about developing a place that's run-down—if it's done right." He put the last of his cheeseburger in his mouth.

She felt challenged. "And you tell me what's so good about tall buildings, besides making big profits for the builder."

He stopped, swallowed, then fixed his dark eyes on her. "Are you against profits, too? I never claimed to be a charity, Alicia. Of course I make profits. That's partly what it's about. And anyone who thinks that's a dirty word—"

She interrupted, contrite. "I'm sorry." She knew she'd become carried away. But still she felt abhorrence for what he was doing. Beginning again on a gentler note she said, "Tropical islands don't look right with tall buildings, Michael. They don't fit together. Why do you have to bring in so *much* civilization?"

He reached across the table and covered her hand. She felt he was patronizing her, and she found herself more annoyed than pleased. She pulled her hand away gently.

He went on, his eyes lingering on the hand she'd withdrawn. "My dear girl, civilization, which you seem to despise so much, has its advantages." Raising his eyes to hers, he added, "Civilization is good roads and indoor plumbing—and jobs for the locals." He leaned closer, compelling her to listen. "When you keep buildings low and spread them all over expensive land like Hawaii you only make the resort costly. Shouldn't ordinary people be able to afford Hawaiian vacations?"

She could see he found this enjoyable; he was testing her, challenging her to put up a good fight.

But she was not amused, and retorted, "It's not a Hawaiian vacation if it looks like downtown San Diego when you get there."

"I suppose you'd vote against inexpensive chain restaurants, too."

Alicia groaned. "Oh, Lord. Why would anyone want to go thousands of miles to eat dinner in his local fast-food joint?"

He shook his head in exasperation. "You're naive, you know it? You have a grass-shack philosophy; if it's native it must be good. Well, I'll take a fast-food cheeseburger, and you can have native Hawaiian poi. You eat it with your fingers, by the way; it's mushy and gray."

Involuntarily she shuddered. Then she thought of her own home. "Michael, in the long run you'll ruin what you're trying to exploit."

He didn't answer. Instead he said, "How about a sundae?"

They ate their ice cream in silence. Afterward he looked at her curiously. "Did you say you were going on in oceanography?" She answered that she was, if everything worked out.

Nodding, he went on, "You grew up in California, Alicia?"

"No," she said. "The Virgin Islands." She waited for his reaction. It was what she'd expected.

"So!" He stared at her long and hard. She knew most men were startled at this information, perhaps not expecting a light-skinned, green-eyed, auburn-haired girl to be from such a place. There was more than surprise, however, in Michael's reaction.

"Yes," he said. "I might have known. I should have figured. It explains a lot. I suppose you were raised in a grass shack."

"Hardly."

"An unspoiled island?"

"Yes."

"So this makes you a campaigner for island virginity."

"It has nothing to do with me, Michael. I'd believe what I said no matter where I grew up. I believe in saving timber, too. And mountains. All sorts of things."

Michael studied her thoughtfully. "Which island are you from?"

"I'm sure you haven't heard of it. No one has. Virgin Gorda. A small place, so small we knew everyone. I was raised by my aunt and uncle."

"And your parents?"

"They died. In an accident."

"I'm sorry."

"It's all right. I was very young. I only know them through my aunt's memories."

He frowned as though trying to remember something. "Virgin Gorda. That's part of the British Virgins, isn't it?"

She nodded.

"I *have* heard of it, I just couldn't quite place it at first." Absently he brushed crumbs off the table. "Pelican Point—that's the resort I was trying to think of. Pelican Point's on that island, isn't it?"

She answered yes, deciding not to tell him that her aunt and uncle ran the smaller resort next door, Seahawk Cove. Compared to Pelican Point it wasn't much—more of a family business, hardly known except by the people who came back habitually year after year. Its very charm lay in its smallness, she thought. She shuddered, imagining high rises despoiling the rolling softness of the land. It would be desecration to touch the island with Michael's brand of development. But it would never happen, so there was no point in bringing it up; she'd already argued with him enough. Besides, all his projects were thousands of miles away...a world away. Virgin Gorda was quite safe from his mad schemes.

He cocked his head at her. "How did you happen to come to San Diego, Alicia? You must have found it hard leaving that place—if it's as beautiful as you imply."

"It was—and it wasn't. In some ways living on a island, even a beautiful island, is confining. I wanted to know more about what lay beyond our little world, and California seemed suitably far away. I suppose I chose San Diego State partly because of the scuba diving, partly because it's a good all-around school. There was so much of the technical stuff I didn't know. You see, I wanted to run our family scuba school someday back home. But as I learned more...oh, I don't know, Michael, it's just that the details about underwater life get more fascinating the more you study them. I find myself thinking about how it's all organized—about the ecological balance, and what will happen if this or that species becomes endangered, how it will affect other species and eventually man. Now I've become more interested in doing something with ecology other than teaching. But I don't know *what*.... It's all pretty vague, isn't it?"

He looked at her intently. "You're an interesting woman."

She laughed. "'Interesting.' I was hoping for

'glamorous'...'devastating'...'sexy' .... But 'interesting' is better than nothing.''

Silently Michael folded his napkin into squares, folded it again, then spread it open. He traced his finger around the geometric patterns. "I've had enough of devastating and glamorous. They don't last."

She felt herself pushed into asking more and before she could stop said, "Your wife...?"

"My wife," he intoned, "was beautiful, not quite devastating, certainly glamorous. She wanted to be a model, and she would have been a good one, but I wouldn't have it. It was a mistake. In the end, beautiful was all she was."

Since he seemed less hostile now, Alicia ventured to ask more. "Where did you meet her, Michael?"

Unexpectedly he smiled. "You're really curious about her, aren't you?"

"It tells me more about you."

"She was just out of high school, a high-school cheerleader, all freshness and bubbling enthusiasm. I was in college then, finishing my last year—I swam for U.C.L.A. Dixie came up to one of the sororities, and I met her at a party. Funny how smitten I was—instantly." He shook his head. "No judge of people, I guess, but then she wasn't the same later. At the time I could only see that she was the most beautiful girl at that party. Not like any of the others. A genuine beauty, every bit of her—nose, eyes, hands. I had to have her, that's all." He stopped abruptly. "We've talked about her enough. I don't like hashing over the past."

"But, Michael, you're still part of whatever's happened to you. Or it's part of you. You don't get rid of things entirely, just because they're over."

"You're right—" he looked at her thoughtfully "—and I'm afraid she's altered my outlook permanently. I'll never feel the same about that sacred institution of marriage. It's a sacrament that becomes a joke. I'm soured and I know it. Permanently. Well, I won't set myself up like that—" He broke off, gazing at a point beyond her shoulder. "Damn the past." His focus came back to her. "I thought you had to study."

She jumped up. "I do. Thanks for reminding me."

He stood and took her arm. "Never play second fiddle to anyone else, Alicia. You don't need to. Be your own self. Be strong—but you are, anyway. I just don't want you to change."

Again she felt his overwhelming presence, his nearness making her tremble inwardly. In some odd way he talked of strength but made her feel weak. How ridiculous, she thought.

They drove in silence back to the diving school where her car was parked. She climbed into her yellow Toyota, as he gallantly held her door open. Putting his hand on her shoulder

Michael leaned toward her. "Alicia...." His eyes fixed hers with a probing intensity. "I want to see you when I come back. I'll be gone two weeks. But then—" he smiled down at her "—come out with me again, will you? There are places I want to take you."

"I think I can manage it," she replied softly.

"You'd better." The words were almost harsh. Abruptly the outside world dissolved. He was half-inside the car, one arm around her shoulder, the other hand lifting her chin. Then his mouth was against hers, hard yet wondrously sweet. The kiss was long with an intensity that threatened to leave her breathless. Finally he released her. For a moment he stared down at her longingly, then quickly walked back to his car.

When he was gone she sat still, unable to do the things necessary to move, her mind spinning like a whirling dervish, her body alive with feeling. Yet she'd learned some things about him tonight that gave her pause. Thinking about this she turned the key and started the car. So he'd been married. Well, that was to be expected, a man like him.

She drove blindly, heading toward her apartment.

Of course he'd been involved with someone, more likely several someones. Other women must have found him as compelling as she did— warm, interesting, exciting. But what about his wife? How long had that marriage lasted and why had this beautiful woman failed so miserably to hold him? And why did he show such bitterness about her? It was the only time she'd seen him close to anger, the look on his face uncompromising. What had his wife done? Or what had *he* done? She realized that all along she'd been assuming the woman was at fault.

She turned down the street to her apartment, a small one-bedroom place in a four-unit, pea green complex. The rather drab two-storey building wasn't improved by the crabgrass embedded in the lawn, the scrub palm trees leaning precariously toward the front door, or the Bird of Paradise flower standing unkempt near her living room window. Other similar apartment units crowded hers, and at times she felt stifled by the closeness of people. It had been a compromise moving here, a matter of money. It was such a contrast from her home on Virgin Gorda that she often felt rebellious just driving up here. This was what happened, she thought, when you tried to put too many people on the land.

This itchy proximity of people...how much worse it would be in Virgin Gorda or Hawaii! Wasn't the whole point of a tropical vacation getting *away*?

She bit her lip. Michael was wrong. As sincere as he seemed, he was wrong. He was in the business of despoiling beautiful places. She sighed, wishing she didn't know this about him.

Her car slid into the open-ended stall and she jumped out, leaving her scuba equipment in the trunk. She unlocked her front door. An ungenerous front door, she thought, obscured by the garage. It almost appeared as if she were sneaking in a back entrance. Someday she'd have a front entrance that *was* a front entrance instead of merely a way to get in.

She laid her canvas purse on the counter, went upstairs to the bedroom and sat down at her small maple desk. Books littered its top, and a notebook sat open on the back corner. She began studying her biology notes, but thoughts of Michael kept intruding. What had he said about women wanting to 'spend'? That was when he'd grown especially bitter. Women and money...plainly a sore subject. Michael obviously had hang-ups—Alicia just hoped she could skirt them.

He said he'd call in two weeks. *Two weeks.* For the first time in years, since she was a child waiting for Christmas, two weeks seemed a very long time.

CHAPTER TWO

THE DEEP VOICE came to her as that of a stranger. For a second she'd been hurried and indifferent. Then he said, "You don't recognize me, do you?"

"Am I supposed to?" she asked, and then, in a burst of recognition, "Michael!"

He laughed. "Have I been gone that long?"

"Yes. I mean no. Well—" she didn't want to admit she'd waited breathlessly for almost three weeks and then, convinced she'd never hear from him again, had resolutely put him out of her mind "—it's just that you sound different on the phone."

"Do I?"

Not really, she thought. *You sound wonderful.*

He went on, "My trip took twice as long as I expected," he explained. "Each day I kept thinking we'd finish, so I saw no point in running up long-distance phone charges."

You couldn't afford a three-minute call? She squelched the question before it reached her lips.

"I'm afraid I'm a little fed up right now," he went on. "It was a rather complicated acquisition, but I won't bore you with that. I happen to have a free day Saturday. How about going to the Del Mar races?"

"I'd love to!" she said. She knew she'd say yes whether she was busy or not.

"Saturday morning, then." And with that he was gone.

In a moment of supreme happiness, she cradled the phone and twirled around the room.

AT THE SOUND of gentle rapping, Alicia excitedly opened her door. Michael stood there before her—with that smile she'd almost forgotten, his dark eyes more compelling than she remembered. In all her thoughts about him these intervening weeks, she found that her memories had not done him justice. Everything about him surprised her, as though she were looking at a portrait that had unexpectedly come to life.

"Hello, Alicia."

That voice. It was so full of resonance.

"You're here," she said, backing into the room. It was all she could think of to say, but the words expressed what she felt. *You're here and it's enough.*

She expected him to look around her apartment, but as he came closer, shutting the door behind him, she realized he wasn't seeing the apartment at all. They could have been any-where. His eyes didn't leave her face.

The moment wore on, a kind of recognition between them, and finally she asked, "Do you want to sit down?"

He sat on the couch and she eased into a chair. He studied her almost curiously now, as though he, too, had been surprised. Finally he said, "You're beautiful, you know."

The words were matter-of-fact, he apparently expected no reaction from her.

She didn't thank him. Instead she found her-self lost in his eyes, as if time had stopped and nothing beyond them existed. She could have re-mained like this indefinitely, not touching him but utterly absorbed in him.

She wished nothing would change. But change was inevitable. It was Michael who broke the spell. "I've missed you, you know that?" The words were lighter now, the deeper layers of feeling removed, and she sensed he was making a deliberate effort to surface from emo-tions that had overwhelmed him.

Smiling, he stood and took her hand. "Come on, Alicia. We don't want to lose any of this day." And pulling her gently, he led her outside and helped her into his car.

As they drove north toward Del Mar, he tilted his head in her direction. "Have you ever been to the Del Mar Thoroughbred Club, Alicia?"

"Only past it. Not in it."

He smiled. "They get the world's beautiful people there. It's quite the thing to be part of the racing set."

"Oh," she said, glancing down at her cotton dress. She was wearing a pale turquoise sun dress and sandals and she wondered if she was properly outfitted. "I suppose movie stars come, too."

"They do. Some, like Greer Garson and Desi Arnaz, are regulars. I confess, I go half to see the horses and half to people-watch. Of course we pretend not to see them; we've all learned to look through our ears." They both laughed. "When I was a little boy," he went on, "I could get away with openmouthed looking. Discreetness comes with long pants."

She turned to see the grin breaking into his strong profile and guessed she was seeing a Michael who had been part of a society she hardly knew existed. Just how important was his family, she wondered.

The freeway curved inland slightly. The terrain was hilly and the road at times carved a deep slash into the hills. As they came over a crest they looked down into a richly green valley where palms, eucalyptus trees and homes filled a wide swale. At the bottom, toward the ocean, was Del Mar.

Michael swung off the freeway and toward the fairgrounds that stretched away from the track. Once inside he found valet parking.

Walking toward the clubhouse on Michael's arm, Alicia felt a sense of excitement at being here with him. Michael made her feel right and wonderful. He gripped her arm firmly, pressing her wrist into his side, his attitude possessive and masterful. She walked with her head high, loving it.

They went through a turnstile, and Michael smiled. "Private Turf Club," he said. "Members only."

Inside a man in uniform inclined his head in Michael's direction. "Afternoon, Mr. Mac-Namee."

She turned to look at Michael's face, surprised. This man *knew* him?

Michael nodded back. "Hello, Ken. We've got a good one today, eh? Lots of sun. Any tips?"

"Yes, sir." The other leaned a little closer. "Bally-Hi in the third!" He raised a significant eyebrow.

"Oh, good." Michael stopped and stared at him in mock seriousness. "An inside tip, is it?"

"Yeah." The man grinned. "From the horse."

Michael laughed and gave him a friendly nod.

Though Alicia heard their exchange, her attention was elsewhere. She was captivated by the people milling about in Fifth Avenue elegance, a crowd so beautifully dressed it took her breath away. Women wore tailored linen suits and classic wide-brimmed straw hats. Simple organdy dresses swished gracefully around shapely calves. The men all wore suits and ties. The look wasn't high fashion but classic and understated. In her cotton sun dress Alicia felt woefully underdressed.

As they moved through the crowds she forgot herself in this atmosphere of rarefied air. She sensed she was seeing movie stars everywhere, though out of context like this she couldn't be sure. And she kept hearing Southern accents. She whirled around once to locate a loud heavy drawl. It belonged to a man in a blazing white linen suit and a hat that was a cross between a five-gallon Stetson and a white boater. The man was as big as a building; he went past them like a wall of white.

Following her glance, Michael commented with amusement, "Racing's big in Texas. Almost as big as oil. People from Texas and Arizona always bring their horses and make the season."

"A few more Texans like him," Alicia quipped, staring after the disappearing behemoth, "and there wouldn't be room for anyone from Arizona!" She added, "Everyone here looks...rich!"

"They are," Michael admitted. "Most of them are so rich they don't know what to do with their money." The tone was disparaging. "When you have too much it can be a burden."

"Do you have too much, Michael?"

He whirled on her sharply and she knew she'd made a mistake. "No, I don't have too much. I know how to handle it—and that includes knowing when to save it, too. Money is one thing I know how to deal with."

"Then why are you so sensitive about it?" she queried.

For a moment he didn't seem to know how to take her. He paused with his hand on a post, frowning. But to her relief the moment passed and he shrugged. "I guess I am touchy on the subject. Conditioning, perhaps. I've been taken advantage of a few times by both men and women; it makes you wary. Dixie used. . .favors to get spending money. We each had something the other wanted. When I caught on, it became repulsive. I've never felt sex should be for sale."

"I'm sorry Dixie has made you so cynical. Not all women are like that, Michael."

"I suppose not. Well, Dixie wasn't like that at first, either. . . ." He fell silent for a moment. "Why are we talking about *her*? This is our day, Alicia, not Dixie's." His eyes sought hers and he smiled.

Another set of stairs and they arrived at an open-air dining room. Rows of tables draped in white linen cloths and decorated with bouquets of fresh flowers faced the track. The maitre d' led Michael and Alicia to a choice table. Below, the track was in full view and at a distance Alicia caught a glimpse of the ocean.

When they were seated she exclaimed, "This is wonderful! Weren't we lucky to get this table?"

Michael's smile was ironic. "It isn't exactly luck. My family's had this table for thirty-seven years."

Her eyes widened. "This *same table*?"

"As long as we're members of the Turf Club. It's reserved for the MacNamees." He cleared his throat and explained dryly that his father, a founder, had belonged to the club since he was a young man. "This table is one of the privileges you get for longevity. Even money won't buy it anymore." Under his breath he added, "My stepmother would like to set up permanent residence here."

"You must love it."

"I should. Actually, some of my best afternoons have been spent in the main area, talking to the old racetrack habitués. Their commentary is often choice. They say what they think."

A waiter appeared with an ice bucket and wine. Michael held up his glass, extending the white Riesling toward Alicia. "To you, lovely lady!"

Smiling, she lifted her own glass. "And to you, Michael—the master of high finance and to the table born."

The races began as they started their dinner.

Michael placed careful bets after studying the racing forms. Alicia noticed that his horses usually placed somewhere, though not necessarily in the order chosen, so he was neither making nor losing much money. "I'm too conservative," he explained.

Fascinated, she began reading data on the horses, trying to assemble their record of past wins and losses. Finally, with Michael's bills thrust into her hand, she got up to bet on the sixth race. But once at the window she became confused. Having stammered out her bets she realized moments later that she'd reversed the order of her choices. *And after all that studying, too,* she thought with mild regret. But she kept quiet about it. No need for Michael to know.

He took her ticket thoughtfully. "Well, let's see how you do," he said.

She watched the race with growing curiosity. Mid race she saw a dark-maned filly edging up on the outside, and Michael threw Alicia a quick surprised glance. "Hey, your horse is gaining!"

Alicia smiled.

The filly pulled even and Michael stood up. "This is something of a long shot!" he said with rising excitement. "That horse wasn't supposed to do this well!"

She nodded, amused.

"Come on, Harvest Moon!" Michael's hands formed into fists, and his eyes followed the race with the intensity of a longtime bettor.

Alicia's filly was leading by a few inches, its nose just a fraction out in front of its nearest competitor. The distance grew no larger as the race went on.

Alicia stood, too, jumping up and down as they galloped into the finish, her dress swinging around her legs. Around them other diners stood and cheered.

The race was over.

Alicia asked, "Which horse won, Michael?"

"Yours," he laughed, giving her a one-armed hug. "And your second-place horse came in second, too." He smiled into her eyes. "Go up and cash in your tickets. You'll be surprised at how much it is!"

"How much?"

"Go and cash them!"

Obediently she went. Poker-faced, the man at the window counted out two hundred and twenty-eight dollars. All this cash for a mistake!

When she got back to the table she handed Michael the money. "Your winnings," she smiled. "It was your betting money."

"But yours were the shrewd decisions." He smiled, then gave her a doubtful look. "Though I wonder if it was shrewd or merely unconscious. You couldn't have known what you were doing."

"Oh, sure I did," she grinned. "Didn't you see me studying the forms?"

On the way out, Alicia ducked into the ladies'

room. She stayed longer than she intended, combing her short wavy hair and putting on fresh lipstick. The mirror reflected the pink glow in her cheeks, the sparkle in her eyes. Happiness had given her an unexpected radiance. She wondered if Michael would think her beautiful.

When she emerged she couldn't find him at first. He wasn't where she'd left him. A second look down the long corridor revealed him to be standing next to someone, a woman. His posture was inclined toward her in a way that suggested intense interest.

They were some distance away, but even from where Alicia stood she could see dark hair, a narrow-skirted pink suit, long shapely legs and high heels. The woman carried a wide-brimmed black hat. Alicia walked toward them slowly, feeling her glow fade. The closer she came the more the woman spelled sophistication. Dark, mysterious sophistication. That she was fascinating to Michael was obvious. Moving nearer, Alicia heard him say, "I'll tell you later, Elaine."

Alicia picked up her pace but never quite caught up to them. The woman gave Michael a quick kiss on his cheek, then with rapidly clicking heels disappeared into the crowd.

Michael turned and noticed Alicia's approach. A smile lit his face...genuine, it seemed. He took her forearm and led her through the door. It was twilight outside, still warm. They strolled slowly toward the parking area. He didn't try to explain who the woman was. And Alicia never asked.

Driving home, Alicia quickly put the woman out of her mind. Michael seemed unaccountably happy and she felt a warmth radiating toward her.

He led her to her door. "You're an unusual woman, Alicia. Utterly different." He said something under his breath about "spirit," and she could only guess what he meant.

Then they were inside, the door closed behind them. In the light from the simple fixture above her dinette table, she saw his dark eyes fixed on her face. He stood with his shoulders against the doorjamb, one hand still on the doorknob, as though he were trying to decide whether to stay or go. Behind the calm mask of his eyes she could sense a conflict brewing, a decision being made.

She found herself riveted by his gaze, wanting more from him than she dared admit, afraid that she'd be drawn into something she'd be powerless to stop. Michael compelled her as no other man had ever done. She knew that a long day spent with him had merely raised her level of trust and lowered her instinctive barriers. She yearned for him yet at the same time felt excessively vulnerable.

He stared at her across the few feet of distance. "Alicia," he said softly, "I should go." But he made no move to do so. "You're a beautiful woman," he whispered, and extended his hand to her.

When she didn't take it, he stepped across their small invisible barrier and grasped her bare shoulders. "Why do I stay?" he whispered, staring down at her, his eyes mirroring her desire. "It's dangerous to have me here."

"Dangerous?"

"Perhaps less to you than to me."

"Why, Michael?"

He shrugged, leaning over her now, so close she could feel his hot breath on her face and the warmth emanating from his body. His nearness was an exhilarating thing. Unconsciously she drew in a deep breath. His presence touched every nerve and fiber in her body.

"You're crumbling my resolve," he whispered, and his arm went around her as his face came down to meet hers.

He began to kiss her and the moments went by strangely, as though time had stopped entirely. She felt his lips moving against her mouth, felt his hands, strong, drawing her ever closer to him as though to weld them both into a single permanent entity.

After a while he drew away, his lips traveling caressingly to her throat, his breath hot against her sensitized skin. "Oh, Alicia!" he moaned, and the words were the cry of a drowning man.

She felt weak, overwhelmed by her desire for him. Without his sustaining hands she knew she would fall. She leaned against him and he caressed her hair. It was a caress of possession, a languid touch that told her every part of her body was precious to him.

He kissed her forehead and eyes, then drew away again, brushing his fingertips across her brows. She raised her eyes to meet his and saw the look of yearning filling his gaze, as though she were an object to be sought yet never gained, cherished but somehow unreachable.

He bent to kiss her nose. She watched as his hands moved down and slowly undid the first button of her sun dress. She wanted only for him to go on this way, undoing every button until her dress fell away and the entire length of her body was bared and touching his. But as his hands began their sensuous exploration, an alarm sounded in her brain. Her mind and body fought a brief and terrible battle. She whispered into his hair, "No, Michael. No."

His hand fell away from her buttons.

"You want it as much as I do," he whispered back.

"I do," she said. "Oh, yes. But I don't want it now."

Her response jarred him. He backed away a little and stared down at her, his black eyes so full of desire she could hardly bear to look at him. Blushing, she turned away. He mirrored too much of what she felt.

"What do you mean?" he asked.

"I can't make love like this," she breathed. "I don't want it. . . alone."

"Alone?"

"Just. . . just the physical. There has to be more."

He brushed back his hair, which was now tousled and damp. "There *is* more than the physical. My feelings are genuine." He was still staring down at her. A soft smiled crossed his lips. "I *will* respect you in the morning."

She smiled back. "It isn't just that. "

"No? Then what?" He left her and sat down on the couch.

"Michael, we've only begun to know each other."

"Alicia," he said imploringly, "you're lovely. Not just lovely—you're beautiful. Sensuous. Wondrously beautiful. And you have internal beauty, too."

Warmth flooded her, and desire, too, making her almost ready to succumb. But she held on to her control. "When it's time for lovemaking," she said, "we'll both know. Please, Michael. . . I've never wanted to give in to anyone so much. If you don't go, I'll. . . I'll lose. . . ." *My resistance,* she thought, *and more.*

He smiled, sliding his arms around her waist,

pressing her close. Again, passion swept over her.

"I could make it impossible to resist. I could do it, Alicia."

"I know," she breathed. "Please don't."

Yet his head bent over hers again, the touch of his lips casual at first, then with renewed urgency, as though he could never get enough of her. *Oh, Lord, help me,* she thought, *I can't resist.*

But abruptly he drew back and said, "I won't force you. It isn't in me. But God, Alicia, you torture a man."

And then he left. Suddenly, without turning back for a moment.

Trembling, Alicia wrapped her arms around her own shoulders and stood huddled, staring out the window, as though by hugging herself she was hugging Michael.

Even as she watched the green Porsche drive away she asked herself if she had done the right thing.

CHAPTER THREE

FOR THE NEXT FEW MONTHS, Michael dated Alicia whenever he could. Though his business trips were frequent and often lasted days—sometimes weeks—he always called the moment he got back. She came to regard the telephone as her lifeline to happiness. The sound of his voice touched her day with magic.

Yet as much as Alicia wanted to be near him, their moments of closeness were becoming almost painful. With increasing urgency, Michael pressed her for what she knew all men wanted from women. Yet he never made any promises, never told her he was committed to her. With almost stubborn determination he resisted any suggestion that they belonged to each other.

As the weeks passed, Alicia felt that she was holding back the whole rising tide of emotions for both of them and that she would soon fail. Or lose Michael while she held on.

One day when she returned from class she found a note stuffed into the crack of her door. It said, "Sorry I couldn't reach you before I left. This trip was unexpected. Save me the

Saturday after next. See you then. Michael.''

She stared at it dismally. Another week and a half without seeing him! These sudden absences depressed her. She felt like an old iron kettle, warmed slowly until heat filled every pore, then left to cool. Just when she wanted to see Michael most he disappeared. Today her longing for him was almost tangible, an aching insistent thing keeping her on edge.

Putting away the groceries she'd just bought, she decided a week would give her time to cool down. Perhaps it was for the best.

The phone rang. Alicia hurried to pick it up. Michael, perhaps! But no, it was a woman.

A cultured voice intoned, ''I'd like to speak with Alicia Barron, please.''

''This is she.''

''Helen MacNamee,'' the woman said. ''Michael's mother.'' Alicia noticed she didn't say ''stepmother.'' ''I'd like very much to see you. Can you come to my home this afternoon?''

''Oh.'' Alicia was caught off guard. What could this possibly be about? She'd never met Michael's stepmother, and she had no idea why she was being summoned. Michael had said little about his stepmother, except to tell Alicia casually that his own mother had died when he was fourteen and his father had remarried. ''He married *up*,'' Michael had explained sardonically. ''At least that's what my stepmother keeps telling him. She's one of those high-society

types—sent her daughter to Sarah Lawrence and then to France. They're an Eastern family—lots of position. Their names are always in the papers, that sort of thing. Status seems to be important to her, and if dad doesn't mind...."
He had shrugged, dismissing the subject. It was clear to Alicia that Helen MacNamee had captured the father but not necessarily the son. She wondered now what this request was about.

"I'm sorry, I have a class this afternoon," Alicia demurred. "I really shouldn't miss it."

"Come *after* class, my dear. I have all the rest of the day. And Michael's out of town, as I'm sure you know. Of course, if you have a date—" She stopped abruptly.

Alicia sensed the woman was probing, and she resented it.

"I don't happen to have a date tonight," she said, intending to tell her nothing. "But I should study."

"Surely you have an hour or two you can spare." Mrs. MacNamee's tone was coolly imperious. "You'll want to hear this, I'm fairly sure. It wouldn't do for us to talk over the phone."

Alicia's growing misgivings about Helen MacNamee tempted her to invent a better excuse for not going. But her curiosity was growing, too. She was, after all, constantly driven to find out more about Michael. Maybe this would be an opportunity.

Alicia said she'd come, and Helen MacNamee gave her directions.

Later, she asked herself why she'd given in so easily. She had handed the woman the satisfaction of manipulating her. She sensed they were natural enemies. In what way she couldn't be sure—but enemies beyond a doubt. Otherwise Helen MacNamee would never have tried to contact her behind Michael's back.

She sighed to herself. These days Michael was on her mind all the time, and all other subjects seemed to pale in comparison. Even her studies, she realized ruefully, were fading into unimportance.

So why pretend she could resist finding out what Helen MacNamee had to say?

In her little Toyota, a gift from her aunt and uncle, Alicia drove out to the suburbs of San Diego. A winding road took her up a large hill, where the homes changed gradually from modest to imposing. She saw houses with high roofs, Grecian columns, elaborate stone facades and balconies. At the very top she arrived on a street where all the homes commanded a distant view of the ocean.

She found herself walking toward a two-story red-brick Georgian mansion with tall white columns. It was a classic and suggested a kind of Eastern permanence. It had obviously been built years ago.

She stood back, ruminating. So Michael had

grown up here, she thought, ridden his bicycle up and down this street, perhaps thrown a football out here with his father. Or played on a vacant lot, for surely there were lots here then: his home was clearly the oldest on the street.

She paused for a moment trying to imagine Michael in this setting. . .a young boy growing up on the top of a hill. . .a lonely childhood, his friends all living at a distance. . .the boy slowly becoming the self-sufficient man she knew now. She saw him leaving for college, his time taken up in swimming, then in his senior year smitten by a beauty, a bubbling effervescent type who was everything he wasn't. Yes, it all fit, she decided. This hilltop had played its role in molding his character.

At last Alicia rang the doorbell.

After a long while the door opened and she found herself staring at a tall imposing woman.

Helen MacNamee was at least four inches taller than Alicia. Her carriage was erect and her figure marvelous. Her silvery white hair was swept back on either side of her face, but the face was not what Alicia would have called "older." Rather it was beautiful—aristocratically beautiful—as though Helen MacNamee had once been a movie star and time had done nothing more than change the color of her hair.

In her first quick glance Alicia took in the other's softly pleated lavender dress, its folds casually draped over her bosom. Though Mrs. MacNamee appeared outfitted for a party, Alicia supposed this was the way the very rich dressed at home.

Suddenly she felt plain. Her blue jeans and loose-fitting beige cotton blouse, appropriate for college, seemed out of place here. An image came to her of a small freckled child standing tongue-tied at the door of an overbearing queen.

Discomfited, she held out her hand. "I'm Alicia Barron."

The other seemed not to notice at first, and the hand hung in space unacknowledged. Alicia had just decided she'd made the wrong move when the woman unexpectedly reached out to shake hands with her, but the delay had its effects. Alicia's discomfiture increased.

"Come in," Helen MacNamee said, smiling, her eyes sweeping subtly over Alicia. "Please." She moved back from the doorway.

They entered an elegantly furnished room. Pale blue damask chairs were placed on one side of a glass-topped coffee table, which was adorned with a bouquet of yellow roses. Along the other side of the table a cream-and-blue flowered damask couch nudged up to a marble-face fireplace. At the distant end of the room an enormous picture window framed by blue velvet draperies looked out over the San Diego Harbor.

Alicia could see that this room had recently

been redecorated. The classical dining-room furniture near the picture window—red brown fruitwood with blue velvet chairs—looked as though it had never been used.

"This is a lovely home," Alicia said.

"Thank you. My decorator's good."

Alicia's eyes alighted on an oil portrait over the mantel above the fireplace, obviously Michael's father. He seemed to be merely an older Michael: the same heavy brows and firm chin, but extra flesh rounding out his cheeks and more gray than black in his hair. Still handsome, she thought, missing only a suggestion of humor in the eyes, and she wondered if the lack was in the artist or in the man.

"Michael's dad looks just like him, doesn't he?"

"We prefer to think Michael resembles his father," Mrs. MacNamee corrected. With a wave of a finely manicured hand, she enjoined Alicia to sit in one of the chairs.

In the brief moment of silence as Mrs. MacNamee settled onto the couch, Alicia thought, *so Michael grew up with more money than I ever imagined, but where does he stand now? Is his own business so successful, or was part of it this?* He had said so little about his work. It was as if he wanted to keep the various parts of his life separate.

Mrs. MacNamee was speaking. "You've known Michael a long time?"

"A few months. Two or three."

"Really?" Perfectly shaped eyebrows rose with the question. "He began speaking of you only this last month. I'd no idea it had gone on so long."

Alicia wasn't sure what Mrs. MacNamee meant. She almost said, *nothing has gone on,* but she didn't.

"You're about what I'd imagined. A little smaller, perhaps. You *are* quite tiny." The words were faintly deprecating.

"Five-four," Alicia replied flatly.

"You're also younger than I imagined." When Alicia said nothing, she went on, "Michael is twenty-nine, you know. I'd say he ought to confine himself to ladies at least twenty-five, don't you agree? You're not twenty-five, my dear."

Alicia gave her a stony look. "No, I'm not." She'd expected a cold woman, but not one who was so overtly nasty.

An awkward silence ensued. At last Helen MacNamee broke into a warm laugh. "I'm sorry for what I've said. I didn't mean to embarrass you, honestly. It's just that you caught me by surprise. You weren't what I expected—neither your size nor your age. But I suppose these things aren't so terribly important, really." She brushed an imaginary eyelash off her cheek. Then, her tone pleasant, she asked, "What does your father do?"

"My father's dead."

"Oh." In that instant Helen MacNamee looked genuinely stricken. "I'm sorry. I didn't know."

"You don't have to be...I was very young. I only barely remember my parents." When the older woman leaned forward, obviously interested, Alicia went on. "They died in a boat...in a hurricane...off Tortola Island. I was only five. Nobody knew what to do with me until my father's brother and his wife found out a few days later. They took me right away. They've been like my parents." Alicia smiled, more relaxed now that Mrs. MacNamee seemed warmer. "They've been better than most parents I've seen. Kind. Good. Always understanding. I've had a special childhood. You don't have to feel sorry."

"Well. That's nice." Helen MacNamee stood. "I'm having a glass of sherry. Will you have some?"

Alicia hesitated. She never drank during the day. Then she thought, *why not,* and said, "Yes. Please."

She watched Michael's stepmother pour the amber sherry out of a crystal decanter. Handing her a long-stemmed crystal glass, Mrs. Mac-Namee took a sip and sat down. "I'm glad to hear about your childhood. I'm sure your aunt and uncle have helped you become the sensible woman you obviously are. I expect you'll be able to understand what I'm about to say. And above all, my dear, I don't want you to take this personally. It isn't meant that way.''

Alicia stiffened.

"I think it's only fair that I warn you about Michael. Especially now that I see you're so...well, rather young. Michael's not in this...this relationship for the right reasons, you see. He hasn't wanted to make any lasting commitments since his marriage, and I'm sure, from what he's said to me, he really wants...." She let the words hang in the air and pushed at her silvery hair with a well-manicured hand. "My dear," she began abruptly, "you wouldn't want an older man *living with you*! You don't want to be somebody's mistress!"

Alicia stared at her coldly. "Can't Michael speak for himself?"

"I just thought a little warning might be welcome." She smiled, but it reminded Alicia of heatless sun on a winter day. "And there's something else...." Mrs. MacNamee cleared her throat delicately, holding the glass away from her. "How shall I say this? Michael is involved in a very...high-level business. A business where meeting the right people and having the right personal contacts can mean everything. And this means having the right background, too. You understand what I mean?"

She took another tiny sip of her sherry, and

Alicia watched her, thinking, *yes, I'm beginning to understand what you mean.* But she said nothing. She merely put her glass on the table and gazed across at Mrs. MacNamee unblinkingly.

The other went on uncomfortably. "What I'm trying to say is that his wife's background is important, too. He's dealing with...well, people like the Rockefellers and the Mellons and the Duponts. These people have to take him seriously. His wife is an integral part of those relationships, or she certainly will be."

Meaning, that Alicia didn't measure up! She felt suddenly conscious of the inelegance of her clothes. Coldly she inquired, "Did Dixie have the right background?"

Helen MacNamee froze. Her glass went down on the table with a loud clink. "Dixie has nothing to do with this! She's no longer part of Michael's life, and God knows he'll never tangle with another Dixie."

Suddenly Alicia felt sorry for Dixie.

"If we must be blunt about this, Alicia, I'm wondering how Michael can handle a liaison with a girl from an insignificant place like the Virgin Islands."

Alicia stood up, furious. "The Virgin Islands is as good a place to be from as anywhere I know of, Mrs. MacNamee. And a lot better than most!"

She marched toward the front door. Her hand

on the doorknob, she whirled around to glare at Helen MacNamee. "I wouldn't change what I had and the way I lived for ten of this! How lucky Michael had grown up before you got here!"

She closed the door firmly behind her, resisting the urge to slam it, and half ran to her car.

It was only partway down the hill and fishtailing around the curves that she burst into tears.

ALICIA NEVER QUITE UNDERSTOOD why she went shopping. But she did. She took one thousand dollars of her inherited money out of the bank and went to the nearest shopping mall. In no time at all, she'd spent all her money on seven of the most elegant dresses she could find. She was determined that the next time Michael saw her she'd be worthy of any Rockefeller he cared to dredge up! She'd show them—Michael, Helen and that old man hanging over the fireplace!

She paid for the dresses with an abandon that surprised the salesgirl. All the time she realized she'd gone a little crazy with anger and resentment, but she couldn't get that horrible Helen MacNamee out of her mind. Oh, she'd show that high-living stuck-up woman who was worthy and who wasn't!

Back in her car she rushed home, her spirit of vengeance still propelling her as she pulled into her parking stall.

She threw the dresses carelessly across her

living-room couch, then went upstairs to study. But it was a useless endeavor. Her mind kept going over old ground. What if Helen was right? What if Michael wanted nothing more than a mistress? Certainly he'd already decried marriage! What good had she done with her wild shopping spree?

Finally she put her books away and went downstairs to make herself a small supper. Then she took a warm shower.

At last she felt calmed down. She climbed into bed with a copy of *Time* magazine until she felt drowsy. As her mind drifted into sleep, a voice inside her asked, *tell me what you really want, Michael.*

Dreams brought forth colorful visions and ringing sounds, first a street vendor ringing the bell on his little pushcart, then a vicar in a belfry ringing Sunday's church bell. The church bell wouldn't be denied; its insistent ringing finally dragged her out of the depths of sleep. Reality took over. She realized the sound was here, in her apartment.

She struggled awake. The ringing went on, *dingdong,* pause, *dingdong.* Her doorbell?

She sat up. It *was* her doorbell!

Sleepily she sought out the windows and saw by the edge of light rimming her curtains that it was daylight.

When the doorbell rang again, Alicia jumped out of bed, snatched her yellow terry-cloth robe from its hook and stumbled down the stairs. At the door she called out, "Who is it?"

"Michael!" came the answer.

Oh, dear, no, she thought, *I look a mess! And this room...all those clothes....* But she knew from her confused dreaming he'd already been there a long time. "Please wait a minute, Michael!" she called, then rushed to the bathroom. She ran a comb through her hair and took a hasty drink of water. A quick glance in the mirror reassured her, and she ran back to the door and opened it quickly.

Michael was on the front stoop regarding her quizzically. He was wearing a dark blue lightweight business suit with vest, a blue-and-brown diagonally striped tie and a light beige shirt. She'd never seen him in a suit before and found herself staring as though at a stranger. He looked so incredibly distinguished! Then she saw his eyes and realized they were heavy with fatigue.

He stepped forward smiling. "Well...are you going to let me in?"

She hesitated, glancing down at her disreputable yellow robe, and once again felt less than gorgeous. She stepped back into the room as he approached.

"You weren't supposed to be back yet," she said lamely. "I thought next week—"

"That's right." He closed the door. "But my meeting was canceled yesterday. There was no point in staying, so I took the night plane home and arrived early this morning. I was even nice enough to kill some time before coming here. You have no idea how much I've wanted to see you, Alicia." The dark eyes bore into hers, and her heart lurched. "I've wanted to be here ever since I left. I wouldn't have taken that miserable red-eye otherwise." He yawned. "But I might as well have waited. I've been standing on your doorstep for twenty minutes, ringing that insignificant little doorbell. It's worthless; it makes about as much noise as a wind chime."

She backed into a chair and sat down.

"I heard it," she admitted. "But I kept dreaming it was a church bell. I was getting married and the bell rang and rang but somehow I never made it to the altar." She smiled ruefully. "I have very vivid dreams."

"Not unusual." He looked at her thoughtfully. "Our dreams are usually our wishes or our fears."

She hoped he'd say more, but he didn't.

He turned then, looking for a place to sit, and for the first time noticed that the couch was fully occupied. Her new dresses, tags dangling, filled all the available seating space and spilled onto the floor. Seeing his puzzled frown she jumped up and pushed the clothes to one side.

He sat down, looking sideways at her purchases. Piled up like this, there appeared to be even more than seven dresses.

He said in a flat voice, "I see you've been shopping."

"Yes." Her chin went up.

He lifted one edge of the pile slightly. "It must've taken you quite a while to buy...all this."

"Actually, it didn't."

"Were you so short on clothes?"

"Why do you think I bought them? Are you suggesting I didn't need them?" The defensive edge to her voice irritated her, for she knew unwanted feelings of guilt were showing. Still, what business was this of his?

He stood up. "Let me see your closet, Alicia!"

Horrified, she said, "No! I won't show you my closet! It's *my* closet." Full of defiance she stood blocking the stairs, her eyes challenging him to come closer. And even as she stood there she pictured her closet jammed with clothes, a sight that would doubtless inflame him more. She was a hopeless saver, and some of those clothes dated back to high school. But it wasn't his affair.

"Sorry, that was thoughtless of me." He sat down again, this time edging away from her purchases as though they were contaminated. But he couldn't seem to get his thoughts off them, for in a moment he muttered under his breath, "If you bought these so quickly, what would you do in a whole day?"

"What?" she asked, not sure she'd heard him right.

"No good," he said, his head shaking in discouragement, his words intended more for himself than for her. "It won't work. It's the same old pattern."

"What do you mean?" she demanded, thinking she knew too well what he meant.

"Exactly like Dixie." The words were uttered bitterly. He looked at her pityingly. She felt demeaned. "You're as bad as Dixie...and I've already had one Dixie too many. The Lord preserve me from women with misplaced values." He rose from his seat.

"What makes you think I'm like Dixie?" Alicia threw back at him. "What right have you to make such a comparison? This is the first time—"

"It's obvious, isn't it?" he broke in, his hand waving over the pile of clothes. "Nobody but a shallow, immature woman would go out and do a thing like...a thing like this!" His words were so filled with loathing he seemed to be actually reviling her purchases.

"You're overreacting," she said, stunned. She knew she'd been intemperate with her shopping, but that didn't justify his outrage. "What does 'shallow' have to do with me? You're just tired! You can't possibly mean what you're saying!"

"Oh, I sure as hell do. I've been through it

once." His eyes went down to her clothes. "Binges, sick binges."

She recoiled from his words, amazed. Who was this man? Obviously what she'd done was symbolic of larger things, triggering emotions he couldn't control. Yet it was all so out of proportion, so unreasonable. Until now he'd seemed fairly levelheaded. She continued to stare at him, wondering if she knew him at all.

At the end he stopped shouting and became icy cold. She saw a face as hard and impenetrable as stone. He stared back at her and it affected her terribly, chilled her straight to the bone. She felt defeated, utterly lost.

If he'd gone on yelling, she thought, she might have been able to deal with that. But not this. Against this coldness she had no defense.

She saw him moving toward the door. "I'm sorry, Alicia," he said impersonally. "I thought it might work." Then the door opened and quickly closed.

She sank back into a chair, wanting to block him out. Instead she found herself listening as the Porsche sputtered, started and rapidly gunned away.

CHAPTER FOUR

ALICIA FOUND the next few weeks almost unbearable. Losing Michael had been bad enough, but losing him the way she did, over a mad spree in a department store, was all so pointless. Worse, it didn't reflect what she really was. She had never been on a shopping binge before, and she'd done it more in a spirit of revenge than desire for the clothes themselves, though she wouldn't tell Michael that. Yet Michael had given it so much importance, transferred so much of his old resentment toward Dixie onto her. How much larger the event loomed in his mind than hers! Bitterly Alicia reflected on what a long and terrible shadow had been cast by a stranger named Dixie.

Well, at least Helen MacNamee had got what she wanted, though she couldn't have dreamed it would work out as it did.

After a few weeks Alicia decided there was no point in thinking about Michael any longer; he was never coming back. And it was odd, she thought sadly, because she was sure Michael cared for her. He'd shown her tenderness and concern, those dark eyes often fixed on her with an expression she could only read as rich in feeling. And always, her interests seemed to be his interests.

She stood at her sink doing dishes, carelessly putting plates away half-dry. True, she thought, they'd disagreed about some fundamental things—the way land ought to be developed, the desirability of marriage. But they'd laughed together, too, more than she'd ever laughed with anyone. With him there was always a magnetism stirring up feelings in her that nearly made her lose all track of time and place, of rightness and wrongness. Only by the fiercest exercise of will had she fought back her own cascading emotions.

And what irony that she'd lost him over something that had nothing to do with their frustrated yearnings.

In the next weeks she picked herself up, resolutely setting about the task of forgetting. She tried not to cry.

Each day she went to class, determined to think only about her studies. In two more weeks she'd be finished.

When the call came from her cousin, Alicia had hoped as always that it would be Michael's voice she'd hear, and as always she was disappointed.

"Hi, Alicia!" Brandon had begun. Setting aside her dashed expectations, Alicia decided she was almost as glad to hear her cousin's familiar tones as anyone else's. She'd grown up with her cousin, and his voice brought her memories of a lazy good-natured youth, a boy she'd had fun with because he viewed the world uncritically. When she needed to escape from her own unrelenting sense of purpose she sought out Brandon. He made her happy with simple things.

"How's the weather down there?"

She laughed. "The same as always, Brandon. Warm. Good for scuba diving."

"I may be coming down soon. I'm getting sick of San Francisco."

She read the signals and felt alarm. At twenty-three, Brandon seemed to feel little pressure to satisfy his employer, taking a "mañana" attitude she found alarming. "Your job's not going well?"

"Nah," he said, "no problem with the job, cous'. I don't like it, but they don't know that. Just thought I'd come down for a visit. To get some rays. Up here the sun's never out."

"Well, sure," she said, quite certain this wasn't the real reason for his call. "I'm almost through with school now."

"So what're ya gonna do when you get out?"

She told him she wasn't sure yet.

"Mom's broke her arm, you know."

The words were casual, spoken almost as an afterthought. Alicia now knew the real reason for his call. Alarmed, she said, "Why didn't you tell me right away? What happened?"

"She slipped on the patio last week when it was wet. She didn't want you to know."

"Why not, Brandon? Oh, I can't believe this!"

"She said you'd be upset and I shouldn't disrupt your school. But dad called last night. He said mom can hardly do anything, it hurts her too much. So I thought I oughta call you. But what can you do about it, 'Lish? We're both too far away."

"I know what *I'm* going to do, Brandon." The thought came to her as clearly as if it had been part of her plans from the beginning. "I'm going home."

A few minutes later, after they had said good-bye, Alicia's mind began to whirl with a new sense of purpose. So she was back to square one. Back to her original plan of helping run her family's scuba school. Well, it hadn't been such a bad idea before, and returning to it now saved the necessity of making agonizing decisions—at least for the time being. It would do her good to get away, away from places that reminded her of Michael, and she would have time to make plans...for her career...for her life. In these past few minutes her life had become simplified, and she was glad.

She went into her room, pulled out a suitcase and planned her packing. As she laid a few neglected things in the bag, she thought wryly, *how lucky it was that I talked the store into taking back those useless clothes!*

TWO WEEKS LATER SHE stood in her living room with her suitcases around her. The room still held echoes of Michael's presence. Though he'd seldom been there his vital presence had held its effects. She felt nostalgic leaving this place. In those few brief months she'd met and lost a wonderful man, and she doubted she'd ever meet another like him.

It was obvious that she'd blundered, but she knew it could have happened again some other time—as long as Michael still saw all women through a veil marked "Dixie."

Well, she thought, taking a last look at her living room, *goodbye, San Diego. And goodbye, beloved Michael.*

She was out in her car when she thought she heard the telephone inside the apartment. She held the key away from the ignition, listening. Another ring. Yes, it was the phone. She jumped out of her car and rushed to the door. As she fumbled with the doorknob her purse dropped out of her hands. Bending to retrieve it, she heard the phone ring again. Desperately she clawed the door open and burst into the room, racing to pick up the receiver.

"Hello. Hello." For a moment she listened to emptiness then the dial tone returned.

Flooded with disappointment she put the receiver back in its cradle. Whoever it was hadn't heard her voice. Could it possibly have been Michael?

She glanced at her watch, giving herself ten minutes. She'd wait ten more minutes to see if the caller tried again.

She sat down on the floor. Five minutes went by, and then ten. The phone remained silent. Regretfully she stood up and went back out to her car.

It was truly over now; she'd never know who had been trying to reach her.

THE SMALL PLANE began a short descent through the thick cloud cover, seeking an altitude free of turbulence. Alicia stared out of the rain-streaked windows trying to see the ocean. The black clouds swirling densely just beyond her pane formed an impenetrable screen. She knew that somewhere down below the Atlantic was churned to an angry froth. It seemed somehow fitting that she would be returning to the Virgin Islands on a day in which sea and sky expressed the same tumultuous feelings that raged within her. Leaving had been harder than she'd thought.

It had been irrevocable, a goodbye that afforded no looking back.

She turned sideways in the narrow seat, suddenly caught up in the small plane's pervasive roar. The vibration went right through her, jarring her very bones. She'd forgotten how tiny these planes seemed compared to the cushioned remoteness of the jumbo jets. It was this reawakened memory of the island planes that made her realize she'd been away a long time.

She glanced surreptitiously at the thin, gray-haired man sitting next to her on the double seat. His hands gripped each other where they pressed against his knees, his eyes fixed on a point straight ahead. The plane lurched and he threw her a quick terrified look.

Another day she would have tried to reassure him it was all right, that these island hoppers always behaved like this and always survived—but today she didn't have enough largess of spirit to cope with someone else's misery.

Again Alicia felt the plane veer sharply to one side, and as she looked through the window it seemed the black devil cloud swirling by outside dared them to enter its domain. Fragments of gray and black cloud spun past her window like dark cotton candy and then seemed to rise. The plane had lost more altitude. She glanced at her watch. She was nearly home.

Through a fleeting hole in the clouds Alicia saw that they were passing over Tortola. She took a sharp, agonized breath. Below her, as helpless as a twig, a small boat tossed near the island. The two people aboard were rowing desperately, but they were powerless against the sea. Black waves threw them into a trough, then picked up the boat and swung it around wildly. Even as their oars left the water they continued to row uselessly. She watched, desperately afraid; her throat tightened and her eyes filled with tears.

In a moment of dredged-up memories Alicia cried for the parents she'd hardly known.

Soon the island hopper was approaching Virgin Gorda. The small plane lurched and corrected itself, lurched and corrected again, then turned around the far end of the island, finally under the cloud cover. The last leg, Alicia thought, the last mile to home. Now she could clearly see the land below, the tops of the trees blending into a dark green covering, a lush cloak that made the island bearably cool.

At the south end, rock piles spilled over the land as though they'd been dumped there. Rocks covered everything and spewed downward toward the sea.

The plane lowered and aimed for the small dirt runway that ran alongside the ocean. She could see it ahead of them, a mere path, the hill of rocks on one side, the ocean on the other. It was a terrifyingly narrow target: miss that small thread and you'd hit the boulders or the sea.

Beside her the old man's stoic fear changed to stiff-backed alarm.

"It's okay," Alicia smiled at him. "These pilots can hit it every time. They're good."

The plane lowered, and with a thump the wheels touched dirt.

"You see?" she said.

His thin hands unclenched and he turned to look at Alicia, his face pale. "I'll never come again. Next time I'm going to Miami."

Alicia laughed.

The plane swung abruptly to the left and stopped on a patch of macadam. Peering out the window, Alicia looked for her Aunt Lily and Uncle Bill but could see no sign of them. Then as she left the plane she caught sight of Anselmo, her uncle's gardener. He was alone.

"It's good to see you, Miss Alicia." Anselmo held out his hand, his dark eyes shining. He looked as he always did—the same old straw hat, same light blue shirt and rumpled pants. Laughter lingered in the corners of his eyes, and his grin washed over her, warm and endearing.

"Oh, Anselmo, I'm so glad to see you." She rose on tiptoes and gave the old man a hug. For just a moment he held her, then backed away, embarrassed.

She got into his battered truck and let him start it up before she asked, "Where's Aunt Lily...and Bill?"

"Miss Lily wanted to meet you, but their car isn't working right now and Bill can't handle this truck." He grinned. "It don't behave for anybody but me. But they's so excited I thought maybe they'd try 'n' walk partway."

"Aunt Lily's arm pretty bad?"

"Not so bad anymore—but she's in a cast so it's hard for her to do much. The right arm, you know."

"Yes. Brandon told me. And how's Bill's arthritis?"

"If you ask me, it's getting worse all the time. He's more stooped now, and even settin' down he's pretty hunched over. Been so wet, you know. Miss Lily says he ought to go someplace dry." He shrugged. "They been here so long now, I can't imagine what it would be like not having 'em on the place. . .twenty-seven years I been doin' for them! I do feel right sorry for Mr. Bill."

Alicia's heart went out to her uncle. Her aunt hadn't said very much in her letters—but then she wouldn't. She'd wanted Alicia to finish school, so of course she wouldn't dwell on anything that might bring her home.

Her thoughts went back to her aunt's accident and she shook her head in dismay. "Poor Aunt Lily. What an awful thing to have happen."

"She's goin' to be just fine," Anselmo said soothingly, noting Alicia's sad expression. "I suppose it's lucky it wasn't worse."

He shifted gears and started up a hill. The old truck coughed and almost died, but then it caught hold and surged forward, bumping up the rough road at a good pace. Anselmo grinned. "Me 'n' this truck, we been together so

long we don't need to tell each other where
we're goin'. It just rears up and I wait and it
goes." He gave a hearty laugh.

It's good, Alicia thought. *It's good to be
home.*

The road from the airport looked the same,
trees and shrubs pressing in on both sides, the
oleander and flowering red trees in bloom. But
when they came to her resort, the old wooden
sign that said Seahawk Cove showed signs of
age. The colors had faded and the wood needed
varnish. She supposed that the aging had come
so gradually for those living here that they
hadn't even noticed.

The truck pulled up onto a gravel patch, and
Alicia saw her Aunt Lily and Uncle Bill standing
outside the white cottage, beaming.

She jumped out of the truck and ran into
Aunt Lily's arms.

Her aunt, still plump as ever, grabbed Alicia
and hugged her with the good arm. "My, Alicia, oh, my, I've missed you." Tears ran down
her round cheeks and slipped into the valleys
created by excess flesh. Alicia noticed that her
aunt's hair was now entirely white and the
casual strands waving softly around her face
were sparser than before.

Bill stood by smiling, his back curved in its
permanent distortion. It seemed so much more
crooked, Alicia thought, than when she'd left.
She hugged her uncle and felt his bony thinness

through the loose-fitting shirt. He was much thinner, too, she realized sadly. He shouldn't be trying to run this place anymore. Maybe it was just as well she'd come home.

She looked around her. The nine cottages dotted the beach, all somewhat weather-beaten now. Palm trees stood among them, rustling in the perpetual breeze; the lawns were shaded by lush tamarind trees; the coarse grass was neatly trimmed as always. It all looked good to her.

Their own small house, set far back from the ocean, needed paint on its white clapboards. They went inside and Alicia found that nothing had changed. It was as orderly as ever. She sank into the flowered chintz cushions of the rattan couch. Above her a ceiling fan with large wooden paddles slowly stirred the air, supplementing the light ocean breeze that came in through the screens.

In spite of the fan, Alicia felt too warm in her blouse and skirt. She pulled her blouse away from her body, feeling the perspiration trickle between her breasts. She'd forgotten how pervasive the heat was. Her nylons, now cloying, stuck to her legs uncomfortably.

Her aunt noted her niece's discomfort, smiled and suggested, "Go and change, dear. Take a shower. And get rid of those nylons. We never wear them here, remember?"

Moments later, standing in the shower with suds in her hair, Alicia thought of Michael. She rinsed her hair and slowly lathered the rest of her body. In this moment of solitude came a sharp realization that from now on there wouldn't be Michael to look forward to.

She rinsed the soap off her delicate body. Who would kid her about her little foibles? Who would notice her red hair? Who would make her laugh?

Unwilling to torture herself further, she hurried from the shower and quickly slipped into a pair of white cotton shorts and a tight-fitting pale blue halter top.

As she walked into the dinette, her aunt glanced at her and smiled. Using her good arm to balance plates against the cast, Lily bustled companionably from refrigerator to stove to kitchen table. She placed slices of cool papaya before Alicia, with thin-sliced toast, a cup of vegetable soup and a serving of chicken salad. "It's been such a long trip for you, Alicia. You must be starving."

Her aunt's attentions had their effects. A sense of comfort flooded Alicia and, for the moment at least, put her troubles at a bearable distance. This was home, she thought, with her aunt's kindness and her uncle's easy silences and Anselmo keeping things running. As long as she was here, where she belonged, she could bear Michael's absence.

That night, under another red-bladed ceiling fan, Alicia slept soundly, washing away her weariness from the trip...and some of her regrets.

ALICIA AWOKE TO A WORLD of sunshine. Looking through her slatted blinds she was dazzled with vivid color—the greens of trees and grass and, far beyond, a sparkling azure ocean. *No wonder the world comes here to play,* she thought.

Later, over breakfast, she asked about Brandon. Bill and Lily exchanged a quick look, and neither of them spoke. Alicia felt their tension, saw her uncle's thin lips draw into a bleak line.

Lily poured a cup of coffee and sat down. "His job isn't going well, Alicia. I was so hoping...." She turned her head and Bill coughed loudly.

Lily turned back, staring into her cup. "Brandon hasn't changed much, I'm afraid. We had such hopes for this job, but it isn't working out. He said they were thinking of laying him off. It's a growing company, Alicia. They wouldn't lay him off unless something was wrong. Oh, dear God, he went such a long way for that job!" She took off her glasses and cleaned them while Alicia sat, feeling compassion for her aunt's unhappiness. She nodded sympathetically.

Why, Alicia asked herself, was Brandon screwing up again? He was twenty-three now. He'd always been lazy—sweet, good-natured but disinclined to exert himself. For years he'd charmed her and everyone else into doing his chores.

Her aunt was talking again. "I've been praying for him, Alicia." She smiled shyly. "I'm always praying for one or the other of you kids."

"Don't worry about him, Lily," Alicia said. "He'll be all right." But inside, she wasn't sure.

She sipped her aunt's strong coffee and took a bite of homemade coffee cake. After a while she asked, "What about Seahawk Cove? It looks as though... well, maybe you need help."

Her uncle pushed his chair away from the table and made an attempt to straighten his back. "This is still the best resort on the island, good as that big one and always will be." He jerked a thumb vaguely in the direction of the famous Pelican Point resort. "They'd like to have this and add it to their place. Well, they'll never get it—our customers like us small."

For a fleeting moment Alicia thought distastefully of Michael's high rises.

"Just wish I had the back I used to," he said quietly. He stood up and walked painfully toward the door. His attempts to straighten his shoulders were unsuccessful.

Alicia watched and felt his pain. "You two really do need me," Alicia said when he was out of earshot. "How does he keep going? How does he maintain everything... the cottages and the scuba school?"

Aunt Lily smiled. "Anselmo's been a god-send. He does most of the maintenance now. And Victo, you remember him...."

Alicia smiled. Anselmo's grandson. Of course she remembered him. As a boy he swam like a fish and seemed born in the water. He and Alicia had spent hours of their childhood together, exploring the ocean depths.

"Victo's running our scuba school now. And, oh, Alicia—" her eyes sparkled "—he discovered a new wreck, one of the ships that went down off Peter Island in the big hurricane. You know, in 1867. Can you imagine, a brand-new wreck to your credit?" She laughed, her pride in Victo's achievement as strong as if he'd been her own son.

"As for Bill...." Her aunt shrugged. "Bill thinks he's still doing most of the work here, but he isn't. He's stubborn. You know that. It's funny, when he bought this place all those years ago he had an idea, and he's never let go of it. If anything, his feelings are stronger than ever. I guess Bill figured this bay would always belong to us and to your family, too. It was his dream to have his brother come in with him. He wanted that more than anything, Alicia, and I sometimes still see regret in his eyes. Regret that his brother never became partners with him."

Lily brushed her eyes with her hand. "Oh, my, Bill loved his brother. I thought he'd never get over what happened...their little boat...all that wind...." She made an effort to control her emotions. "When your folks died, it didn't change Bill's stubbornness about this place. And having you just gave him more reason to want to keep it in the family. I've always been glad Bill's got such a strong sense of family and what it means, though it gets in the way sometimes. He can't see anybody on this place but us Barrons and he's dead set against being swallowed up by Pelican Point. But he can't do it anymore, Alicia. He needs to go someplace where it's dry—like Arizona." She smiled wistfully. "I wish I could get him to sell. Sometimes people don't know what's best for them."

Alicia nodded. "Anselmo told me some of this."

"Anselmo. He's another reason Bill stays. He's been with us so long." She sighed, reaching into the edges of her cast to scratch the skin. "We always supposed Brandon would get interested in this place.... And we never wanted you to feel burdened. You always seemed so much more interested in the scuba school than the rest of it. And you wanted to go to college, too."

"Yes. But I didn't *have* to go."

Aunt Lily flared momentarily. "Of course you did!" She set her coffee cup down on the table with a slight clatter and looked pointedly at her niece. "What happened, Alicia? Why did you come home so suddenly?"

Alicia swallowed and thought hard. Why did

her aunt so often see beyond the obvious? But she said evenly, "You know why, Lily. You needed help."

"That's not the only reason, is it?" Lily's eyes probed hers. "There was another reason, something you haven't told me. A man?"

"Well...that, too," said Alicia. "But it was only that I no longer had a reason for staying."

"I thought so." Aunt Lily waited for her to elaborate.

"I...he wasn't just any man." Thoughts of Michael swept over her again, and for a moment she could see his dark eyes, feel the pressure of his hand on her arm. Acute yearning overwhelmed her, and tears welled up in her eyes. "Darn," she muttered, and quickly turned her face. With a paper napkin she dabbed her cheeks. "I thought he...I thought we were doing fine. But we had a fight—a stupid fight really. I didn't think it was important, but apparently he did. He'd been married before and he was so worried I might turn out like his former wife. Dixie was a great spender and it drove him crazy. She was bored, had nothing else to do. He lost respect for her."

"But you're not a spender."

"No. But he thinks I am—or he thought I was. I don't suppose he's thinking about me anymore. I did go out once and buy clothes— too many clothes—because I was angry. Oh, Lily, it's a long story." When her aunt waited patiently, Alicia went on. "Anyway, he took it all wrong. He got angry and left. After that he never called again."

"Were you spending *his* money, Alicia?"

"No. Mine."

"Then what right had he to object?"

"It was the principle, I suppose. The fear that a second marriage might turn out as badly as the first."

Lily gazed at her sympathetically. "But he must have seen the difference between you two."

"Oh, I think he did. And then he sort of didn't. I don't know. I really thought he'd call me again. I kept hoping...." Tears welled up again. "Oh, darn." The comfort of home had vanished, and all she could think about was the emptiness of being here without Michael. She gazed past her aunt to the ocean extending beyond the cottages. It was no longer an inviting tropical sea but merely a vast separation— thousands of miles of emptiness between her and him.

"Maybe you'll see him again," her aunt offered.

"No. No, I won't. He doesn't know where I am. He doesn't even know I've left. It's not possible." She held on to herself, controlling the sobs that threatened her composure. She wouldn't break down. She wouldn't.

Her aunt shifted in her chair. "It's hard, isn't it, losing someone you've cared for?"

"Oh, yes!" The agreement burst out of her, more vehemently than she'd intended. "He was right for me, Lily." Even thinking about him now sent shivers through her, shivers of excitement. He'd always had the power to make her want him. She shook her head. "He was the man I wanted, Lily. But I have to stop thinking about him. It's useless."

"Oh, dear." Her aunt stood up slowly and put her arm across Alicia's shoulders. "We've all been through it. You'll find someone else."

Alicia blew her nose and nodded her agreement. But inside she knew her aunt was wrong. There wasn't another Michael.

CHAPTER FIVE

TIME MOVED QUICKLY. Weeks went by, then nearly six months. At first Alicia worked unceasingly in the gift shop at Seahawk Cove helping her aunt as her broken arm healed. But gradually more of her time was spent in the water, or at the edge of it, helping Victo give scuba lessons to the patrons of their resort and the neighboring Pelican Point. Although Seahawk Cove officially owned the school, the larger resort was happy to offer guests lessons without the nuisance of operating its own school. Victo had had a helper, but shortly before Alicia arrived, the helper left one day without warning. Alicia became Victo's partner. For the time being she put aside her plans for returning to school.

The customers who came to their resort found her attractive, and their attentions gradually diverted her thoughts from Michael. To her surprise, she noticed that occasionally a whole day would go by without a single thought of him.

In those odd moments when her mind replayed the past she wondered what she might have done differently. She asked herself if, at another time, she would have fallen irrevocably into the trap that Dixie had unwittingly laid for her. It was inevitable, she realized, and it could happen again. Until Michael cleared his mind of the past, neither she nor anyone else would have much chance with him.

Well, it was over now. She wouldn't get a second chance. He was gone, and her soul's salvation lay in forgetting him.

But no matter how much her rational daytime self worked at the task of erasing Michael's memory, her more vulnerable nighttime thoughts betrayed her. Unwittingly she dreamed of Michael, felt again the warmth of his lips on hers, spoke his name in her sleep. And when she woke and realized that it had all been a dream she felt an ache inside that sometimes brought tears to her eyes. But she never let Lily see them. Alicia would never cry for Michael in front of anyone else again.

A NEW TENNIS PRO arrived at Pelican Point and soon discovered Alicia. He was tall, fair and blue eyed, with a deep cleft in his chin. Silky blond hair on his arms and legs glinted in the bright sunshine.

David Lindy was affable and lazy, and sometimes Alicia wondered how he gathered the energy to give lessons. He told her constantly,

"It's too hot to play tennis today. Come with me for a swim, Alicia."

"I have to work," she'd remind him in laughing tones.

"Let Victo give the lessons. Come with me."

"This is my job, David."

"Ask him," he'd whisper playfully in her ear.

And if she succumbed, Victo always shrugged and said, "Alicia, I s'pose I can do again what I did before. Go ahead."

Feeling guilty, she'd hurry away to spend a few hours on the beach with David.

Lying there on the sand next to him she'd steal glances at his handsome face, the square-ness of his chin, the way his hair waved away from his face. She felt drawn by his good looks. Most women would find this man irresistible, she would think, and sometimes she'd move closer to him, as though seeking some of that essence of magic she always felt near Michael.

But with him it was missing.

Whenever David caught her looking at him he'd smile lazily and reach for her, and Alicia, wishing with her innermost being that this were someone else, would let him kiss her. But she felt nothing.

Maybe when she had entirely forgotten Michael, she'd tell herself, David would fill a need for her and she'd want him.

One day after he'd kissed her, Alicia rose on one elbow and stared down at him. "Can't you put a little steam in your kisses? Let's have some passion here. This isn't tennis!'' she joked.

He sat up. ''You want me to make love to you, Alicia?''

''I didn't say that,'' she teased. ''I said put a little more into the preliminaries.''

''It isn't worth it in this heat,'' he said seriously. ''Not unless there's more to come.''

''You really don't like heat, do you? What are you doing here on Virgin Gorda?''

He shrugged. ''It's a good job. Some days I don't have to work much. I can lie here on the sand with you. I like to look at you.''

''You do?''

''I've always liked to look at you. You're pretty. You've got charm, too, and you're not silly. You're interested in things. I don't know.'' He smiled at her. ''I like your legs.''

''What else?'' She felt like egging him on. ''What else, David?''

''I don't know.'' He studied her intently, and she could feel her lips curving sensuously. It was fun being admired. ''I like your mouth—it's seductive. The more I look at you . . . you know, you're beautiful!''

''It took you a while to get to that!''

''Yeah? Maybe I never quite noticed. You really *are* beautiful! Come here, Alicia!''

''Come and get me,'' she teased provocatively.

''All right.'' He rose to his knees quickly and

dragged her down beside him. "You want me to kiss you?" he said fiercely against her ear. "I'll kiss you, Alicia!"

She found herself taken into arms suddenly strong, kissed by lips newly fervent, her own feelings of excitement growing to match his. She thought fiercely, *I'll get along without you, Michael. I'll make it. I'll leave you behind forever.*

But in the middle of David's passion something went wrong. Alicia came back to reality, realized in one strong and terrible moment that she didn't want what might happen here, that she didn't love David and anything that happened between them would be purely physical with none of the commitment she would have felt for Michael.

She struggled, wrenched herself free and found herself facing him. David stared down at her. "What's wrong?" he asked huskily.

She shook her head. "I can't do this, David. I—" Lord, she couldn't tell him that thoughts of another man, Michael, had intervened. "Please, David, not now. It isn't right. There has to be more between us."

"What do you want?" he asked, his blue eyes bewildered. "I was doing what you asked."

"I don't know. Please. . .I'm sorry."

Still he stared into her eyes. "Why did you say what you said?"

"I. . .I was half-kidding."

"But not entirely kidding?"

"No. Not entirely. I don't know *what* I want."

"Your signals have been clear until today." She heard a new David speaking. "I've known until today I meant little to you, Alicia. Now you turn me in three directions at once."

She nodded humbly. It had been unfair to him. Lord knows, she thought, he was handsome enough, charming enough. Why hadn't it worked?

She didn't know. But it hadn't.

David stood up. "Let's go back. When you get your mind made up you might tell me. But tell me before you get me going. It's too hot to make half-love!"

They walked across the warm sand to his car parked under a tamarind tree.

Ten minutes later he'd dropped her off in front of her white cottage. As she started to climb out of the car he smiled at her with his old laziness. "It's a funny thing—I still like you."

ALICIA HAD BEEN BACK on Virgin Gorda nearly a year when she began to see subtle changes in David's attitude. He came around more often and was more insistent. When her old yearnings drove her to teasing him occasionally, he turned petulant. One day when she was putting away scuba gear in the little shack down on the beach he stood in the doorway watching her. "You going swimming with me tonight?" he asked lazily.

"I don't think so, David. Not tonight."

"Okay. Tomorrow."

"No. I'm going to read. I'm in the middle of a book. I want to finish it." She looked past him out to the beach. No one was around. She didn't want anyone overhearing this. "David. . . I need to think. You give me no chance to think."

"What do you need to think about?" He came into the shed and lifted one of the tanks onto a shelf for her. "What's there to decide? You like me. And I—" he broke off, taking her shoulders "—I feel more than like for you. I've been considering asking you something else, Alicia." He sought out her eyes with his and she could see the hunger in them.

She felt panicky. He looked so serious. She didn't want to hear what he was feeling, to be responsible for it. She grew tense and rigid.

He must have felt her pulling back, because his tone turned lighter and he withdrew his hands. "One of these days" he said, "you gotta think about marrying."

But not yet, she denied wildly. Not yet.

"You *are* going to get hitched eventually?" He was making light of it now.

She laughed, relieved. "David, you sounded so serious when you started."

"Maybe I was."

"But I'm not ready to get married."

"Well, all right, we'll move the timetable forward. You can have an extra week." He smiled. "But think about it, Alicia."

"Then let me have a few nights to myself." She turned to leave the shed. "And if I decide not to marry you, can't we go on being friends?"

He ran his hands distractedly through his blond hair. "I don't know about 'friends.' 'Friends' is hard. Some day it's gonna be too hard. So don't put me off too long." There was a sour note to his voice. He walked ahead of her up the beach and turned onto the road that led back to Pelican Point.

Was she being a fool to hold him off, she wondered, strolling back up the beach. David was free, attractive, reasonably intelligent, perhaps even passionate—though she'd had only a passing glimpse of that.

I need someone, she thought wistfully, *I need someone. But not David.*

A few days later Alicia walked the quarter-mile to Pelican Point to catch the small bus that would take her to the Yacht Harbor Shopping Center. Usually she took the car but it was having repairs done. She cast an apprehensive look at the sky. Large black clouds seemed to be harboring a tropical storm.

Automatically she glanced down at her crisp white eyelet dress with its gathered skirt, then shrugged to herself. Rain would make it go limp, but there was little she could do about that.

As Alicia waited at the entrance to Pelican Point, the rain began. She ducked under a near-by tree, hoping it would shield her from the wet. But it rained harder and soon the water poured down like a staged storm. She imagined a film crew manipulating its volume, arranging the sheets of water slanting out of the sky and form-ing a misty curtain in front of her.

Gradually she was getting wet—droplets were falling off her red hair and trickling down her neck. In the distance she saw with relief that the bus was coming. Then, to her disappointment, she realized it wasn't her bus, but the van bring-ing the day's new check-ins to Pelican Point. Alicia glanced at them without interest as she brushed a fallen leaf off her shoulder.

At that moment, two things happened at once: the rain stopped, and Michael MacNamee stood up inside the open-sided van.

Michael!

Conflicting desires to rush forward and to pull back tore at her simultaneously. Uncon-sciously she backed away. Her heart began such a fierce pounding she felt it must be visible. In-side her head a melee of emotions fought for supremacy. *Oh, Michael, you're here, you're here at last! You've found me!*

She stood staring, watching him move

through the bus. Instinctively she combed her
fingers through her hair and smoothed her
dress. Still she didn't rush to him, not quite
understanding what held her back.

The passengers at the front of the van stepped
down slowly, and Michael stood waiting. As
Alicia watched, her heart still pounding furiously, a small internal voice ordered her to be calm.
Michael couldn't be coming back to her—he
didn't know she was here! *Be casual, Alicia,* she
told herself. *Play it cool.*

She was almost behind the tree now, still unseen. Slowly she gathered her wits and her poise.
In a moment she would approach casually and
say hello.

Michael had stepped down, and Alicia was
about to move forward to extend her hand. But
then she stopped.

To her horror she saw that Michael had
turned back and was helping a woman down the
high step of the van.

Oh, no, she thought, her heart sinking in
despair. Who could that be? His girl friend or—
her mind could hardly form the word—his
bride. Maybe he had married after all. Maybe
this was his honeymoon.

In a single searching look before she turned
away, Alicia noted that the woman was tall and
elegantly dressed, her rich dark hair pulled into
a loose half-knot. In that same instant she saw
long shapely legs and very high-heeled tan

shoes. Something about the woman looked familiar—but she wasn't sure what.

From a long-buried memory she drew out an image of those same shapely legs and that dark hair. Puzzled, she shook her head once. She'd seen enough.

At a half-run she escaped down the stone path toward the Pelican Point dining room. The last person she wanted to meet in the whole world was Michael's bride. She felt sick, but not just physically undone. Her mind told her that the chapter of her life with Michael was finally, irrevocably closed. With a new bride he was lost to her forever.

As she stopped near the dining room she heard them approaching. She pulled back toward the kitchen, frozen. The woman had her arm through Michael's and was exclaiming with enthusiasm about the beauty of the place. "Look at these red blossoms, Michael! And pink oleanders! I'm so glad you brought me here!"

Alicia stared at Michael for a moment, hoping he wouldn't look her way. His dark hair seemed thicker than ever, his eyes more brooding. Small lines had appeared near the corners, but they only enhanced his features. He wore a blue open-necked shirt and pale blue, almost white slacks. Anywhere, anytime he would make her breath catch. She wondered how she'd ever had the strength to resist his lovemaking.

Abruptly she was sorry he'd come, perplexed that he'd reopened wounds she'd thought healed. As he and the dark beauty stood with their backs turned, looking at the vast open dining room and the ocean beyond, once more she decided to bolt before she was seen. Michael need never know she was on the island. In a week or so, his honeymoon over, he would leave. In the meantime she'd make sure she stayed out of sight at Seahawk Cove.

But Alicia had not considered the effects of the rain on the smooth terrazzo surrounding the dining room. Just as she ran past Michael her leather sandals skidded, her feet sailed out from under her and she landed hard on the damp stonework. Her white dress, like an oiled sled, carried her a few feet across the slick surface before she came to a halt.

A startled cry and several "ohs" of dismay from the woman greeted her fall.

Humiliation combined with fury at her insufferable situation. She sat for a moment where she'd stopped, staring down at her dress. But before she could rise she felt arms around her waist and a familiar masculine voice saying, "Let me help you." He pulled her to her feet. She looked up chagrined and found herself staring into Michael's dark eyes.

"Alicia!" he exclaimed, his surprise so great he almost dropped her. Then his grip tightened, and his fingers pressed into her tiny waist. The pressure of his hands produced both pain and pleasure and called back to memory the unbearable, suffocating fever of his touch.

"I don't need help," she declared stiffly. She knew how ridiculous she sounded because he had already helped her and she had needed it. Apart from the wildly disrupting effects his touch elicited in her, she felt the pain of a bruised hip and ankle that threatened to let her fall.

Pride, pain and desire all fought for supremacy. She wanted to run, and at the same time she wanted to lean against him forever. Finally her pride overcame the other emotions and she wrenched free of his hands. She stared down with dismay at her eyelet dress. It had done an efficient job of mopping up the tile work and was covered with dirt.

"Alicia, what are you doing here?" Michael began.

She gathered herself up, standing hard against the pain. "I'm sliding on my rear for the benefit of the guests," she pronounced sarcastically. "Care to see my next act?"

He grinned, unable to help himself. The dark-haired woman stood at a distance, intrigued, arms folded across her waist.

Then Michael grew serious and beckoned to the dark beauty. "Elaine, this is Alicia. You've heard me mention her."

Alicia froze, remembering. Elaine. That

name, heard so long ago, came back to her in a
rush of memories. Del Mar . . . the racetrack . . .
that was the name of the woman he had been
talking with when she came out of the ladies'
room. Of course! This was the same woman! So
he'd known her even then, she thought in dismay. Even back in the days when she'd thought
him all hers. Her heart contracted. She had a
sense that she had lived out destiny. If Michael
had known this woman then, surely Alicia
would have lost out in the end. How much better that she'd left San Diego and Michael the
way she had instead of watching him slowly
wrested away from her.

All these thoughts flashed through her mind
in a dark instant of perception. She returned to
the present to see the other woman hesitating.
"Alicia?" the woman mumbled vaguely. "I'm
not sure I. . . ."

"But you must remember," Michael prodded. "We've talked about her."

"Oh, the one who bought all the dresses!"
Elaine recovered with a smile. "Oh, of
course."

Michael threw her a warning look.

"There were so many, honey," Elaine explained sweetly, "how am I going to—"

Michael interrupted, pointing toward the
desk. "Why don't you go and see about our
rooms?"

Casting a look of condescension at Alicia,

Elaine swung around on her beautiful tan heels and walked away.

It was Michael who broke the tense silence. "You could have told me you were leaving San Diego."

She reared back, surprised. "Told you? *When* might I have told you? I hadn't heard from you in a month."

"I called you—"

"You didn't call," she said flatly. "I was home all the time, studying for my finals. I'd have known if you called."

"But I did call," he said, and his words were definite and calm. "No one answered. The next time I called, the line had been disconnected."

She rubbed her sore hip, and thought, could that have been the one call she missed? The day she left to come home?

"It was about a month after I last saw you. I'd been out of town nearly four weeks. I called when I got back."

So it *had* been him, she thought with profound regret. How narrowly our lives are changed, diverted down strange paths.

She looked up at him, sadness so intense it brought tears to her eyes. Hoping he wouldn't notice, she asked, "Why did you call, Michael? Our relationship...well, things were over. Between us, I mean." She averted her face.

"*Were* they over?" he asked, gazing at her with his old probing look. "Yes, I suppose you must have thought so, the way I left that day. But I thought everything over, Alicia. That trip gave me time. Long before I came home I'd realized you weren't like Dixie at all.''

"You might have called from wherever you were.''

"I don't usually—''

"Yes, I know.'' Her tone was scathing. "You don't make long-distance phone calls!''

"It's a waste of money.''

"Instead you'd rather waste your whole life. Or someone else's.'' When he glowered at her silently she said, "What I don't understand is why you would take your honeymoon in the Virgin Islands. I hadn't thought you were quite that callous, Michael.''

"In the first place,'' he said, holding up an irritated finger, "since you're so sure things are over, what does it matter *where* I honeymoon? In the second place—'' a second finger raised "—I didn't have the slightest idea you'd come home. You were supposed to be going on in oceanography, remember? And in the third place—'' a third finger went up "—this isn't my honeymoon. Elaine and I aren't married.''

Relief and hope had just begun to flood over Alicia when Elaine appeared again behind Michael, dangling a room key. "Marriage isn't necessary for us,'' she said, smiling. "We have things worked out another way.'' She took Michael's arm in a proprietary grip. "I think I'll go to our cottage for a little nap, honey. I need to cool off and freshen up for dinner...." Her silky voice trailed off as she walked away again, leaving behind an agitated silence.

As they watched Elaine leave, her words, "Marriage isn't necessary for us," echoed through Alicia's mind and dashed her awakening hopes. So he'd found a mistress, she thought, a woman obviously qualified. Her clothes were expensive, her manner cool and faintly aggressive. She was beautiful in a Vogue-fashion sort of way. She was just the sort of woman Helen MacNamee had once implied he needed. She wondered if Helen had arranged it, because the two women seemed curiously alike—a matched set. They probably got along famously, she thought.

With sudden harshness, Michael grabbed Alicia's arm and gripped it as if intending to hurt her. "That was a rotten thing you did, Alicia, leaving without telling me. Giving me no notice, nothing. I thought you'd have a little more faith in us than that."

"Faith?" She laughed shrilly. "Had you given me any reason for faith? Don't be a fool, Michael. You'd said goodbye that day. It was clearer than clear. I do have a little pride...." She jerked away. "You're hurting me!"

Then, finding her anger rising, she went on, "This is where the rich men come." She waved her arm in a sweeping gesture that covered the whole resort. "This is the place where people come who don't mind spending money." She laughed, her misery mixing with unexpected brittleness. "I'm surprised you're here, Michael. It costs three hundred dollars a day! Why would you waste that kind of money when you can find a high rise somewhere and go to one of those fast-food chains for dinner? Why would you ever spend this kind of money? How did you justify this? Did you sell your Porsche or something? From here you might even have to call home. . .*long-distance*!"

The moment she finished her tirade she was aghast. She braved a look at his face and found it frozen, as cold as if he'd been cast in ice.

He was very angry. For a long moment he continued to fix her with those dark eyes, then said firmly, "Maybe I was right, after all." And he walked away.

SHE SHOULD HAVE BEEN the one who walked away first, Alicia thought miserably that night, sitting on the edge of her bed. She'd always imagined it the other way—Michael staring after *her* as she turned on her heel and departed dramatically. And now he'd already managed to walk out on her twice. She'd played it all wrong, she thought in despair. She'd acted like a fool, but she'd had no time to think anything out. She'd simply reacted—reacted in bitterness and disappointment. It was as if she'd poured a year of bottled-up emotion and unhappiness into one hideous outburst. How would she ever explain this to Michael?

Well, she wouldn't. It was too late for explanations.

She tried to sleep but couldn't. In the midst of restless tossing and endless recriminations, Alicia began to understand some of what had prompted her irrational behavior. For the first time she recognized flaws in Michael—small character defects that had little to do with Dixie.

He was too unforgiving, judging her by a strict set of principles that left out a tolerance for human foibles. He was rigid, afraid to take a chance on anyone. In spite of his sense of humor, he failed to see the flaws in his own character. And it was only because she'd had a year to grow that she at last understood what she'd only subliminally observed.

In the dark of night she laughed to herself. In some ways this past year she'd outgrown Michael!

Well, she had to come to grips with the situation now. It was important, she realized, not to let Michael know how much she'd cared for him. Otherwise she'd be vulnerable to his advances—if, indeed, there were any. But she couldn't imagine that happening when he already had Elaine. Surely Elaine was enough for any man!

Restlessly she rolled about in the tropical

heat. Kicking off the sheet covering her swelter-
ing body, she got out of bed and walked to the
screened window. She pulled the slats aside and
watched the moon glinting off the ocean.

She might never even see him again, she
thought sadly, if his stay at Pelican Point was
only for a few days. She refused to consider that
possibility. At any rate, if they met again, one
thing was clear: he would never quite dominate
Alicia Barron.

There was a tiny wall built up inside her now,
a thin bit of something kept in reserve. Whatever happened, she would hold on to that core,
and Michael MacNamee would never have quite
all of her again.

SHE WAS DOWN AT THE DOCK the next morning
filling the gas tank on the boat when David
came to find her. "Alicia, there's a new
manager at Pelican Point. I don't know much
about him—rumors are he's an old guy, and
rich. Anyway, they're having a reception for
him tonight. How about going with me?"

Alicia shook her head. "I already told you,
David, I need time to think about us and—"

He didn't wait for her to finish. "Suit yourself. Just giving you another chance at my beautiful bod." He grinned. "I'm the best thing
around, you gotta admit."

She looked at him in exasperation, then
started to laugh.

"Seriously, Alicia," he went on, "I think you should go. I mean, you'll be practically working for the guy with your scuba school and all."

Alicia hesitated. David was right. Half of her customers came from the neighboring resort and it would be best to get on the manager's good side. Besides, Michael would be there. . . .

She screwed the lid back on the gas can and jumped out of the boat. "Okay, David, you're on—I'll be ready at seven." He turned to go, then grinned over his shoulder. "I knew I was irresistible! See ya, cutie!"

Alicia spent the rest of the morning working down by the dock. By the time she finished it was too early for lunch, so she decided to go for a walk. She needed to think.

A narrow hiking trail led to the top of Cow Hill, the cap of the cliff that rose at an abrupt angle out of the ocean. Rocks cascaded down two faces, one of which became a stern sentinel guarding Honeymoon Beach. As Alicia started up, she felt the oppressive midday heat.

She climbed the hill slowly, her hip still sore from yesterday's fall. The twisted ankle seemed better, but the hip sported an extravagant purple bruise. She climbed upward. Trees bent to brush her shoulders and the lush and fragrant frangipani flowers filled the air with rich perfume. It was quiet and somewhat cooler up here; the dense vegetation overhead allowed only pinpricks of light to filter through.

Following the winding trail as it meandered upward several hundred feet, Alicia was just coming to an outcropping when she heard a soft cry.

She stopped in her tracks and waited to hear the sound again. Nothing. Only silence. She wondered if she had imagined it.

Then, as she took up her walk again, the sound came once more. It was a soft bleating this time and Alicia recognized it as the cry of one of the island's small goats. Looking around, she could see nothing. She shrugged and trudged on. Goats roamed these islands freely, some of them with curious wooden triangles around their necks. The wooden yokes prevented their escape through small fence holes on the rare occasions when they were fenced in. Meanwhile, the effect was considered quaint by tourists.

Farther along the path the soft bleating grew insistent and turned into a pitiful wail. She was sure, now, that the animal was in trouble. She broke through the dense growth and found herself near the top of the rocky point. Ahead of her the tropical seas spread their translucent blue as far as she could see.

Alicia scanned the rocky cliff for the goat but couldn't find him. She realized she was being foolish climbing out on this steep point. She shaded her eyes, searching. Another insistent cry, and she spotted him. The small, light brown animal was partway down a great rock face, its wooden yoke hooked on a tough manzanitalike shrub that protruded from a crack in the stone. The goat bucked wildly, trying to pull away from the offending branch.

Alicia had no idea how long the goat had been trapped by the branch. The tiny thing alternately struggled fiercely, then stopped to rest and cry. Alicia knew that if she left him he'd eventually die. And it wouldn't take long, she thought. All the island goats had ribs that protruded starkly under loose skin. They were left to forage for themselves and she doubted that they ever had enough to eat.

She began to climb down to the little animal, watching in dismay as his brown skin quivered with each despairing cry. All at once, the heel of her sandal caught a loose rock and she slipped, catching herself at the last second. *This is truly ridiculous,* Alicia thought. *The goat should be rescuing me!*

Slowly, slowly, with bruised thigh and skidding sandals, she made her way toward the great rock and the trapped animal. She slipped often and sometimes had to drop to her haunches and grasp at a protruding shrub. She scolded herself for her foolish heroism as she fearfully looked down past the goat to the ocean surging below.

Suddenly, Alicia skidded several feet and fell, caught herself, then sat panting. Her fall had brought her to a great rock. Uncertainly she rose again and searched for footing. The goat stopped crying and watched her approach. Her shoes found the granite treacherous as she took one precarious step after another. A few more feet, a few more shaky steps brought her face-to-face with the animal. Gently, she grabbed hold of the wooden yoke with her hands.

To her horror, just as she lifted his yoke from the branch, the goat bucked and sprang free. His sudden upward motion knocked Alicia off balance. She began falling, her hands clutching the stone, her white shorts catching on the jagged surface.

I'm going all the way down, she thought desperately, snatching at whatever bits of shrub came within reach, *I'm going to slide all the way down this mountain!* Rock, brush, sandy dirt scraped her bare skin as she slid. She reached out frantically for something—anything—to slow her descent.

At last, in the middle of a vast expanse of uninterrupted rock, her foot came to rest momentarily on a narrow protrusion, which slowed her momentum. With a surge of energy she grasped for a small handhold in the rock face, found it and finally stopped altogether.

Still in danger of sliding, she wriggled upward and secured her foot again on the tiny ledge. Then she fell back, resting against the slab. She breathed in deeply and drew a hand across her head feeling the perspiration, the residue of fear, gathered in the roots of her hair. Inside her bra, little rivulets of sweat trickled slowly, inching down between her breasts.

Cautiously she looked around, assessing her situation. She realized there was no way she could move: only her wedged foot kept her in place. She felt like a butterfly impaled on a pin; the rock was holding her prisoner. Futilely she berated herself for starting across the rocks in leather sandals. Only a fool would entrust her footing to tractionless leather.

Far below and off to the right she could see the white sand of Honeymoon Beach, deserted as always. She considered her position. Another fall would send her the final distance to the sea, her body battered senseless long before she reached the water. She could only stay as still as possible and conserve her strength.

When would she be missed, she wondered. Perhaps Lily and Bill would begin looking for her in late afternoon, but that was still hours away. *I must hold on for three or four hours,* she told herself, *at least.* She wondered how long her leg muscles would hold up.

Time passed slowly. After a while, gazing helplessly at the great expanse of blue sky, she began thinking her predicament untenable. Her leg was tiring; she longed desperately to move it. What if she tried crawling away on her hands and knees, she thought. She felt the rock, tested the grip of her hands on the stone, but it was hopeless. Her leg would simply have to sustain her; there was no other escape.

Just as resignation settled over her she thought she heard her name called.

She listened. It came again.

"Alicia!" A man's voice.

In disbelief, she knew someone was on the way. Was she dreaming, or had three hours already passed?

Like the fury of thunder, her name was shouted again. "Alicia!" And this time she recognized the voice.

It was Michael!

Alicia clung to her rock and willed herself to stay calm.

She thought his voice was coming from somewhere below, and she shouted a relieved "Here!" in the general direction of the call, projecting her voice as far as she could.

Then she lay back, resting.

She couldn't have guessed how much time elapsed. Between his periodic cries of her name and her answering "Here! I'm up here!" her mind was occupied more with confused thoughts than the mere passage of minutes.

That Michael should be the one to rescue her was only an ironic twist of circumstance. It could never make any difference to either of them. Yet she found herself longing to see him, aching for these few minutes they'd spend together, as if in this short time she'd find the end to all her yearning. Even as she dared hope, an answering voice told her sternly to stop torturing herself over this man. It was useless; he was already committed elsewhere.

Alicia reached down and massaged her leg. Oh, how it ached. Still, she dared not move it.

Yearning rose in her again and she faced the truth. She *did* want to see Michael, wanted to see him desperately.

Alicia, her inner voice warned, *don't do this, don't do this to yourself.*

Then she saw him.

He'd come up another part of the hill, so she hadn't noticed his ascent. She saw him struggle with the slope. She wondered how he could navigate the hill at all, except that she could see, finally, that he wore tennis shoes.

At last he reached the rock where she lay. He climbed above it, looking down at her. He was panting, and the sweat rolled off the sides of his jaw. His beige shirt, completely soaked, clung to his chest. His hands were on his hips, and he stood with his legs apart, the corduroy shorts tight against his thighs. For a moment he simply looked at her without speaking, trying to catch his breath.

He leaned toward her, his leg muscles taut. "Take my hand, then slip off your sandals. Careful!" he said as she slid a little. He held her firmly while she removed first one shoe, then the other.

Slowly his powerful legs pushing against the rock, Michael pulled Alicia toward him, his hand gripping hers so strongly she felt she was in a vise. At last they stood together, precariously balanced on the rock. Alicia refused to look sideways down the mountain.

As she twisted to gaze up at him she quickly realized he was not only terribly out of breath but angry. His dark eyes seemed full of internal fire.

He took a deep breath. "What in the name of God were you doing up here? I couldn't believe my eyes when I looked up and saw some damn fool on this cliff."

"A goat was trapped," she said quietly.

"A goat?" Incredulous, he frowned, his anger dissipating. "A goat? Am I hearing you right?"

"The little thing...he was caught on a branch and he would have died. *Somebody* had to help him."

He shook his head. "You'd risk your life for a goat?"

"I didn't know I was risking my life. When you're trying to help...you don't stop to think—"

"No, it's obvious you didn't. Well—" his expression softened "—I hope the goat remembers you in its will."

In spite of herself she laughed. The same old Michael.

"Stand still. Let me think."

He didn't release her hand, though, and just touching him like this reawakened old responses. She felt herself overwhelmed once again by Michael's pervasive, compelling magnetism. She should never have allowed this; it was fatal. But what was she to do? Refuse his rescue? No, she would just have to keep her feelings in control.

He turned to her. "Hook your fingers around my belt." When she hesitated, he said, "Come on, Alicia. I'm not that much in love with this rock."

Her hand gripped his belt and she followed him, step after cautious step. He proceeded carefully, guiding her across the rocky slab, then down, over boulders, loose dirt and grassy stubble.

As they put the upper cliff behind them the available footholds were often too narrow for both his feet; with powerful leg muscles and pure will he held firm in places where another might have faltered. Once he caught her as she stumbled, holding them both for a precarious moment.

Concentrating on the descent, Michael didn't speak except for a few brief cautionary remarks—"Alicia, hold on here! It's slippery...easy now, easy now..." —until at last they reached a short drop-off, the last obstacle to the small beach she'd seen from above.

Michael jumped down first and turned to help Alicia. He reached for her and she sprang into his arms. She expected he'd release her, but he didn't. He held her close to him, so close she could feel the exertion-driven thumping of his heart against her flesh. For a moment they stood thus, and Alicia had the sensation that all life had stopped, that everything possible had ceased functioning while she was cloistered in Michael's arms. She had waited for this so long!

She willed the moment to last forever, savoring his embrace. But he dropped his arms and reality broke in on her.

She took a deep breath and looked around.

She'd been to this beach before, though not for years. White sand stretched from one jut of land to the other, so the beach was accessible only by water. Or by some goatlike approach such as theirs, she thought wryly.

Just then she spotted a powerboat wedged into the sand above the waterline. Michael must have been out exploring. "You came by boat?" she asked.

"The first time, yes," he smiled. "It's the preferred route." He glanced at the towering cliff behind them. "I'm not into overland trips, as it turns out."

She laughed. "Michael, you're a nut."

"Really? I thought I was a lover."

A warning flashed in her head. "You were— once." Then, lest he get the wrong idea, she explained, "This is called Honeymoon Beach. You and Elaine can come here later."

"Maybe we will," he replied.

Suddenly his mouth tightened. He took her by the arms and spun her around. "What makes you think I'm not still a lover?" The words were almost harsh.

"Michael—ouch!" For the second time in two days she jerked away from him.

But instead of relinquishing her, he renewed his grip, pulling her toward him. His eyes sought hers. "You owe me for this afternoon."

"Owe you what?" she asked.

"Just this," he said, and enfolded her in his arms.

He kissed her as though he'd waited years for this. He couldn't get enough of her, it seemed— nor she of him.

All her defenses, her restraints crumbled, and she felt herself swept away on a crest of joy.

Fiercely, Michael's lips moved over hers, the craving so intense that Alicia could only melt against him. Again and again his mouth bore down on hers, devouring her, and when his lips were finished there they sought other places— her neck, the palm of her hand, and finally her breasts. How tenderly he lifted her shirt, slipped his hand beneath the bra and pushed it aside. He bent his head, and his moist lips caressed the sensitive nipples.

She cradled him against her shoulder, stroking his hair.

She found herself yielding to him with all the unspent passion of the past year, all the yearning she'd felt expressing itself in her hands and then her kisses.

He pulled back once to look at her, said huskily, "Alicia!" in a way that made her want to cry.

He still cares for me, she thought wondrously. *He does, he does. He's missed me as I've missed him. Oh, I could live without food, without sleep, without anything else, just for the eternity of his arms.*

She never knew what made her pull away finally, though she guessed it was a mental image of Elaine. Or perhaps it was the small bit she was keeping for herself, that core she'd promised never to yield—not until he truly loved her and was willing to commit himself to her. Until then that part of her must be protected.

She drew back reluctantly. "I'm sorry, Michael, I can't do this. Please don't hate me. You belong to Elaine."

He stared at her. "What's she got to do with this? What brought her up?"

"It isn't just her."

"Then what?"

She shook her head. She couldn't demand that he love her, so what was there to tell him? The self she was protecting had its own need for anonymity.

She said finally, "Don't press me. When you really want to know, you will. You'll have to figure it out for yourself, Michael."

"Oh, I've already figured it out." He spat out the words, and Alicia flinched at their harshness. "I've figured out plenty—that you're saving yourself for a guy with a bunch of promises." He ran long fingers through his hair and turned away from her, staring out at the ocean. "Well, don't expect that from me—you're not going to get it. Not you or anyone. You can take what I'm offering, and if it's not enough—"

"It's not enough, Michael..." Alicia pronounced firmly. She felt tempted to add, *it would never be enough without love,* but pride kept her from blurting it out. She turned away from him, her face ashen and pained.

Suddenly he wheeled toward her, eyeing her with a cold fury. "It's enough for me and I know it's what you want, too. I'm not blind, deaf and dumb. I can feel, Alicia. I can feel you wanting me."

She shook her head. Her mind registered his words but refused to absorb their meaning. *Not like this,* she said to herself. *Not like this.*

His eyes began their slow descent down the column of her neck and the slope and curve of her breasts. She felt as if he were undressing her. But his scrutiny was clinical; she felt cold under his gaze.

She wrapped her arms around her body protectively. "I don't think you know me at all, Michael. Not at all."

Slowly he approached her, pulling her to him and pressing his mouth hotly to hers. His grip on her was strong and she could feel him overpowering her. She sensed how effortlessly she could melt beneath his powerful embrace, but she knew for her own sanity she would have to resist him. Calling on both her mental and physical reserves of strength, she pushed him away. He stumbled backward, momentarily shaken. As he came near her again, she retreated.

"You don't have to be afraid of me, Alicia—I just want you so much," he explained softly. He paused and reached out to stroke her hair. "When you're ready, Alicia, when you're ready to come to me you will. I won't force you anymore. Sometime when you can't help yourself any longer you'll come to me. You'll be transported beyond your wildest imaginings. You'll see, Alicia." He sat back smiling, his gaze warm and tender.

"Take me home," she said, but his words had already done more to arouse her than he could have dreamed. She knew instinctively that everything he said was true.

"Please, Michael. Take me back to Pelican Point." Let him think she lived there. What difference did it make? She began to walk toward the small boat, knowing he'd follow.

She unwound the rope from a post driven into the sand for that purpose, holding it out to him. "I'm ready, Michael."

Without expression, Michael took the rope from her hand. "Get in!" he said, and pushed the boat into the water. Seconds later he climbed in after her, but he didn't sit on the same seat; he treated her as if he was the captain and she a paying customer.

Gradually the motor picked up speed, propelling them violently over the water. The bow, where Alicia was sitting, leaped up, then slapped back down on the water, nearly throwing her out of the boat. Over and over it rose, only to come crashing back against the swells with a hard thump. Up, down, *bang,* the pattern repeated itself. She held on to the side, watching Michael surreptitiously as he guided the boat over the vast water. His jaw was set into the wind, his hair blowing ragged across his face. He was utterly, darkly masculine.

The wind buffeted the back of her neck and washed over her arms, cooling and soothing her.

Expertly Michael guided the boat, veering once to avoid the wake of a much larger vessel, then changing his heading again toward Pelican Point. If he had wanted to speak to her, it would have been nearly impossible. The confused cacophony of wind, slapping water and pulsing engine drowned out all other sounds. She understood that he wouldn't try. Yet she found it almost unbearable that he wouldn't look at her, either.

He does this well, Alicia thought. *He does everything well. God, I could ride with him on and on to a distant shore and let him make love to me as beautifully as he guides this boat.* Had she been a fool, she asked herself. Maybe she should have given in back on Honeymoon Beach. But she knew she had been right. The physical part wasn't enough. She wanted him forever, not for a few moments on a lonely beach. She had to know that he loved her. She had to know that it was something more than a Saturday-night love—that it was a Monday-morning love, too.

But would it ever happen? She shook her head against the fierce wind, felt its coolness washing over her face. *I don't know,* she thought. *I just don't know.*

CHAPTER SIX

ALICIA DRESSED CAREFULLY that evening, knowing she was dressing for Michael but pretending to herself she wasn't.

She'd found a new shipment in their small gift shop, and in it was a halter dress of pale green crepe de chine. When she put it on, she saw with satisfaction that the soft green material clung to her hips smoothly and swirled in a graceful flare at her knees. The top crossed her breasts in easy folds and tied behind her neck. The dress was simple and elegant, unadorned except for a narrow silver belt.

Alicia put on very high heels, silver pumps with thin straps across her tiny ankles.

With a discriminating eye, she stared into the mirror. Her thick and wavy hair framed her face as it always did—the waves swept away from her small ears into gentle upturned strands at the side of her head.

She smoothed a bit of blush onto her cheeks, then added a touch of peach lipstick to her full lips. Her eyes, darkened slightly by long lashes, needed no additional makeup.

She took a final look in the mirror and tried to imagine how Michael would see her. Then she frowned. Why did she imagine anything had changed since the afternoon? They had parted on a strained note, and no doubt the awkwardness would continue. Would he even be there, she wondered. Shrugging, she went out to join her family. As she came into the living room Aunt Lily said, "Oh, my! You look lovely, dear! Really lovely!"

Uncle Bill grinned at her, a rare smile illuminating creased cheeks. "Pretty good, Alicia. Hope David knows what he's got!"

Alicia threw a quick look at Aunt Lily. Lily knew Michael was on the island, but she had promised to say nothing to the others. Lily's answering glance was an affirmation of her promise to keep her niece's secret.

Alicia sat down on a rattan chair, waiting for David. Just then her eye fell on a letter. Brandon.

Aunt Lily followed her glance. "He's doing better in Dallas, Alicia—much better." She reached for the letter and opened it. "Let me read you this. He says, 'I've got something big in the offing, which I can't tell you about yet. It's a make-me or break-me deal, but if it comes out right it'll be big. Really big.'"

Alicia asked, "What did he mean, 'break me'?"

Bill shrugged. "Brandon makes a big mystery

out of things. Always the big deal... even things that never work out.''

Lily smiled. ''That's how salesmen are.''

''When's he coming home?'' Alicia asked.

Before anyone could answer, the door burst open and David bounced into the room. ''Ready, Alicia?'' She stood up and he grinned, his eyes wide. ''Wow! *Magnifico*!''

Twirling, she spun around to be viewed from all angles. ''Do you like this, David?''

''Oh, yes, ma'am. I didn't know I rated quite this high. But I never ask questions. Take what you can get, David, and enjoy!''

Alicia felt the twinges of remorse. Poor David, she thought. How could she tell him that there was no longer any hope, not since she had seen Michael again? But she smiled at David and took his arm, telling him how handsome he looked in his cocoa-brown sport coat.

''Have fun,'' said Lily, and Alicia thought she detected more than the obvious in her aunt's simple statement.

As they walked toward Pelican Point David said, ''You'll like the new manager. I met him, Alicia, and he's not an old codger, after all. He's young, and he has ideas. He wants to make this place grow....''

Alicia only half heard what he said. Pelican Point had had a succession of managers since she'd been home, and none of them had changed anything. Resort managers came and went with astonishing regularity, but the resort stayed the same.

"This new guy may even want to enlarge in your direction," David continued. "Seahawk Cove has that terrific bay. I'm sure he's got his eye on it."

She shivered thinking how Bill would take such an idea. But David was talking nonsense. Owners were the ones who made policy and talked expansion, not managers. But why argue with him?

They had left the main road now and turned into the side road leading to Pelican Point. "I suppose it would be best for Bill if he sold," Alicia said. "Aunt Lily's been working on him, pushing Arizona. But I swear, David, he'll never budge...." She stopped walking to face him. "How do you convince an old man he's wrong?"

David shrugged. When he didn't answer, she resumed walking.

"He's stubborn, that Bill. God, he's stubborn."

Still David said nothing. She realized he was already thinking about something else.

"There's the band," he said suddenly. "Reggae tonight." Sounds of a steel band came to them through the trees—delicate, tinkling music. Alicia felt David walking faster. "Come on, we gotta make the reception before the new manager's all talked out." He now walked so fast she was half running to keep up.

"I don't need to meet him *this* badly," she laughed.

They came to the Pelican Point terrace, an extension of the dining room that looked down over the bay. Candles glowed softly on tables in the open-air room, and in front of them lighted palms were a backdrop for the steel band. Alicia could smell the sweet scent of blossoms from the Jerusalem-thorn trees.

For a moment she and David stood watching the band—five men were beating sticks against large red-painted oil drums of various sizes. On these instruments the five tapped out music that was melodic and rhythmic. The sound had a haunting, almost hollow quality that she suspected could not be easily duplicated.

These men had grown up with steel drums. Alicia had seen them playing here for as long as she could remember. She marveled at their technique. They never looked where they tapped, but knew by memory which area on the drum's surface produced which note. And they never looked at one another, either, though each man was in perfect synchrony with his fellows. The music seemed to go on indefinitely. How they all knew when to stop was a mystery to Alicia.

Tonight, as always, the air was balmy. A soft breeze that was neither too warm nor too cold brushed Alicia's bare shoulders. Weather would be just as pleasant here in June as in December.

She looked past the band to the ocean beyond. Moonlight frosted the placid bay; only the slightest ripples on the surface revealed this was part of a vast living ocean instead of a cleverly executed painting. She searched the dining room for Michael but didn't see him.

David seemed to feel the beauty of the scene and squeezed her waist lightly. Alicia leaned toward him for a moment and touched his shoulder with her head.

He whispered, "Let's get down there," and brushed her hair with his lips.

She started and shivered.

With his hand on her waist, David guided Alicia down the wide stone steps to the beach below, where the manager's reception was held.

Tall flaming torches lodged in the sand lighted the beach. A short distance away Alicia could see a circular wooden table built around a tall palm. On it, generous platters of hors d'oeuvres were spread out.

The reception line moved slowly and Alicia became impatient. Politeness dictated that each person say a few words to the new manager and his wife and to the woman who was head of reservations. With shuffling feet, the people ahead of her inched forward. The reception line became visible.

For the first time Alicia felt curiosity about the new manager. Wondering what he looked like, she sought out his face in the shadowed light. Suddenly she drew in a quick startled breath.

Standing calmly at the head of the line was Michael!

Involuntarily Alicia drew back, drawing closer to David.

Not Michael, she thought. It couldn't be. Why hadn't he. . .?

Michael was watching her.

Flustered, she saw that his smile was disarmingly casual. He was amused by her surprise.

She drew herself together. She didn't like Michael laughing at her.

As she waited her turn to shake his hand, a mental signboard flashed urgent questions. Why wasn't he still working in Hawaii? What made him sign on here as manager?

Then she was standing in front of him, staring into the face of a stranger, his smile enigmatic, his manner curiously detached. He offered her his hand. "I'm Michael MacNamee. Nice to have you with us tonight."

"Alicia Barron," she said, keeping her voice casual. "Thank you, I'm glad to be here. Good luck in your new job, Mr. MacNamee."

"Job?" His eyebrows went up.

"As manager of Pelican Point."

He smiled. "I'm afraid you have it wrong, Miss Barron. The manager hasn't changed. I'm the new owner."

"Owner?" she gasped, incredulous. Michael was the owner? Of Pelican Point? The idea was so shocking that for an instant she felt weak.

The second surprise of the evening almost overcame her. "Oh," she said falteringly. And when that didn't seem enough she fumbled out, "Well, good luck in that, too."

Behind her she heard David mutter, "Guess I got it wrong."

She gave Michael a small dismissing nod and moved on to shake hands with the woman who was head of reservations at the hotel. Laughing, the woman leaned toward Alicia confidentially. "What was all that stuff, Alicia? Didn't you know he was the new owner?"

"No." Alicia shook her head. "Nobody told us this place was for sale."

The lady took her aside momentarily. "It's been very quick and very hushed up. The prior owners didn't want a lot of publicity. And neither did Mr. MacNamee."

"Well, it's certainly been a secret—even my aunt and uncle don't know." She nodded quickly in Michael's direction. "What's he like?"

"Nice. Decent. You'll like him."

She moved on. So Michael was the owner of Pelican Point, she thought, trying to absorb the news. He was committed here, then. She could see that their destinies might be interwoven for some time to come. The realization gave her pleasure—but a pleasure mixed with pain.

Elaine would be here, too.

Then a new thought came to her. Was Pelican Point about to become a Caribbean version of

Hawaii? Was Michael planning high rises and fast-food restaurants and all the other unpleasant aspects of a densely packed resort? She turned around to stare at him and felt herself frowning. A man with his philosophy could ruin this place for all time. He could turn it into all the things she hated. Watching him smile at each guest in turn she felt he was deceiving them all, about to ravage what they'd come here to find. And all in the name of profit. Even as she watched him she found her feelings toward him changing. It was one thing for him to destroy places she'd never been; it was something else to come here and desecrate her home.

Turning she found David at her elbow. "Why didn't you tell him you lived at Seahawk Cove?" he asked. "You acted like a ding-bat guest."

"He wouldn't care about that."

"Sure he would. You gotta let him know you're part of the organization. You gotta start buttering him up. He's bread and butter for you, Alicia. C'mon—" he pulled at her "—the line's gone. I'm gonna tell him who you are."

"No, David. I can tell him later."

"Don't be a fool. The sooner he knows the better. And you look gorgeous tonight. Now's the time to tell him."

"David!" She gave him a warning look.

But he ignored it, and she found herself in front of Michael once more.

"Alicia didn't get a chance to tell you, Mr. MacNamee," David began, "her family owns a resort here. It's one of the oldest resorts on the island." A jerk of his head indicated the direction of Seahawk Cove. "She also helps run the scuba school—where we send our guests."

To Alicia's satisfaction, Michael's eyes shot open in surprise. He started to comment, then apparently thought better of it. Instead he murmured a distant, "Is that so?" as though the subject were only mildly interesting.

Alicia became extravagantly gracious and played along with him. "Yes," she said. "We've been here a long time. Do come and see our little resort—it's lovely." And without waiting to see his reaction, she headed toward the hors d'oeuvres. Had she looked back, she would have seen Michael staring after her.

Alicia tried a cracker-and-cucumber tidbit, then gravitated to the shrimp.

A male guest, a sandy-haired portly man, had arrived before her. He turned toward her appreciatively. "Can't beat this food," he enthused, dipping a shrimp in cocktail sauce. Then he took another. And after that a third and a fourth. With his mouth full he asked, "Is it always this good?"

Alicia nodded, intrigued by his blatant gluttony. "Around here shrimp is just for starters. The rest gets better."

"Really? Boy, I can't believe this resort has

existed all these years and I didn't know about it.'' He cleaned his fingers with a red paper napkin, but the shrimp lured him back. ''You've obviously been here before,'' he mumbled through another large mouthful.

Alicia hesitated. ''Yes,'' she said finally. ''Many times.''

''Lucky you.'' Looking at her curiously he asked, ''Rich husband or rich boyfriend?''

Before she could answer, David was beside her with two drinks. ''Rich tennis pro,'' she grinned wickedly, and led David away, leaving the man to wonder what she meant.

''Who was that klutz at the food table?'' David asked, ''The one pigging out on shrimp?''

''A guest. A very friendly guest.''

''You do attract 'em, don't you? I noticed Mr. MacNamee—'' He stopped suddenly. Michael was coming up behind them, talking to someone about tennis.

''David, will you explain your lessons to this lady? I know you're part of the tennis program.'' They turned to find an athletic-looking woman in her forties trailing Michael. ''I was trying to explain the rating system, but I got in over my depth.'' He laughed pleasantly, nodding at Alicia. ''Maybe your friend—Miss Barron—would tell me more about her scuba school.'' His eyes, focused intently on her, were at odds with his casual words.

"Now?" she started to object. "We have brochures. . . ." David shot her a warning look.

"Surely you can spare a few minutes, Miss Barron." Michael's hand was already on her elbow, steering her toward the beach.

They walked down by the ocean, where the water came up and soaked the sand. Alicia took her shoes off. Barefoot, she held her shoes in one hand and tucked the other under Michael's arm. He gripped her hand tightly.

"You look lovely, Alicia." He turned to study her face, touching her cheek gently. "Beautiful," he murmured. They strolled along the quiet beach. "There's a lot we don't know about each other," he said after a while. "We both got surprises tonight." When she didn't answer he went on, "I looked for you on the employee roster. I thought maybe you worked here. This explains why I never found your name. You never have worked here, have you?"

"No." She shrugged and smiled. "But I'm over at Pelican Point a lot—for various things. Half our students are from here, of course. And sometimes our family comes for dinner." She changed the subject. "When did you buy Pelican Point, Michael?"

"I've been negotiating for it almost six months."

"But you never came here—"

"I did, once. Two months ago. I only stayed

two days. Lord, Alicia, I wish I'd known you were here. It would have—"

"It would have what?"

"Made a difference, I suppose. I've been wondering about you so long. Ever since you left."

"You have, Michael?" Hope rose in her. "What were you thinking?"

"That I'd left us adrift, the two of us—that everything was unresolved between us. We'd only begun to know each other. And now it was too late. I hated seeing the relationship struck down just as it was starting. I was restless. I needed to finish that last argument." He smiled. "It wasn't an argument, was it? You must have seen it as a tirade. I had it in mind to apologize, but you can't apologize to an empty phone—to a recording."

"I made some mistakes, too."

"You knew they were mistakes?"

"Doesn't one always know? Of course I knew. But they were only mistakes, Michael. They weren't me."

They walked on in silence. After a while he asked, "Do you like teaching, Alicia?"

Her eyes lit up with enthusiasm. "Oh, I do. I love it!" She turned to face him. "I like introducing others to things I care about." She paused, thinking. "Here, where the water's warm, the world under the surface is beautiful. Full of things that astound you. Just today I saw a school of tiny fish, all a vivid shade of bright yellow with dark blue edges. They were miniature, no bigger than a thumbnail. I swam among them and I was tempted to take one home in my pocket—'' She stopped. "Am I boring you, Michael?"

"No. Never, Alicia. And look—I don't know how to say it, but I'm sorry. About this afternoon. I got a little carried away. It was stupid of me."

She stiffened slightly. "It's okay." She was hoping he'd say more but he didn't.

They walked along the beach quietly, listening to the peaceful wash of the wavelets as they licked the shore, smelling the odors of blossoms that drifted to them on the balmy air. After a while, Alicia felt utter contentment. Just being close to Michael, feeling his arm around her waist and sensing the strength of his physical body next to hers, was a joy she wished would continue forever. Beside him she felt protected and cared for. She had never felt this with any other man.

"So you came back to your scuba school, Alicia?" Michael asked.

"Not mine. My aunt's and uncle's. It's part of their resort."

"What's the resort called?"

"Seahawk Cove."

For a moment he seemed unbelieving. "You're kidding, Alicia! Seahawk Cove?" He stopped walking and turned to her. "That's right next door! It belongs to your family?"

"Since I was a little girl. Why, Michael? What's so strange?"

He shrugged, passing it off. "Odd you'd turn up being part of a place I've heard of as far away as San Diego...." He drew her away from a lapping wavelet. "That bay's famous, supposed to be owned by a—" He stopped, embarrassed.

"Go on, Michael. You might as well say it."

He smiled at her. "Well, I never learned his real name because everyone called him Old Seahawk. He has a reputation in the industry. They say he's impervious to money, doesn't care how much is offered; he won't even talk about selling. He's also been called stubborn and eccentric. Or worse. Sometimes his sanity is called into question."

Alicia laughed. "That's my uncle. Wait till you meet him. I'll have to admit he's stubborn. Not insane, though. It has more to do with his loving the place and not wanting to see it ruined. I'm afraid you'll find me just as single-minded. And my feelings extend to the whole island— maybe the whole Caribbean. You may think me a little strange, too."

She glanced sideways when he didn't answer and saw his face had hardened slightly. When he said, "Look at the moon, Alicia," she knew it was an effort to change the subject. She wondered at the rest of his thoughts, convinced that he'd told her only a fraction of what he was thinking. The rest of it lay like a forbidding shadow between them.

They had reached the end of the cove now and could wander no farther. The rocky steepness of the land cut them off like a wall. Without comment, Michael sat on a rock and pulled her down beside him. He took her hand, holding it in both of his. In warm silence they gazed at the moon-sprinkled water.

After a while he asked, half-serious, "Alicia, if I promise to keep my raging lust under control, will you show me the Crawl at Spring Bay tomorrow?"

She turned to him. "It's rather a private place, Michael. Won't your girl friend mind?"

"My girl friend?" He paused, as though giving it great consideration, then laughed, his voice deep and pleasant in the darkness. "You must mean my *bride*—Elaine! Funny how that lady keeps popping up everywhere we go. Back in San Diego I never noticed her incredible omnipresence. Tell you what I'm going to do. I'm going to run right home and ask Elaine if I can go."

She kept silent.

He paused. "Didn't I ever tell you she's my stepsister, honey child?"

"Your stepsister?" Her eyes widened in surprise.

"When my dad married Helen, Elaine came with the territory. She wasn't around much at first. Her mother obviously hoped the two generations would start a tradition."

Alicia nodded grimly. So *that* was why Helen had tried to run her off. She might have guessed....

"Actually," Michael went on, "the two ladies are rather alike...except Elaine is much more to my liking."

Alicia nodded. They were alike, she thought. No wonder Elaine reminded her so instantly of Helen. They were a matched pair, just as she'd guessed.

"If you're wondering what she's doing here, she's acting as my hostess. She has the right social touch, always exactly as charming as she needs to be. We understand each other. And she's not interested in marriage, so we get along fine in that department, too." He rubbed the back of his neck thoughtfully. "I can't say she's unappealing, either. You saw her...she does have her charms." He laughed. "Let's leave it at that, okay?"

But Alicia couldn't let it drop. "For that kind of relationship she's awfully...possessive."

"Sure she is. Why wouldn't she be? She likes things just the way they are. Frankly, Alicia, you make her nervous—you and anybody else I show an interest in."

That wasn't what Alicia wanted to hear—that

she was just another of the many women who'd appealed to Michael. But pride silenced her budding protest at being lumped with the girls in the chorus.

A voice came to them from the distance, breaking into her gloomy thoughts. "Alicia!" It was David. They stood up and started back.

When David reached them, Alicia and Michael had pulled apart and were walking silently again. "Alicia, they're already serving dinner," David said. "Oh, and Mr. MacNamee, the lady you came with...she's been looking for you."

"Elaine...yes, I suppose she would wonder where I'd gone."

Unhurriedly they strolled back to the dining room. The members of the steel band were taking their places again behind their drums.

From a table in the dining room a tall dark-haired beauty stood up and came toward them. It was the first time Alicia had seen Elaine since the day they arrived. She was dressed elegantly in a clinging wraparound dress of dusty rose with a plunging neckline and a provocative slit up the side.

"Michael," Elaine said coolly, ignoring the others, "where have you been? The reception's over: I've been waiting for dinner. I'm hungry."

He smiled soothingly. "There were other matters to see to, Elaine." He gestured casually.

"This is David Lindy, our tennis pro, and Alicia Barron—"

A hint of malice flickered across Elaine's face. "I know her. I believe the last time I saw her she was on the floor, sliding across the terrazzo. You *are* that same person?" Her words, a forced attempt at congeniality, fell flat. Her smile was frosty. She looked merely nasty.

David turned toward Alicia, puzzled.

An angry flush crept over Alicia's cheeks as she replied, "How nice of you to remember, Elaine."

Michael broke in quickly. "How about the two of you joining us for dinner?"

As Alicia opened her mouth to refuse, David said eagerly, "Great idea! Right, 'Lish?" He draped his arm possessively over her shoulder.

Alicia was convinced dinner for the four of them was a terrible idea. Then, glancing from Michael to Elaine, she quickly changed her mind. Elaine's eyes had grown hard and cold at Michael's suggestion of dinner, and now Michael seemed disturbed as he stared at David's arm across Alicia's shoulders. Perhaps this dinner would serve a useful purpose after all, Alicia thought. Here was her chance to show Michael she didn't need him. Quietly she said, "Thanks, Mr. MacNamee, we'd love to."

David sat down next to Alicia and put his hand on her knee. "Happy, Alicia?"

"Sure," she said, and smiled into his eyes.

When she looked back across the table, Michael's face was deep in the menu.

The dinner proceeded as Alicia had hoped, the four acting out their roles predictably. The more David showed his attentiveness to Alicia, the more Michael withdrew.

Well, what did she owe him, Alicia asked herself. He didn't have a claim on her.

Elaine, sitting across the table from David, appeared bored. Dessert came and she stirred, leaning across the table and smiling engagingly at David. "Dance with me, David?"

David's face lit up with interest.

The minute they were out of earshot, Michael turned to say, "I don't like games, Alicia."

"I'm not sure what you mean."

"You're not? You've been acting the fool, buttering up to that tennis pro. What's with you two?"

Alicia gazed back at him. "David and I are friends," she replied simply. "I'm not sure you have any cause to complain."

"The way you're carrying on with him is ludicrous."

"Oh?" Her eyebrows went up. "I wouldn't call our friendship 'carrying on' or 'ludicrous.' I don't even know what you're referring to. Why don't you tell me what you mean?"

"If you don't understand, I can't explain."

"I'm sorry, Michael." She continued to regard him coolly. "I see nothing wrong with my behavior." She turned to watch David and Elaine dancing cheek to cheek. "If you ask me, Elaine's the one making a play. Look at her—she's burrowed into David's arms like a tunneling mole."

"That's just Elaine's way. That's what she always does."

"Well, I'm the one who should be jealous. She looks like she's trying to make David forget me for all time."

"Don't worry. Next time she'll be snuggling up to someone else."

"Does it with you, too, huh?"

"On occasion. Elaine likes men."

"Yes," Alicia frowned, "I can see."

"In her insincere way, though, she's sincere," Michael explained. "She'll do anything for me, and I appreciate that."

"Including fight for you tooth and nail?"

"On occasion." He leaned across the table and took her hand, his mood warm again. "Did I tell you you look beautiful tonight?"

"Yes." She smiled. "But feel free to say it again."

"You are, Alicia. I suppose it just galls me to see another guy—any guy—with his arm on your shoulder."

Then make me a promise, she wanted to beg him. *Ask me for a promise—and I'm yours. But until you do . . . don't expect me to wait around.*

As soon as Elaine and David returned to the

table, Alicia stood up. "My first scuba lesson's early tomorrow, people. I have to get home."

As she and David started to walk away, Michael called after her, "Don't forget—you're going to show me the Crawl tomorrow."

She hesitated, all at once not sure she wanted to go off with him. What was the point in this when Michael seemed so casual about dangling Elaine before her eyes, the immutable barrier to his ever making a commitment? Always another woman coming between them, she thought half-bitterly. First Dixie, now Elaine.

"No, Michael," she began, but her eye fell on Elaine. There was pure hatred on the other woman's face. The deep red lips had hardened into an ugly line. Her eyes flashed. She was jealous, pure and simple.

In that moment Alicia changed her mind. "Sure, Mr. MacNamee," she said lightly. "I can't wait. You'll see the Crawl—and a lot more!" Her smile was sly and deliberately sensuous. The two men laughed appreciatively.

Elaine stood hard as a stone.

On their way back toward Seahawk Cove, David asked, "What was all that between you and Elaine? Sounds like you've been enemies for years. Didn't she just get here yesterday—with Mr. MacNamee?"

Wildly, Alicia tried to think of something reasonable to tell him, but nothing came to her. She didn't want to tell him the truth—at least, not yet—and anything else would sound impossibly farfetched. The silence dragged and became uncomfortable. And then a novel idea struck Alicia. She didn't have to answer every question. Let David think whatever he liked. Lightly she said, "Elaine and I were enemies in another lifetime." She laughed, and to her relief David let it pass.

They turned onto the main road, and David took her hand. As they walked along in the warm night, Alicia listened with half an ear to David's comments on her success with the charming Mr. MacNamee and how he might be the best thing that had ever happened to this resort. Then her attention sharpened because a querulous note had entered David's voice. "'Course you might have overdone it."

"You think I did, David?" she asked lightly.

"I don't know." He backed off a little. "For a moment I coulda sworn you two...something about the way he looked at you...but it's probably because you're so darn pretty. I've always thought so." In the shadowy tropical night she could feel his eyes on her. "And say, Alicia...you've never given me an answer."

"I'm not ready with an answer, David. I still need time. All I can say is I'm fond of you, I really am. You're decent, good-looking...." Her words trailed away as she tried to think of an honest way to reassure him. Why wasn't she ready to give him up, she asked herself, when she knew she could never pretend a love she didn't feel?

They rounded a corner, nearly back to Seahawk Cove.

At her front door he held back, staring at her longingly. Then he put his hands on her shoulders. "It's been sweet, Alicia—short but sweet. You can be so charming when you want to be. How's about a little charm for me, huh?" He leaned toward her, grasping her shoulders eagerly. "A little charm for the tennis pro?"

With a quick motion she gave him a dispassionate kiss on the lips, then slid out from under his arm. "David—thanks!" She blew him a second kiss as she reached for the doorknob.

"Geez!" He stood looking after her, his disappointment gathering in a frown. "Hot and cold. I'll bet that dark one back there—" he inclined his head toward Pelican Point "—is a real volcano compared to you. I saw fire in her eyes. Maybe I'll cultivate her."

If he had been trying to make Alicia jealous, he succeeded in arousing only the slightest twinge. To be really jealous she would have to care for him a lot more than she did. But in deference to his feelings she said quietly, "Don't chase her too hard, okay? Good night, David."

CHAPTER SEVEN

THE NEXT MORNING the sky was its usual intense blue, but massed clouds hung over the sea in the distance, marking like an arrow from the sky the location of a neighboring island.

With a sense of anticipation Alicia raced through the scuba lesson she was giving to a young honeymooning couple, then ran back to her house, arriving out of breath as Michael pulled up in one of the Pelican Point jeeps. The resort's distinctive logo was painted on the side—a pelican in a steep head-down dive. It was appropriate, she thought. She'd spent hours herself, watching the local pelicans making their dramatic fish-seeking dives into the ocean. It was always with a sense of awe that she observed the bird's graceful flying motion suddenly change to a swift perpendicular dive, the bird breaking through the surface like a thundering stone. How that heavy-billed creature attained such fierce sudden momentum was beyond her. But the pelican was a successful fisherman: he seldom came up empty.

Michael jumped out of the jeep. He was

dressed in navy blue swimming shorts and a navy-and-green-striped cotton shirt, quite unlike the formal suit and tie of the previous evening. "Hi, Alicia," he smiled. "Ready?"

"Come in and meet my aunt and uncle," she said. She held the door open for him, and Michael ducked under her arm into the small living room. Alicia looked at him in wonder. He seemed to fill the room.

Bill stood up immediately, his twisted back allowing him to attain his full height only by degrees. Lily beamed happily as she pulled her ample body out of a chair.

Bill extended a thin hand.

"Mr. Barron," Michael said. "I've always wanted to meet the man who had the good sense to find the best bay on this island." He grinned disarmingly.

Pleased, Bill nodded. "It's sure that. I always did know a good thing when I saw it. For years I've had calls—people trying to get me to sell." He shook his head. "But I'm never going to. This bay belongs to the Barrons. We shoulda named it Barron Bay, I guess, 'steada Seahawk Cove. But whatever, the coral and the fish—you can't equal 'em anywhere else. I used to snorkel myself, every day—till my back got so bad. Sometimes I just push myself and do it even now."

Alicia was amazed he'd said so much. Bill rarely opened up to strangers. Then, seeing

Michael's expression, the way he listened so intently, his eyes never leaving Bill's face, she could see why a shy man like her uncle might find himself saying more than usual.

Her aunt said graciously, "Alicia's told us about you. You met in San Diego, didn't you?"

Swinging half-around, Michael grinned at Alicia. "We sure did. A hundred years ago. When she was a mere lass."

Alicia playfully stuck out her tongue. Reaching for a large bag she asked, "Do you have snorkel gear, Michael? I have extra."

"Pelican Point had some stuff."

Minutes later they were in the jeep heading for Spring Bay.

"What do you know about this island, Michael?" Alicia asked as they neared the small town. They drove on the left side of the road, British-style, traveling past homes that were hardly more than shacks. Some had tin roofs, a few were red-tiled, but universally the houses beyond the resort area bespoke poverty.

Michael shifted down for an awkward rut. "This jeep could use better roads," he said dryly. "I suppose if I break an axle I'll find it could use a good garage, too. By the way...*is* there a garage here?"

She smiled. "*You* wouldn't think so. Our local handyman has his setup in his backyard. He has a gas pump and a shed with tools. But if you mean hydraulic jacks and that sort of thing...no. It's amazing how he keeps us go-ing, though.''

"Hmm," Michael grunted, keeping his eyes on the road. When she lapsed into silence he said, "Well, go on...."

She pointed. "We're just getting to Spanish Town. It's very old. It's sort of scattered across a square mile of land, on this narrow part of the island. Actually, the yacht harbor and its little stores are as much the center of town as there is." Her attention shifted to a black farmer shooing his cow out of the road. "You'll find there's a looseness here, probably because the weather is so soft and warm that nobody feels a very big sense of get-up-and-go," she said, try-ing to suppress a yawn.

He threw a sideways glance at her. "You're reflecting the spirit of the place very well. Can you stay awake long enough to tell me some of the history?"

She laughed. "Sorry. Well...I guess you'd say the greatest energy people ever expended in these islands was fighting over them. It's been a pretty bloody history, Michael. Way back the early Arawaks had to defend themselves from the fierce Carib Indians, who migrated from the Amazon region. Later, in 1493, Christopher Co-lumbus gave these islands the name Las Virgines after St. Ursula and her 11,000 virgins. Then the Spaniards came and opened up the copper mines. After that, for years, it was a sort of free-for-all.

"Sir Francis Drake came much later and threw out the Spaniards. They named Sir Francis Drake Channel after him.

"For the next four hundred years, these islands were always at war. The English, the Dutch, the Danish, even the French battled for them at one time or another. And things got worse after slavery started. There were terrible slave uprisings and mass murders of whites. It took years before there was anything close to peace."

Michael scanned the countryside. "Looks peaceful enough now."

They had passed the small settlement and come out into open land, where thin cows grazed near the road and the houses became even more scattered. Out here the vegetation was sparse and random.

The half paved, half dirt road grew steadily worse. At times the ruts were so deep that Michael had to come to a near stop, shift into the lowest gear and creep across the break. Alicia watched him handle the jeep and felt a rush of pride that he did this, as he did everything else, so well.

She glanced at his strong profile—the nose and chin aggressive and determined, the forehead perfect with dark hair blowing across it. She wished she could sit and stare at him without his knowing. *Oh,* she thought suddenly, *I'd love to seduce him.* And it could happen. At the end of the Crawl there was an isolated beach.... She shivered. Why was she taking him *there?* What did she want to happen?

After a while Alicia broke the silence. "I love this island, Michael. It's so unspoiled. We haven't talked about this much since you got here—" she looked at him sideways "—but I'd like to know what you have in mind for it."

"I'm not sure you do want to know."

She frowned. "Try me."

He threw her a challenging look. "Tell me, how would civilization hurt this place? You like these rotten roads? And look at the way the people live—all struggling with their poverty."

"But they—"

"They don't know the difference, that's all. Don't tell me they like having the rain pour in through their rusty roofs. And their cattle and goats starving to death—and maybe their children, too."

"How is your fine civilization going to solve *that*?" she asked testily.

"Civilization brings people, and people bring money. This place is so exclusive only a few tourists can afford to come here. And their money all goes to the resorts and pays for the elegant services they demand. How much of it filters down to these poor souls, I ask you? Not a damned lot."

"I suppose you're going to bring high rises!" she said, unable to contain her anger.

"High rises?" He turned to look at her. "Is that a dirty word, Alicia? Because you say it as if it is! You tell me what's intrinsically bad about buildings being more than one story off the ground! It's just your old-fashioned notion that buildings must be low and spread out all over the place, using up the land. You tell me what's so basically rotten about a ten-story building!"

"If you don't know," she said scathingly, "I can't tell you. You said something like that to me the other night, remember? Look around, Michael! It should be obvious how wrong high rises would be!"

"I *am* looking around, and I think my eyes are seeing it all a lot better than yours. You're blind, lady! You've been here too long!"

Angry, he stepped on the accelerator. With a great jolt they bounced over a rut that threatened to throw them both out of the vehicle.

"Slow down!" she yelled.

He did, but his chin remained set in hard angry lines. She saw his anger and didn't care. He was a fool, and suddenly she couldn't stand him. For his own reasons, and not for the sake of the islanders, Michael was here to spoil her home, of that she was sure. He obviously thought tall buildings would be profitable for Pelican Point. He pretended they'd do something for the populace, too. But she knew better. Bringing in the kind of bustling civilization she'd seen in San Diego would only disconcert these people, uproot them in the long run and alter lives they'd found comfortable for centuries. But Michael was blind and stubborn and too set in his ways to change. All her arguments merely angered him; they didn't change him.

Hating what he stood for, she found herself hating the man, too. When they turned onto a dirt road, Alicia fervently wished that she hadn't come. How had she ever thought she could love such a blind, obstinate man?

To her surprise, she found herself wondering if David might not be the better man for her after all. A simpler, uncomplicated person, at least David wasn't destructive. This one...Michael...threatened to ruin not only her way of life but the lives of hundreds of islanders, too.

The road continued upward for a short distance, then opened onto a kind of high meadow, where coarse grass spread out into an area the size of a football field. From up here they could see the ocean.

They followed a kind of rutted trail across the meadow that ended abruptly at a small grove of trees. Another jeep was already there, parked under a spreading turpentine tree.

"Stop anywhere," Alicia said crossly.

Michael jumped out of the jeep and helped her down. She took his hand grudgingly and let go the minute she was on the ground.

He stood back and surveyed her. "We're

here," he said, "so we might as well try to enjoy ourselves."

"*You* try, Michael. I don't feel like it."

"Shall we turn around and go back?"

"If you like."

"Okay, then." He climbed back into the jeep and started the engine, waiting impatiently for her to get back in by herself. Gone were all remnants of his former courtesy. He shifted gears and started back across the rutted road.

At this point a sense of sadness overtook her. She had a despairing feeling that she might have had a wonderful day and it had all been spoiled— and for what? Yet she could never pretend to feel differently than she did, and her sense of impending disaster would never quite go away as long as Michael was on this island. That he couldn't even begin to understand her views left her ineffably sad, for she knew his attitude would remain one more barrier between them.

She shook her head, her eyes filling with tears. Michael was so wrong. Why couldn't he see it?

She noticed the jeep slowing. He was looking at her. "You're crying."

"I'm not."

He pulled over and stopped, then turned and took her chin in his hand. "You *are* crying. I'm sorry."

She shook her head, denying it, even as a tear coursed down her nose.

"Look," he said quietly, "let's do what we were going to do. It doesn't have to stop us, does it, this difference in philosophy? We just won't talk about our differences. We'll call a moratorium for today, okay?"

"If you like," she said dully.

"Don't give me that," he growled. "You and I are going to go back to the Crawl and we're going to enjoy it!" Less harshly he added, "I'm declaring enjoyment the rule of the day. You *will* enjoy the Crawl! That's an order!"

The absurdity of it made her smile. "All right," she said, "I will enjoy it."

Ten minutes later he was helping her out of the jeep once more, and this time he reached into the back for a red-and-white cooler. "The hotel packed us a lunch," he explained. Taking half the snorkel gear he set off, striding ahead of her as though he knew exactly where they were headed.

"I haven't told you where to go," she called after him.

With a hint of impatience he answered, "There's nowhere else you *could* go. I see only one trail."

Still walking so rapidly that she almost had to run to keep up with him, he led her into the grove, where the rutted path, sometimes merely a crevice between boulders, took a steep downward tilt, ever deeper into the forest, then made a sharp turn. In here, where the sun scarcely penetrated, the air was cool and damp. Each time Alicia had come here she'd had the feeling that she was invading a sacred antiquity. At its darkest point, the jungle was as dark and murky as dusk.

Abruptly the path gave way to brilliant white sand and the dazzling turquoise ocean just beyond. But the beach was unlike any other on the island. To the left and right of where Michael and Alicia stood, enormous piled-up boulders, some the size of igloos, others as large as buildings, gave the impression that they were spilling down the hillside and tumbling forward into the water. Together these two rock walls formed a private beach.

The look on Michael's face expressed his astonishment.

Smiling, Alicia pointed to the right. "This is just the beginning. The Crawl is that way."

As they climbed over the boulders, Alicia could see the beaches ahead of them. Each one was an entity separated from the others by rock clusters. After a little walk they came to Spring Bay, a large white-sand beach with its own protected swimming area. The inviting cerulean waters were almost entirely enclosed by rock formations, with only a narrow channel leading to the ocean. "It looks like someone's private swimming pool," Michael commented.

"The kids and grandmas love it. It's just *like* a swimming pool—always placid like this."

Alicia spread a towel and sat down in the shade of a palm tree. "This is one of my favorite places. I'm glad no one's here today." She sighed, crossing her slender legs in front of her, wiggling her toes in the warm sand.

"Why?" Michael asked, grinning. He put a hand on her upper leg and she shivered, involuntarily, wondering that his touch could alter her feelings so quickly.

Smiling, she said, "It's peaceful. I like having it to ourselves. The boats come here all the time, though. The peacefulness may not last."

With his hand still on her leg, Michael gazed down at her. To her discomfiture, she sensed his eyes on her even after she'd looked away. Finally he broke the mood and asked if she was hungry.

When she said she was, he opened the cooler and took out cold Cornish game hens wrapped in foil, red and golden Delicious apples, squares of cheese, two small containers of potato salad, a packet of black olives, tiny pickled cobs of corn and chocolate cake. A large thermos contained iced tea.

"I can't believe there's so much," Alicia said, unwrapping one of the small hens. "It's a feast."

Michael nodded and began to eat. After a while, gazing at the chocolate cake, he said, "I'm glad to see the food is so consistent." He took a bite of cake. "You can bet some things about this resort will stay exactly the same."

"Good," she murmured, and hoped he wouldn't continue.

But he wiped off his chin with a napkin and said, "At the risk of getting into dangerous shoals again, I think it's safe to tell you, Alicia, I plan to use solar panels for heating water. Energy on these islands is apparently hard to come by and we have to conserve it. And we plan to improve the desalination plant, too, building bigger cisterns for catching rainwater, some of which we'll filter and purify for drinking and bathing. And we may add horses, though I'm not certain of that yet." He paused to look at her quizzically. "Okay, so far? Have I said anything inflammatory?"

She smiled. "No."

"And we'll pay our employees well. Give them a bigger part in management, moving them up as fast as we can."

When she looked at him, waiting calmly, he said, "Pelican Point has lots of possibilities, but maybe we'll both feel more like discussing it another time."

She thought, *I don't think so, Michael,* and was glad when he lapsed into silence.

They both sat in the warm sand, feeling the sun's heat broken by a breeze, staring toward the rocks and beyond to the open sea. She tried to pretend, then, that they still had the easy camaraderie of their days in San Diego before so many issues had crept between them. Heaven knows he still cast the same spell over her now as then, if only she could force herself to forget what he stood for.

"Alicia—" Michael reached into his kit and took out suntan lotion "—put this on my back, will you? I'm burning. I forget how quickly you cook in the Caribbean."

She took the lotion and began rubbing his shoulders. As she smoothed the cream into the light brown skin, touching his muscles, feeling the strength and tightness of his body, her mind gradually turned away from conflict and toward desire. Her fingertips brought her a sense of his masculinity; soon her whole body ached with wanting him. Odd and wonderful, she thought dreamily, how the body could overwhelm the mind.

Slowly, softly, she massaged his shoulders, his back, around the edges of his blue trunks, caressing him as she'd longed to do over the past months, shivering with the sensation of touching him, stroking him. The longer she smoothed and rubbed the greater the sensual desire he aroused in her, until finally she realized her breathing was heavy against his neck.

He sensed her arousal as he leaned back against her breasts and fitted himself into the shape of her body. Her tiny rose-colored bikini was no covering at all. She felt naked.

"Put some on my chest, Alicia," he murmured. She reached around him, touching, feeling the hairs on his chest, the hard muscles of his upper arms. Within moments he was driving her crazy. The intensity of her longing grew so overwhelming she felt she must either have him or run.

"Michael, I'm burning up," she said abruptly, not caring how he interpreted her words. Gently she pushed him away, jumped up and ran down to the water. She threw herself into the depths of the pool. The cool water closed around her deliciously, and she felt the heat dissolve from her body. Languidly she lay back, her head half-submerged in the salty liquid, staring at the intensely blue sky, then closing her eyes as her body lifted easily, floating along on the ripples of the ocean. The water encased her body and soothed her. Now she could think rationally again.

"Michael, come in!" she called, then opened her eyes to find him standing beside her, staring down at her.

"Why did you run away like that?" he demanded.

"Oh, Michael." She let her feet find the sandy bottom and dug her toes into it. Standing, she shook water out of her hair. "I had to...to cool off."

"Are you referring to the sun—or me?" His smile was teasing.

"You ask too many questions. Far too

many." She took his hand and pulled him back out of the water. "Let's get our snorkel stuff. Then I'm going to show you the most astounding things."

"Really?" he asked, teasing again.

She laughed. "Come on, old one-track. Let's get going." In a minute she was rummaging in her snorkel bag, pulling out a black face mask, then two fat green flippers and a blue snorkel tube. She stood up, ready to enter the water. Michael was already there, bent over his fins, one trim hard leg holding him steady while the other was raised, slipping into its fin. Poised as he was his body never wavered. She marveled at his steadiness and his perfect physical condition.

"Follow me, Michael," she said. "I'll point out what I want you to see." She spit into her mask to prevent fogging, pulled it over her eyes and nose, pushed the free end of the snorkel tube up through the face mask's rubber strap— which kept it in place—put the mouthpiece in her mouth and headed out.

Moving gracefully, Alicia led him through the gap at the far end of the secluded pool and out to the ocean, where rougher water lapped against the hovering rocks. Now they were away from the shoreline, floating free, their faces submerged.

For a few minutes, Alicia swam slowly, looking at the floor of the ocean, astounded as always at the fullness of the world she saw down there. It was exactly as if she were hovering over a miniaturized version of the dry world outside. Below the surface of the water she saw small trees, tiny shrubs of all colors and little rock gardens.

Most of the plant life, she observed, was not what it seemed, but endless varieties of coral, both hard and soft. Some took the shape of stiff leafless branches; some became great peach-colored flowers. Yet another variety assumed the shape of feathery wands and wafted slowly back and forth. Hard grayish mounds of brain coral were scattered here and there like under-water tumors. Fish darted in and out of the gardens. Since Alicia and Michael were still in shallow water, perhaps only eight or nine feet deep, the fish below were mostly small. Reef butterfly fish, about the size of Alicia's hand, hurried about like square saucers, their black stripes vivid against yellow bodies. Quickly she pointed out to Michael a four-eyed butterfly fish that seemed to be swimming backward. As a means of confusing its predators, this fish sported a pair of altogether false "eyes" near its tail, while its real eyes enjoyed relative anonymity at the other end.

Briefly, Alicia raised her head and looked around her. They were now leaving the rocky area near shore. Here boulders invaded the sea and formed endless watery caverns, secluded pools and partially enclosed beaches. Waving

Michael on, she dropped her head again and swam out to greater depths. Beneath her, she could see the mountains and valleys of the darker regions and found they were about to float over a virtual "Grand Canyon." Down in that channel, larger, less colorful fish evolved from the gloom. One fish, perhaps two feet long, approached her mask momentarily, then with a quick flick of its tail disappeared behind a rock. She pointed quickly and turned her head to see Michael give an answering wave. They followed the channel until it grew wider and opened into a cavelike area—deep and dark, with spiny dirty-white plants barely visible on the ocean floor. Here the richness of color disappeared and the sea life became nearly monochromatic.

Alicia lifted her head from the water again. She took the snorkel out of her mouth. "Follow me! I'll show you the Crawl." Not waiting for his answering nod, she dropped into swimming position again and stroked expertly back toward the piled-up rocks. Rounding the bend she found it: a narrow channel of water between two steep rock walls, perhaps twenty feet high. The trough was two and a half feet wide, and as she treaded water, waiting for Michael, she remembered her first journey between the walls. On that day, years ago, she'd wondered if she might somehow get trapped in this long passage whose sides were too steep and slippery to allow escape. Or worse, she'd asked herself, what if another swimmer came through from the other direction? There wouldn't be room to pass.

Oddly, it had happened. She'd been halfway through, barely able to see the light at the far end, when she came face-to-face with another snorkler. He was as surprised as she. Both of them had hugged the edge of the rock, pulling themselves past each other with handholds of stone, and in a second the emergency was over. She'd emerged with a kind of heady excitement at having made it through.

Now she gestured to Michael to go first. Following him along the curving passageway, she became acutely aware of his long muscular body floating easily on the surface of the water, the sinewy strength of his legs as he propelled himself forward, the exquisite narrowness of his hips. How indelibly his college swimming years had left their mark! She followed him willingly, wishing herself days of nothing but this.

Swimming lazily, they emerged at the far end. She pulled up her face mask and grinned at him. "That's the Crawl; isn't it spectacular?"

He smiled back. "Everything around here is. Where to next?"

"You'll be surprised." She motioned with her hand. "Follow me." In and out among the rocks she searched for that smaller version of the Crawl and finally found it. Swimming rapidly, Alicia pulled through the narrow channel and saw ahead a minuscule white-sand beach. Touching her feet to the bottom she ran duck-footed to the sand, where she shook herself all over like a wet puppy and pulled off her fins.

As Michael came to stand beside her she said, "Wish we had towels."

He moved closer and answered, "Who needs towels?" For a second he stood unbearably close, staring at her hungrily, his dripping hair lying in a dark tangle across his forehead.

Then, before she could say anything, he had her in his arms, his wet body encircling hers, water compressing between their stomachs, running and mingling along their entwined arms. He kissed her, and she tasted the sea and his hot mouth all at once. Seawater dripped off his hair and ran into her face, but she scarcely noticed. Over and over he kissed her, pulling her ever tighter against his warm wet body, the slipperiness of water adding a dimension that heightened her awareness of him.

I shouldn't have brought him here, she thought. *I should pull away now, this minute, but, oh, God, I can't, I can't. I want him so much.*

She felt herself surrendering, then growing tense with her own yearnings.

His swimsuit, his stomach, his legs pressed against her forcefully. One of his hands held her wet head, proclaiming ownership, while the other moved along her back and caressed her hips. Then his fingers slipped under the strap holding her bikini top and quickly released its hook. He held her away slightly, pulling the straps off her arms and letting a scrap of rose-colored material fall to the sand.

She tried to raise her arms to cover her breasts, saying, "No, Michael! You mustn't!" but he only laughed at her, grasping her wrists firmly and holding them down.

Unabashedly he looked at her, staring as though he must store the sight of her breasts for all eternity. Her tiny pink nipples swelled as he bent to kiss each in turn. She felt weak, hardly able to stand. He pulled her against him again in a long tender embrace, then, without releasing her, dropped to a sitting position and took her onto his lap, holding her momentarily as if cradling a child. As last he pushed her back onto the warm sand, and his mouth again searched hers, his lips bearing in on hers with a craving he couldn't seem to satisfy.

"Alicia," Michael whispered hoarsely in her ear, though there was no one else to hear, "Alicia, I want you. I've waited too long. Alicia, my God, come to me."

She wanted to protest and tried to pull away momentarily, but her limbs refused to obey the commands of her mind. His passion carried her on a wave of elation she was helpless to stop. She felt his breath on her neck, his lips against her ear, his hands warm and sweet where he held her body. She seemed to feel him everywhere at once.

She knew his insistent kisses would soon propel her to something she'd never been through before. As he stroked her thighs and breasts, his breath hot against her skin, she felt awe, love—and lust. She felt beloved, as though she were his, always had been, always would be.

In another moment it would be true, and whether he truly loved her or not, it was no longer within her power to resist. She felt his hand tugging at her bikini bottom.

Then, as though from a dream, she heard a distant splashing. Michael suddenly pulled back his hand and sat upright, bursting out with an astounded, "God, I don't believe it!"

Instinctively Alicia seized her bikini top and sprang to a sitting position.

Swimming down the little passageway toward them were three snorkelers, their faces still submerged in water. Quickly Alicia pulled the sandy top over her tiny form, trying to get enough of it untangled to cover the relevant spots.

Scowling, Michael drew his legs up in front of him, his expression dark and brooding. "Where on earth did *they* come from?" he muttered. Angry, he took a handful of sand and slung it toward the water. "Their timing is incredible!"

The two watched as the snorkelers reached the shore and at last stood up.

Two pear-shaped adults and a young boy stood on the beach. The woman, her hair bedraggled and her one-piece flowered suit inadequately covering her lumpy body, stared around curiously. The man, his baggy blue trunks clinging wetly to his legs, grinned at them. The young boy, blond, knobby kneed and skinny, seemed annoyed. It was the lady who asked, "Does this beach go anywhere?"

Michael, unsmiling, waved a brief hand. "You see it all. Here it is." Then he added, "Did you get lost?"

Suddenly aware of what they had interrupted, the man smiled knowingly. "It seems we did. Sorry, folks." He turned back toward the water. When the rest of his family hesitated, he said, "Come on, Mabel, for heaven's sake!"

But Mabel glanced toward Michael's waterproof watch. "What time is it?" she asked.

"Four-thirty."

"Oh, my. I can't believe it's already—"

"Mabel!" Her husband sounded exasperated. "Come back in the water!"

"Coming. I'm coming!" Her voice grated unpleasantly. "I'm coming, Harry!" She waddled back into the water, the flowered skirt floating briefly around her like an inflating lily pad. The boy had already run past his ample mother and was swimming ahead of her down the channel.

Michael and Alicia watched as they disappeared beneath the crystal water. Michael turned to Alicia and threw back his head and laughed, the laughter absorbing him until Alicia, too, saw the humor in it and found herself giggling irrepressibly.

"The man knew he'd stumbled onto something—he couldn't wait to get out of here!" Michael grinned. "He looked as if he'd accidentally opened the door on a bordello!"

"Probably the guilty look on my face," Alicia murmured. Then she looked down at her bikini top and found out what the man had seen: in her hasty attempt to cover herself, she'd left one breast peering out at the world unabashedly.

Michael noticed at the same instant and broke into renewed laughter. "So *you're* the one who tipped him off! Well, next time you're in a delicate situation, Alicia, remember—always put your best breast forward!"

She made a face at him, covering her bosom with crossed arms. "At least the woman didn't notice!"

"She wouldn't," Michael said wryly. "She wasn't the type. By the look of her, the lady wasn't into breasts and thighs, she was into chocolates."

Alicia began trying to rearrange her suit. "How did you undo this top so fast? I can barely fix it when I can see what I'm doing."

He grinned at her lazily. "I'm good with my

hands. You'll see." And with a new look of hunger he put his arm around her again, trying to pull her close.

But Alicia drew away. "No, Michael. No." At his perplexed expression she said softly, "I wanted it to happen, you know I did. But I'm glad now it didn't. Michael, if we're not—"

She wanted to tell him that without his love— his as well as hers—it would never be right. She could never face herself, knowing that with him it was merely physical gratification. She wanted Michael, all of him. His tenderness, his understanding—but mostly his love.

At her hesitation he stood up, shucking off sand. "You have to have a ring on your finger, is that it?"

"No, Michael, that's not—"

"Well, I don't expect to have to buy everything. Lovemaking shouldn't be for sale!"

"Michael!"

Bitterly he brushed sand out of his hair, off his broad shoulders.

She stared at him dumbfounded. He hadn't understood at all. Now she knew he'd never understand, not if he saw her in that light—as trying to hold out for a ring. It was love she wanted. Commitment. Without that, what they had nearly done would be an empty act.

She felt suddenly infuriated by his lack of insight.

"You're blind, Michael MacNamee!" she

shouted. "You haven't a clue! I thought you understood me, but obviously you don't. You don't know the first thing about me. You—" Too angry to find the needed words, she jerked her bathing suit top off, uncaring, and shook it out and put it back on. Then she turned the hook to the front to fasten it. She didn't care now what he saw; she was too angry for modesty.

Watching her, the furious head bent over the strap's hooks, the determined set to her shoulders, he remained silent. At last he came up behind her, patted her gently on the shoulder and said softly, "Someday...." He looked down at her without a smile. Then he put on his snorkeling gear and led the way back through the narrow passage.

Going home in his jeep they were both silent. Michael drove as before, slowing for the worst bumps, then gradually picking up speed again.

Alicia folded her hands in her lap and waited for him to say something, but he drove with his eyes straight ahead, his expression withdrawn. She wished she could talk to him and explain her feelings. His silence, with its implied disapproval, made her feel left out, as though they were strangers.

She threw him a sideways glance. The strong face was relaxed, not hostile, yet all the way home he shared nothing of his feelings. She felt rejected. Her physical yearning, still unspent, simmered inside her just outside of conscious recognition.

She stared at him and thought, *I care about him. Oh, Lord, how I care. Why is it all so wrong? What's the matter? Why doesn't he feel the same about me?*

Her hands twisted in her lap; the misery she felt sought expression in her fingers. She wanted to touch him again, to feel his warm skin. She wanted to run back to the sun-washed beach and lie down with him.

Confused, she climbed out of the jeep in front of her little house. She let him peck her on the lips, let him hand her snorkel gear to her silently. Then with her back to his departing jeep, she opened the screen door to her house.

CHAPTER EIGHT

THROUGH THE GIFT-SHOP WINDOW the next day, Alicia saw the side of the jeep as it passed by the small window, its pelican logo momentarily visible. Her heart picked up its pace.

It's Michael, she thought.

An impulse told her to run outside and greet him, but an answering sense of reserve held her where she was. She forced herself to go on pricing T-shirts. Expectantly she waited, knowing he'd come into the shop momentarily.

When she heard the approaching footsteps she looked up. She recognized they weren't Michael's firm steps but the feminine pickety-pick sound of Elaine's high heels.

In one quick glance Alicia took in Elaine's simple loose-fitting silk dress, white with pale lavender flowers. A mandarin collar stood up casually around her throat. Lavender pumps assured that she was overdressed—but elegant as always.

Alicia, conscious of her plain yellow gauze sun dress, forced a smile.

With a faint nod and quizzical raised eyebrows, Elaine looked past Alicia to survey the interior of the shop. "My," she said, "it's nice. Cozy." Alicia knew what she was thinking: *how very small. How very insignificant.*

The crowded little room was lined with shelves on three sides, which weren't adequate for all the merchandise. A fourth wall housed both a dress rack and the glass counter on which the cash register rested. Ingenious shelves in the center of the room displayed gift items in four directions. Yet there simply wasn't room for the many items Lily would have liked to carry. They were limited to small baskets, little handmade wooden trays, drug items, a smattering of pottery, some jewelry. The selection of clothing was eclectic. Still, their stock, chosen with care, was attractive.

Elaine bent over the glass counter. "I like your logo," she said, pointing to the tiny gold charms shaped like coral branches. "Who designed these?"

"I did," Alicia answered proudly. After she'd returned home from San Diego, she'd found a man in St. Thomas who worked gold expertly. He had created the pelican logo for Pelican Point, and he willingly translated Alicia's coral design into a small elegant gold charm that represented Seahawk Cove.

"Do you work here every day?" Elaine asked, straightening up. "Isn't it. . . confining?"

"No," Alicia answered stiffly. "No. I usually teach at the scuba school. I'm just helping out my aunt today."

"Oh, of course. I forgot." She continued to look around, stopping first at one shelf, then another. "I was looking for a gift for my mother," she murmured. Instinctively Alicia knew this wasn't true. Elaine wouldn't shop here for the queenly Helen MacNamee, not when she had the large gift shop at Pelican Point. She waited to hear why Elaine had really come.

Fingering a display of hand-crafted pottery cups, Elaine asked offhandedly, "How was your trip to Spring Bay and the Crawl?"

The question was so casual that at first Alicia thought Elaine was merely making conversation.

"Fine," answered Alicia. "The sea life is always interesting. I love to snorkel and—"

"The out-of-sea life is interesting, too, don't you think?" Elaine's caustic quip caught Alicia by surprise.

Her head flew up and she felt a deep flush burning her cheeks. Memories of Michael lying on the warm sand and kissing her breasts came to her so strongly she was afraid the scene was imprinted on her face. What had Michael told Elaine? Was she his confidante, discussing Alicia intimately behind her back? Feeling Elaine's probing eyes, she hid her face by stooping to arrange a necklace in the glass case, hoping Elaine hadn't already observed her confusion. Under her unrelenting scrutiny Alicia felt as naked as she had yesterday on the beach. How much did this awful woman know?

Regaining her composure, Alicia heard herself asking coolly, "What was that supposed to mean?"

"Take a guess, honey. I think you know what it was supposed to mean." Elaine's silken voice barely disguised her anger.

"I'm not into guessing games. If you want to explain what you meant—" Common sense caught up with her. "Whatever Michael and I do or don't do is our affair," she said coolly. "I can't imagine that you'd stoop to ask! Really, Elaine, it's beneath you!"

"My, my! So huffy all of a sudden." Elaine picked up a small teacup and examined it as if the little item was of utmost importance. She appeared unruffled, her patrician features composed. After a moment, apparently satisfied with the response she had elicited, Elaine laid the teacup down. "Unusual craftsmanship."

Alicia didn't answer.

A moment's silence followed while Elaine surveyed the store without interest. It seemed she had nothing more to say. Then her eyes narrowed and fixed on Alicia. "Did you know that Michael has left?"

Startled, Alicia paused before saying, "No." Immediately she was afraid the pause had given away too much. But it hurt her that he'd left without mentioning it to her. She busied herself again with the jewelry. Masking her disappointment, she asked, "Where did he go?"

"On a business trip. He left last night. He has

interesting plans. He's talking to a firm of architects in Florida. They build high rises.''

Alicia's mind turned over the information and she felt a sense of loss. So he was really going to go through with it. High rises. She could think of nothing worse. She took a deep breath, then released it.

Elaine was still talking. ''Michael's very restless, you know. He goes from one thing to another.'' Coolly she added, ''He never settles on anything for long.''

Or anyone, Alicia thought, understanding perfectly and hating the malice behind Elaine's words. She didn't answer but instead slammed her jewelry case closed and picked up the previous day's receipts.

Elaine wasn't finished. ''Michael and I... we've known each other a long time.'' She tucked her rich dark hair behind her ears. ''We understand each other. We both know what we want, and we don't make too many demands on each other. It's perfect.'' She smiled. ''And he comes to me when he needs to talk, so of course I know what he's thinking. Well. I felt I should tell you, in case you thought that little romance in San Diego meant anything. You're still awfully young, aren't you? In all fairness, someone had to level with you that he wasn't serious.''

Alicia flared in spite of herself. ''Is that what he told you?''

Avoiding a direct answer, Elaine went on

smoothly, "Young girls tend to be overly romantic."

"You're not talking to a young girl, Elaine."

"Well, he's used to women falling for him. He's had them chasing him from one continent to another, ever since Dixie. But he'll never marry again. Dixie made him wise." The smile turned wickedly saccharine. "That's what makes our relationship so special. I don't want marriage, either. We each have what the other needs most. It's a relationship you can't hope to upset. So show him the island, Alicia. But don't try to show him too much. You'll just look foolish."

Too angry to answer, Alicia stared at her coldly.

Elaine appeared not to notice. Heels clicking toward the open door she added, "I have a tennis lesson in half an hour. I must change." When Alicia continued to glare with lips clamped tight, Elaine smiled. "Don't worry. David's still yours."

She had said it all, Alicia thought furiously— Elaine had warned that she had full territorial right to Michael and suggested that she could have David, too, anytime she wanted. Oh, the woman was nastier than she'd ever imagined! She'd shown her full stripes today. Alicia felt a wave of helpless anger that she could think of no way to get even. Well, one sure way would be to run off with Michael!

As she thought of Michael her anger changed, turning to a kind of nostalgic regret. Their ill-

fated trip to the Crawl had obviously been one
thing for her, another for him. She sensed a
kind of animal hunger in Michael that had little
to do with her as a person. That he wanted her,
insistently and immediately, was obvious. That
he loved her was not so clear.

For Alicia, passion was only true and good
when it came with love. And love could only be
shared with one man. She would have to wait,
stilling her insistent yearnings, until the man
returned her love in kind. She was the monoga-
mous woman, she thought ruefully.

Was it so different for Michael? Did he close
his eyes and find all women alike? Did he and
Elaine. . .?

She shuddered, imagining the possibilities.
Elaine had painted an ugly picture, a picture of
his duplicity, of easy moving from one woman
to another. If she meant to put Michael in the
worst possible light, she'd succeeded.

It was deliberate, of course. But was any of it
true?

Alicia couldn't be sure.

Still troubled with anger, fear, doubt and
sinister imaginings, Alicia was unprepared for
the ringing telephone. When a long-forgotten
male voice asked hesitantly, "Alicia?" she had
to collect her thoughts before responding.

"Brandon!"

"It's really me, Alicia! Gosh, you sound
great!"

"Where are you, Brandon? You can't be calling from Dallas! I'd swear you're practically next door."

"I *am* next door." He laughed. "I'm at the airport!"

"You're at the airport!" she echoed. "That's wonderful! I'll be right down. What are you doing—"

His soft languorous laugh filled the phone. "It's a long story, cous'. I've got some good news. I'll tell you all about it when I see you."

They said goodbye and Alicia ran to the house, a few yards away. Flinging the screen door open she called out, "Aunt Lily! Bill! Brandon's home!"

Aunt Lily appeared from the back of the house. Her expression, ordinarily warm, showed concern. "Brandon's back?" she asked. "Oh, my...." Her hand went to her mouth. "Is something wrong, Alicia?"

"I don't think so, Lily. He said he had good news. He sounded great—like normal."

"Oh...well, then." Her aunt beamed. "Go and get him, honey. I'll have Bill here when you get back. Hurry, now—I can't wait to see him."

The small car made its way down the last rutted section of road. Alicia drove toward the blacktop and saw Brandon right away, lounging against the edge of the small stucco building. He was tall, about six-two, and excessively lean. She used to laugh that he had so little in the rear she didn't know what he sat on.

She saw immediately that his hair hadn't changed. The tight blond curls he had hated as a young boy clung to his head in a thick mass. He'd long since given up trying to do anything more with his hair than comb it.

As Alicia pulled up to the building it struck her that even her cousin's lazy pose revealed much of the inner man. He was obviously in no hurry, nor inclined to waste energy standing upright. The comfortable stance, a kind of trusting adaptation to the contours of the building, was a reflection of his naive, gullible nature.

All these images flashed through her mind as she turned off the motor.

Brandon smiled and waved, drawing himself up and strolling to her car. His loose checked shirt billowed momentarily around his cream-colored cords. He poked his head through the window and kissed her cheek. "Gosh, it's good to see you, Alish." He smiled broadly, and she saw his perfect teeth and his incredible smile.

"You look great," she laughed, getting out of the car. "Where's your luggage?"

He waved vaguely toward the sky. "Coming on the next plane. It's supposed to be here in ten minutes." She nodded, understanding. This often happened. The little island hoppers were too small to accommodate more than about eight people, and if they had much luggage, two planes were required. The rest of the passengers had obviously gone on to Pelican Point.

She asked if he'd been through customs yet. When he said he hadn't, she started to remonstrate with him, then thought better of it.

He knew what she had been about to say. "Sure, Alish, I could have been doing customs. But why rush? The luggage isn't here anyway."

She wondered briefly, as she had from time to time, how he'd managed these past three years on his own. Well, he hadn't, not at first. He'd lost one job, then drifted. But he was a few months short of twenty-five now and had kept this job for some time. And he'd done it without her quite well.

They sat down on one of the benches that lined the walls. "What's your good news, Brandon?" she asked. "I'm dying to hear."

He grinned impishly. "No point in telling you right now. I'd just have to say it all over again for mom and dad. Wait'll we get home."

"Just give me a hint," she begged.

"No, cous'. You can wait." And that was that, she knew. Brandon, for all his gullibility, could also be stubborn as a mule.

"You know—" he turned to give her a quick appraising glance "—you did a good thing, coming home to help mom and dad. It made me feel better about being away. They sure needed someone. Sometimes I felt guilty, being stuck way off where I couldn't help. But I never had enough money to come trotting home regularly. And it's kind of a good job I have now, not too hard. I didn't want to lose it."

"You never have liked hard work," she laughed.

He smiled. "Does anyone?"

"It's funny," Alicia said, "because Lily and Bill have always worked hard. You'd think some of it might have rubbed off on you."

"They worked too hard!" he declared vehemently. "They don't know how to live. I used to wonder why they did nothing but work, work, work all day long. I wouldn't live like that, not me. I want to have some fun out of life. Well—" his mood lightened somewhat "—I'm going to be able to help them finally. They won't have to keep slaving all the time."

"Tell me, Brandon. Please?"

"Be patient, Alicia. You'll see."

THE FAMILY GATHERED in the living room to revel in Brandon's return. Even Anselmo had come up to their cottage. Now they all sat under the idly turning fan, drinking iced tea and waiting to hear what he'd say.

"What brings you home, son?" Bill leaned forward, then, finding this uncomfortable, quickly sat back against the chair, clasping his knees with blue-veined hands.

"News," Brandon said, beaming at them. "Good stuff. Wait till you hear! 'Lisha's been bugging me to tell her but I made her wait."

He took a big gulp of his iced tea, then set it down, pausing to look at each face in turn. Alicia sensed the drama in the way he did this,

his effort to get everyone's attention before he dispensed his news. At last he announced in a triumphant voice, "My company wants to buy Seahawk Cove!"

If he had expected them all to be overjoyed, Alicia thought, he must have been utterly flattened. The effect was electric, but not as he'd anticipated.

Anselmo's open face grew tight; his eyes narrowed. But he said nothing.

Aunt Lily, expressionless at first, blinked in surprise and folded her hands in her lap, waiting.

Bill turned white and stared at his son.

As for Alicia, she felt confusion and uncertainty.

"What do they want it for?" Bill asked finally.

Brandon shifted in his chair. "To develop, dad! To make something of it! But you haven't heard the best part yet."

Bill growled, "I've heard all I want to hear."

"Dad?" Brandon strained to catch the old man's eye. "Listen...." When Bill continued to stare resolutely at the floor, Brandon went on, "They're making me a vice-president!"

Aunt Lily finally smiled. "Is that so, Brandon?"

"Yes," he said, "and there's more. I'm going to be one of the managers and they've promised me stock, too. Stock in the company. As manager I'll have some say in what happens, so I figured you'd like that." He turned to Bill eagerly. "Dad, I've been wanting to call you ever since it came up, but they thought I should wait till I got here. What do you think?"

Bill shook his head. "You're just a salesman . . . why would they do all that?"

"I've been in the development end of the company for a while now. They must figure I'm good, don't you think?"

"Sure, sure," Bill said doubtfully. "That's what they must think."

"You don't sound glad."

"You know I never wanted to sell this place."

"But, dad, you're getting—"

Alicia heard the word "old" reverberating in the room, but Brandon didn't say it. Instead he said, "tired," finishing lamely. "You can't go on working the way you've been doing, dad."

"We're managing okay."

Anselmo stood up, unsmiling. "Good to have you back, Brandon. See you folks tomorrow." He laid his iced-tea glass on the coffee table, and the screen door banged softly behind him.

A long uncomfortable silence followed.

"I know you're wondering about all this, dad," Brandon began again, " 'cause I've never been that high in the company. But knowing you don't want to sell—I guess they figured if I persuade you, it's worth something."

Bill's expression was uncompromising. "So it's kind of a bribe, is that it?"

"Bill!" Lily was shocked. "You're acting as if Brandon was worth nothing. They wouldn't offer him the managership—"

Bill held up a thin hand. "Hold on, Lily. Hold on. I'm just suspicious, that's all. I always look beyond a person's obvious motives. You have to in this world. If you don't like 'bribe,' call it a business deal. They get the resort they want, and Brandon gets some say in the way it's run, which they figure will please us. Well, it doesn't. I'm not pleased."

"Oh, Bill," Aunt Lily said, "you could at least *think* about it." She gave him an anxious look. "Brandon's got to have this chance—it may not come again. And us...we're not as young as we once were." Compassion came to her eyes. "You ought to be someplace drier, dear. For your sake, too, Bill, we should do it."

"Is this what you want, Lily?"

"Honey, I can't always be thinking of what I'd like. Of course I want to live here and go on the way we've been—it's home to me. It always will be home. But life changes, Bill. We aren't young anymore. And Brandon needs the chance—something bigger than he's had."

Bill looked around at all of them. "I'm being outvoted, I can see that. For the first time you're all gunning me down."

"It isn't that..." Brandon began.

"Bill, please." Alicia went over to him and laid her hand on his shoulder. "Think about it."

After Brandon went to bed, the three sat in the living room talking. Bill, stubborn and uncertain, would not say with finality that he approved of the plan. The more Alicia and Lily argued, in fact, the more his negative resolve strengthened. "What if this company of his ruins it? The whole goldarned place could be nothing but a big city."

"It could," Aunt Lily agreed, "except for Brandon being the manager. He'll see it stays nice."

"Yeah, if he keeps the job!"

Quietly Alicia interjected, "Maybe he will."

Bill squinted at her. "I always thought *you* might take over Seahawk Cove, Alicia."

She shook her head. "I'm not a manager, Bill. I'm not—well, I love the scuba school, but I don't see myself running the whole resort."

"Then there's no other way it can stay in the family, is there?" The old man sighed. "Since we won't live forever." After a few minutes' silence he stood up. "I'll think about it more tomorrow. Going to bed, Lily." He shuffled off toward their bedroom.

Companionably, Alicia and Lily sat in silence. The lazy wooden paddles above them flicked by endlessly, creating the soft whooshing sounds of a slight breeze. The night air, only a few degrees cooler than daytime, washed across Alicia's bare arms with comforting relief. She wondered, sometimes, how people ever lived here without fans.

"You know, it is funny—" her aunt broke the silence "—them offering Brandon so much to get this place. I wouldn't admit it to Bill, but I do wonder if they have ulterior motives. I've never heard of an ordinary salesman getting a vice-presidency, stock and managership all at once."

"Lily, I was thinking the same thing."

"I smell a rat, honey. It's just too much." Lily paused, grimacing. "You and I...we've both come to the same conclusion, haven't we? I hope we're wrong."

"Me, too." Alicia sighed.

After a while her aunt went on. "You know, Alicia, I guess I haven't said it often. You've made my life so rich. I'm not good at saying things like this, but I've loved you so much. It's been years since I even remembered you weren't my little girl right from the start. But I forget to tell you. I just take you for granted."

"You never had to tell me, Lily. I always knew."

CHAPTER NINE

FOR THE NEXT FEW DAYS Alicia found little time to yearn for Michael. Her cousin's behavior mystified her, though she couldn't put her finger on the reason why. Curious, she watched as Brandon pressured his family relentlessly—as relentlessly as he was capable of doing, Alicia thought, considering his natural bent toward laziness. For Brandon, pressure meant he brought the subject up frequently, though when his father and mother quizzed him in detail, he retreated and seemed unwilling to argue. It was as though he wanted to say only so much and no more.

Alicia had the feeling there were things Brandon wasn't telling them.

The third day at breakfast Brandon blew up. "You don't want me to get ahead! You people don't care! I never should have come home! All you think about is protecting this lousy place!"

"Of course we care!" Lily soothed. She reached out a hand and touched Brandon's arm, explaining that they merely wanted answers to questions, that was all. "How could we not care about you? You're our son! We're just naturally a little suspicious. Surely you can see that!''

Brandon calmed down. "Sure. I guess I understand.''

That afternoon Brandon took Alicia aside. "Come to the yacht harbor, 'Lish. I have to talk to you. We can sit in that little courtyard by the stores.''

They left the car in the parking lot next to the small shopping center and walked in silence to the courtyard. This little center, as close to a mall as existed on Virgin Gorda, consisted of an outer square of small specialty shops offering crafts and clothes plus an ice-cream shop, a liquor store and an art store. The shops formed three sides of a grassy square. In the center a spreading cashew tree shaded a wooden bench. It was hot in the square, and the only open side faced the parking lot. Alicia sat down on the bench wishing the ocean breezes could get through.

"I had to get you away, Alicia," Brandon began. "I'm tired of arguing with mom and dad.''

"I know.''

"Neither of us is going to take over Seahawk Cove, so why is dad so stubborn? He may not get exactly what he wants, but it's better than nothing. It's all he's going to get, 'Lish—you and I know that. If I can help run the place...." He shrugged. "What's he holding out for?''

Alicia turned to him. "You never answer their questions, Brandon. They want to know more, and I don't blame them. What is your company going to do specifically?"

When he turned away without answering, she said, "I can see why they're a little suspicious."

"Well...." He hesitated, then said evasively, "The place needs everything, you know that— paint, carpentry. I even heard Anselmo talking about leaky plumbing."

"Yes." She studied his face, not convinced. Why was he grabbing at straws?

They were silent, staring past the parking lot to the sea. She wished she knew what he really was thinking.

"Even if it was sold," Brandon went on, "you could still keep the scuba business. We could make that separate, 'Lish, keep it out of the deal. My company wouldn't care, I'd be willing to bet."

"Well, that's the way I'd want it."

"Then why don't you persuade my folks, Alicia?"

She hesitated, running her fingers through her hair. "Because I have doubts, too, that's why." With Brandon talking to her this way she was reluctant to make accusations, but still she wondered.

Abruptly her cousin put his arm around her waist and pulled her close. "Don't you think I can do a good job, Alicia? Is that it? Are you afraid I won't do it right?'' His blue eyes pleaded for understanding.

"No, Brandon, no.'' She looked toward the parking lot and absently noted a car circling slowly. He let go of her and now it was her turn to encircle his neck with her arm, giving him a gentle squeeze. He'd always needed reassurance. This was no time to show a lack of confidence.

"I know you'll do the best you can, I'm sure of it. You'll do a fine job.'' She gave him a quick kiss on the cheek.

He stood up. "You'll talk to them?''

"Sure,'' she said. "Sure I will.'' As they walked out of the little square she thought, *what else can I do?* All Brandon's arguments were logical and maybe he wasn't holding back anything after all. She had forgotten that Brandon never liked to argue, even as a boy. When pressed he had always reacted the same—always shrugged and changed the subject. He'd never been a fighter, that kid.

Anyway, she thought, selling to Brandon's company certainly seemed wise on the face of it—for him, and for Bill and Lily, too. They just had to trust Brandon, that was all.

They'd almost reached the curb when the car she'd seen earlier streaked by them, its engine howling in sudden acceleration. Instinctively they jumped back, Alicia feeling Brandon's arm thrown across her protectively. As they watched the car roar away Alicia caught a sudden glimpse of the driver's face. It was Michael!

Dumbfounded, she stared after the fast-disappearing car, her shock turning to anger. What in God's name was Michael doing, driving like that? Where had he come from?

A thought struck her. How long had he been back on the island?

Questions without answers raced through her mind.

As Alicia shook her head, Brandon's outburst brought her back to the present. "...the devil is the matter with that guy? He could have run us over. Then he had the nerve to glare at us, as if it was our fault!" Angrily Brandon shook a fist in the direction of the madcap driver. "Fool!"

Alicia groaned. "I hate to tell you who it was, Brandon. It was the new owner of Pelican Point. He's sort of—" she paused, unwilling to have her cousin dislike Michael "—unpredictable."

"Unpredictable!" Brandon spat out the word. "Crazy's more like it."

"Yes, I guess that was crazy."

"I mean weird." Brandon stared at her. "He's buying Pelican—"

"Bought," she corrected. "He's already bought it."

"Boy, we *gotta* sell,'" Brandon glowered. "We got a maniac living right next door!"

Later that afternoon Alicia, Brandon, Bill

and Lily gathered in the living room to talk. Abruptly Brandon announced he was treating the family to dinner that night at Pelican Point. "Morris Mark's band is there. The dinner's on me." He looked at each in turn, giving them his broad smile.

Brandon does have charm, Alicia thought, and with him it was genuine.

Lily smiled and stood up, patting her white hair. "This calls for a shampoo!"

Bill grinned at his son affectionately.

Then Alicia thought of what had happened in the yacht harbor parking lot and wished she could back out. She'd see Michael tonight, it was inevitable, and she wanted none of his black mood. At Spring Bay he'd been chillingly silent. Now, a few days later, he was behaving like a maniac.

Had it been only a few days ago? It seemed a lifetime since he'd left her in front of this house with a thoughtful kiss. His mood then had been unreadable; now it had turned ugly.

She felt uncomfortable. How was she to deal with Michael tonight? Not going with her family would create more havoc than going, she finally decided, so she made up her mind to be as beautiful as possible. Then she could ignore the man and they might somehow be "even."

As Alicia showered and dusted her slim body liberally with fragrant bath powder, she though of Michael's passion on the beach. She shivered.

Her body had been so nearly part of his. How strange, she thought. These past few days she'd seen three sides of Michael—his tender passion, his sarcasm and his explosive temper. Who was Michael, anyway, she wondered. Would the real Michael MacNamee please stand up?

At last, willing herself back to the task at hand, she chose a pale pink full-length dress, knowing it would highlight her auburn hair and fair skin. The dress was simple, beltless, flaring gently around the bottom. Its soft lines shaped themselves to the contours of her slender body, and the neckline plunged slightly to reveal the edges of her breasts.

Around her neck she wore a string of pearls— a gift from her uncle. Each pearl was small and perfect, and the soft glow emanating from them drew even more attention to her bosom. When she was almost ready, she decided to wear her hair up. Working carefully, she brushed her short curls upward, forcing them into a graceful mass at the crown of her head, then secured it with a silver comb. A few loose curls escaped and fell around her ears. The overall effect made her appear sophisticated yet with a flirtatious innocence she hoped would be irresistible. At least to Michael.

THEY STOOD IN THE DOORWAY of the Pelican Point dining room waiting to be seated. It was such a beautiful place, Alicia thought once

again. Even in its grandness it had an atmosphere of intimacy. The architect who had
designed the three open-air rooms had favored
dramatic shapes and natural materials. Massive
wooden beams planted in the ground met thirty
feet overhead to form high V-shaped arches.
The floors of gray white terrazzo were polished
to a pearllike luster and, at each table hurricane
lamps spread a soft glow over the white damask
tablecloths.

Alicia's eyes darted around the room, searching among the diners for Michael, but she didn't
see him. Instead she noted how elegant everyone
looked. The men wore jackets, the women back-
less or low-cut dresses in flowered silks, pale
shantungs and soft voiles. In the pale light from
the candles it was remarkable how years fell off
faces, the old becoming younger, the young
more glamorous. Alicia was glad she'd taken
the time to force her hair into its upsweep and
apply understated makeup to her eyes.

The headwaiter found them a table, and they
had just opened their leather-bound menus
when Michael and Elaine appeared at the entrance to the dining room.

Alicia looked up in surprise and took in a
quick breath.

Michael's arm was around Elaine's waist.
Even as Alicia frowned at Michael's apparent
intimacy with Elaine, she was struck by his easy
good looks. He was wearing a pale blue dinner

jacket, expertly tailored to his broad shoulders. Its light color was a nice contrast to his dark navy slacks. She'd never seen him look more dashing.

Though she seethed inwardly at seeing Elaine once more—and especially in Michael's grasp— Alicia had to admit that the other woman's artfully made-up eyes and dark chignon above the white silk dress made a breathtaking study in contrasts.

Michael spotted them and steered Elaine toward their table.

Alicia saw Brandon look up and catch sight of Elaine. His blue eyes grew saucer round with appreciation, and his lips formed a silent whistle.

Damn, thought Alicia, *I won't have her working on Brandon.* But Elaine had already noticed Brandon and given him her most engaging smile—a smile so ingenuous Alicia could have choked. Brandon met the smile with his own pleasant grin, and Alicia knew it was too late to warn him off Elaine. The spider had already woven its web and trapped its victim.

She glanced at Michael. His eyes were on her, but instead of looking *at* her, he seemed to be looking *through* her. The coldness of his impersonal glance was unmistakable. The moment of hostility was only momentary, but in that instant Alicia realized that her plan to ignore Michael had been futile. He'd put her down first and done it with an expertise she found devastating.

Michael leaned over her aunt and gripped Lily's hand warmly. Bill stood up, shook hands, then eased back into his chair. After Michael's warm greetings to her aunt and uncle he introduced Elaine, who seemed intent on being charming tonight. She favored each in turn with a warm smile.

Michael turned to Alicia, muttered a brief, "Sorry about this afternoon," and inclining his head toward Brandon said curtly, "Introduce us to your friend."

Alicia found herself growing angry. As Michael arrogantly demanded his introduction to Brandon, she had a sudden, almost uncontrollable urge to stand up calmly, turn her back on him without answering and walk off. It was what he deserved, she thought. Her feet itched to carry her away and leave him standing there watching after her.

The silence and the tension grew. Her mind battled within itself. Oh, Lord, how she want to do it, to humiliate him in front of everyone. But a second voice inside strove to be heard. *You can't run away, Alicia, you can't create a scene. There are others here besides Michael, and you will only spoil everyone's evening. No one will understand.*

She saw her aunt frowning, puzzled.

"Well?" Michael asked.

Alicia fought for control and finally inclined her head toward Brandon. "This is my cousin. . . Brandon." Her voice was as cold and distant as she knew how to make it. She didn't smile. Then, excusing herself, she stood up and turned toward the ladies' room. Whatever they thought, she had to get away. Behind her she heard voices, a sudden laugh from Michael and an answering laugh from Brandon.

God, how gullible the kid was, she thought.

In the ladies' room Alicia splashed cold water on her face, then cupped her hand under the faucet to take a drink. But none of these things cooled her anger.

She fussed with her hair, not caring any longer how it looked. She stared into her own eyes in the mirror above the sink. Black fury stared back at her. A face hardened in anger wasn't exactly beautiful, she decided.

She leaned against the wall, her mind stopping momentarily to dwell on her last outing with Michael. Suddenly she was overwhelmed by a sense of relief that she and Michael had stopped short of where they'd been headed. Oh, how close they'd come, she thought. How close!

As she stopped to stare once more in the mirror and attempt a half-smile, the door opened and Aunt Lily came in.

"Are you all right, dear?" Lily asked. "Michael suggested I ought to come and see. You seemed so—'' Her aunt broke off, her eyes searching Alicia's face.

"I'm all right, Lily. I was just angry for a moment."

"Anything you can tell me?" When Alicia didn't answer, Lily said, "Well, never mind, I shouldn't be prying. I don't know what this is all about, honey, but I can only tell you it happens. It's normal. It seems the more you care about someone the more they can hurt you. Whatever it is, it can't be terribly important, Alicia. He's a good man."

"How do you know?"

Her aunt laughed. "Oh, my girl, it's plain to see. His character's written all over him. I'm a good judge of people—I've seen enough of them. I can almost tell you ahead of time who will leave the cabins neat, who will try to fudge on the bill. Michael's decent. I suspect he has a temper, but he's basically honorable. Anyway, he and—'' her aunt made a small, almost imperceptible grimace "—Elaine have joined us. Will you come out now?"

Back in the dining room, Alicia found herself trying to accept what Lily said, that Michael was basically a good man. Yet seeing him there, sitting at the head of their table, made her feel tense again.

Michael looked up when she sat down four seats away and gave her a gracious smile.

"You're back." His earlier aloofness had disappeared as if by magic.

Alicia's eyes flicked over him briefly, coldly, and then turned elsewhere. He'd have to do more than smile.

For a moment, picking up her menu, she wondered at the capricious nature of the man. Utterly frosty one moment and strangely charming the next. What had happened while she was in the ladies' room to alter his mood like this? Was it something to do with Elaine? But no, that was impossible. Elaine was now sitting next to Brandon, listening to him with rapt attention. She saw that Brandon was talking nonstop, loquacious even for him.

Well, nothing was predictable tonight. Bill was talking and Michael was listening to him as though he were a prophet. Only she and Lily were silent—and they were usually the two most talkative people at the table!

Alicia stared at her menu, determined to concentrate. Appetizers included salmon pâté, oysters Rockefeller and fruit cup de menthe. Soups: crab bisque, vichyssoise. Salads: hearts of palm, shrimp *remoulade*. Entrées: rack of lamb, roast London prime rib au jus, pompano with slivered almonds, coq au vin.

She pondered her choices, aware that at Pelican Point every item would be delicious.

In hushed tones Michael discussed the wine list with the waiter, pointed at the menu and ordered wine. A few minutes later two wine buckets were brought to their table. The wine lay on its side packed in ice, each bucket on its own little stand.

Bill abandoned his conversation with Michael, and Michael addressed the group at large, regaling them with stories.

As Michael talked about his trips, launching into humourous tales of travel mishaps and management blunders, Brandon was more charmed than anyone, obviously unaware he was being upstaged at his own party. He'd apparently forgotten the "maniac" of this afternoon, Alicia thought. Brandon's behavior was typical of a naive, trusting person.

The longer Michael went on charming Brandon, the more annoyed Alicia became. After a while she began staring into space, hoping Michael would notice her irritation.

But he apparently didn't. His expansiveness diminished not a whit, and there was doubt that he even noticed her foul mood, for he seemed set on not looking in her direction.

Before long Alicia realized her cousin was quite taken with Michael. She realized Michael had succeeded in endearing himself to everyone.

Alicia's sulky mood persisted until the band started up. In spite of herself, the steel drums captivated her. Each note was a small percussive delight and she began tapping her toe to the sensuous beat of "Jamaica Farewell."

She looked up to see her cousin asking Elaine to dance. Elaine graciously consented, fixing Brandon with the full radiance of her perfect smile. He took her hand and led her onto the terrace overlooking the bay. Alicia had to admit they looked good together—both of them tall and slender. As she watched, she realized Brandon had learned a passable fox-trot, good enough to concentrate on holding Elaine close when the music slowed.

Michael was on his feet, then, hovering over Lily. "Come on, Lily," he asked invitingly, holding out his hands.

"No, no, Michael," she laughed. "You young folks go and dance. I wouldn't be able to do it anymore." Pleasure molded her face into two round pillows.

"Lily, I'll bet you'd dance up a storm. Come on."

Laughter shook her ample stomach. "Michael, you dear, there's no one I'd rather dance with. Except Bill," she amended quickly. "We gave it up so long ago, I wouldn't know which foot to put in front of me first." Chuckling, she waved him off.

He's coming, thought Alicia. *It's inevitable. I must dance with him or be rude.* She sat up a little straighter, her eyes fixed on the dance floor in an attempt to ignore him.

He was in front of her now.

Softly, so only she could hear, he said, "It

had to come, Alicia. Stand up, honey. You can't ignore me forever.''

She stood, averting her eyes.

He took her arm, holding it hard, almost too hard, and propelled her out of the dining room to the terrace. Feeling his strong grip, her hostility began oozing away like sap from a maple. *Why, oh, why,* she asked herself angrily, *does he always affect me this way?*

The music was fast, a samba. Letting go, Alicia began to sway rhythmically back and forth in front of him. Sambas, she thought for one hesitant moment, simply couldn't be done halfheartedly. She would have to do it right or sit down. Without looking at him she undulated forward, then back. Slowly the pace picked up until she felt a part of the music and its rhythm.

She felt him looking down at her. After a while she could no longer hold out against his insistent downward gaze. Unsmiling, she at last tilted her chin and found herself swallowed up in his moody stare. For a second they danced, staring, until the samba finished.

''You didn't accept my apology,'' he said abruptly.

''It wasn't genuine,'' she replied.

''Oh, it was. I meant it.''

''Not at that moment you didn't.''

''I thought Brandon was your *lover*!'' he exploded. ''I saw you holding each other. What was I to think?''

Suddenly conscious of other dancers nearby, he pulled her off to one side. "When I saw you kiss him in the courtyard, I lost my reason. Honest to God, Alicia, I wanted to run you down, both of you—I couldn't help myself. I'm sorry."

Smiling grimly she answered, "You almost managed it."

"No." He loosened his tie, and for the first time since she'd known him he seemed embarrassed. "I wouldn't have hit you, Alicia. I could see you were back from the curb."

"Well, we didn't appreciate it. I could hardly believe it was you." She brushed an auburn curl away from her face. "I had to try to explain to Brandon that you were unpredictable. He didn't buy that. He said you were a maniac. But—" her expression was ironic "—it doesn't matter now, does it? You've won him over. Wrapped him around your finger as though he was a mindless fool. Frankly, I find it despicable."

"What could I do?" He shrugged. "I didn't want Brandon hating me. I hope someday he'll—" The music began again, swallowing his words.

For a moment they stood, their emotions teetering.

The band swung into its compelling rhythm and Alicia felt the music invading her senses.

He cocked his head at her, grinning. "Dance with me?"

She shrugged. But she wanted to.

"Is that your best answer?" he laughed, then took her hand, leading her into the fox-trot.

Immediately Michael molded her body to his with his free hand. The other gripped her right hand near his chest.

It was maddening, she thought, how the nearness of him changed her. Crowded among other couples, she felt his body warmly envelop hers. He guided her around the terrace flawlessly, their feet moving without effort.

Alicia closed her eyes. The exhilaration she'd felt during the samba mellowed to a deep pleasure. His closeness was like a perpetual caress; the feel of him filled her with wonder. Love, beauty, excitement were all magnified by the music. Eyes still closed, she seemed to be floating away from the earth...carried away on tapping steel drums...losing all sensation save the vibrant nearness of Michael. Even as she was aware of his body, treasuring his possession of her, she knew he was aware of hers, too, knew that he was unable to release her, even for a moment. Immersed in heady sensation, she felt herself losing touch with reality.

When the music stopped, she felt his breath on her face. Hot. Forceful.

"I can't take much more of this," he murmured against her cheek.

She didn't answer but touched his face gently.

The band announced they were taking a break and the spell was quickly broken.

He guided her back to the table. They found that her aunt and uncle had gone to the gift shop. Brandon and Elaine were talking, absorbed in each other. Seeing that the others wouldn't miss them, Michael suggested they sit on the patio, where they could cool off and watch the ocean.

He held out a chair for her and sat down on the other side of a tiny metal table.

Michael leaned across the table earnestly. "So...." He paused. "I'm not much for apologies, Alicia. In fact—" he shrugged "—I haven't done it twice in my life. Try to understand about this afternoon. I was kind of crazy, that's all. You wouldn't believe all the things I was thinking. You and Brandon looked...to me you looked intimate. I couldn't believe you'd picked up someone that fast. I was stunned. You might say I went...berserk."

"It's okay, Michael," she said. "It's okay. You didn't kill us, did you? Anyway, in some nutty manner of thinking I suppose it was a compliment."

Almost angrily he said, "It's not like me, I can tell you that. I never figured *any* woman would make me act like that."

She smiled at him, inwardly pleased. If she could affect him like this it might almost be enough.

Together they turned toward the ocean, watching the moon's trail on the water. On either side of the silvery streak the ocean was dark, but in the moon's light small ripples flickered and danced. "Like a trail to Heaven," she murmured.

He put his arm around her and she drew close to him. He bent and nuzzled her neck with his lips. "You smell good."

Backing away again, his eyes swept over her hungrily. "That dress...it's...." Words seemed to fail him. "I don't usually notice women's clothes. Most men don't. Women either look good or they don't. We men can't tell anyone, later, what a woman wore. So I don't know what you'd call that dress, but I wish you'd wear it for me often."

Lightly she mocked him. "I'll wear it swimming, I'll wear it dancing...I'll wear it to bed."

He laughed. "You do that."

Silence, a comfortable silence, tucked itself around them like a soft blanket. Conscious of his hand on her arm, she felt peace and love coming to her through his touch. At this moment she needed nothing more. She hoped she would remember this night in all the years to come. She felt she should store the moment, a tiny jewel of a thing, in case her love for him never came to anything.

When he spoke again it was with a startled,

"Oh!" He pulled away. Surprised, she stared at him.

"God, Alicia, I almost forgot. I've been carrying this with me everywhere." He was fishing in his pocket, searching for something. At last he withdrew a small square black box tied with a single strand of white yarn. "I got it for you after the Crawl," he said quietly. "Yesterday I came close to tossing it in the ocean—which shows how foolish even an iron-core, cold-blooded, all-American man like me can get." He handed her the little box. "Please open it."

She sat staring at it, trembling. Could it be...was it...she dared not form the words. No, of course not.

"Come on," he prodded.

Slowly she pulled the yarn off and removed the lid to find a puff of cotton. Her heart gave a quick extra beat.

Carefully she removed the cotton. In the box lay a tiny gold charm—a pelican.

Beautifully made, the bird's great beak was pointed down, so that when she wore it, the pelican would be caught forever in the act of diving for fish.

For a flicker of an instant as he sat watching her, disappointment welled up inside her. It wasn't an engagement ring...now she could admit to her dashed expectations. But she masked her feelings quickly, hoping he hadn't noticed, and threw her arms around his neck.

Tenderly she kissed his lips, then pulled away. "Michael, it's beautiful!"

"You expected something else," he accused.

She lied. "I didn't! Honestly! Michael, I love it. I'll wear it always." She held it against her chest. "I'll wear it here."

"Well, that's where it belongs," he said brusquely. "Sorry it wasn't what you expected." Before she could protest he stood up, saying, "Come on, the others will think we've deserted them."

As they walked back across the floor, tears stung Alicia's eyes. Perceptive Michael. He'd known what she'd been thinking.

Why, she berated herself, why did she have to think of an engagement ring just then? Why? Everything was ruined, and she had only herself to blame. She wanted too much and he knew it. She would never get it now. Michael thought she was trying to close in on him and all he would do was run. *Oh, you fool, Alicia. You hopeless, blundering fool.*

Still castigating herself, she let Michael push in her chair. At the far end of the table she heard Elaine chide him gently. "You were gone a long time, Michael."

He didn't answer.

Brandon was having a second dessert, but in front of the others the table had been cleared. Bill looked sleepy, slumped down awkwardly in his chair. There was a long silence.

At last Lily said, "Tell us what you plan for Pelican Point, Michael."

Alicia looked up sharply.

Michael caught the look and lifted one eyebrow. Without any sign of discomfiture he mentioned a few innocuous changes—the desalination plant, horses, better wages for the employees—things he knew wouldn't upset Bill and Lily.

Watching him skirt controversy, Alicia listened carefully. If Bill had any inkling of Michael's intentions, he would hate him. But he didn't.

With a genial smile, Michael changed the subject. "This is a vacation, Brandon?"

Brandon hesitated. "Sort of," he said. "Sort of yes and sort of no. I'm actually here—" he threw a quick look at his father "—to see if I can persuade dad to let my company buy Seahawk Cove."

For a split second Michael's eyes revealed a heightened interest, even surprise. But he quickly regained his composure. "Oh?" he commented in a tone of casual politeness. Yet Alicia knew his first reaction had been genuine.

Bill sat up straighter now, his sleepy lids drawing apart.

With both men looking at him, Brandon began to talk freely. "My company would like to buy our place, you see, and frankly I think it's the best possible answer for Seahawk Cove.

They're a multimillion-dollar company—based in Dallas, if Alicia didn't tell you. And I'd have quite a stake in the project: a vice-presidency, some stock in the company and part managership of our resort." Pride made his words come faster than normal.

He stopped and smiled. "They've got lots of plans, all kinds of ideas for improving the place, and as I told Alicia yesterday, I think it *needs* improving. I mean, windows are practically falling out, their frames are so rotten. It needs painting, and the plumbing—"

Michael broke in, "Those things are minor. You don't need a million-dollar company for projects like that!" His tone was scornful.

"Well, no, but they're going to do a lot more than...." His voice trailed away and he looked around in sudden confusion.

"Than what?" Michael asked.

"Well, just some things that need doing," Brandon finished lamely.

He looked a little desperate, Alicia thought, like a small rabbit caught by a fox yards from its hole. She glanced at Michael and saw that his eyes had a faint gleam, a grim intensity she'd seldom seen there.

"What sort of things?" Michael persisted.

Brandon shrugged.

"But you know what they are." Michael's tone was pleasant, conversational again, yet he wasn't going to give up, Alicia sensed. She felt sorry for Brandon. Whatever Michael might prompt him to say would come out reluctantly...and wouldn't bode well for her cousin.

With everyone's eyes on him, Brandon shifted in his chair and pulled at his collar. The silence grew thick. His words, uttered at last, came out in a rush. "Sure, but some of them I'd never approve of, not if *I'm* manager."

"What things?" It was Bill asking now. His eyes were stern, his thin mouth tucked in upon itself as if the set of his lips could fend off the world.

"Uh...." Brandon was trapped. "Some buildings, that's all. Just a few extra buildings. But I'm not going to approve the six-story condominium—I've already told them that. I told them my family would never—"

"Six-story!" Bill stared at him. "Six-story!" he repeated, shaking his head as though the words were incomprehensible, a catastrophe beyond his understanding. "There'll never be any six-story building on my—"

"It's all right," Lily broke in. "Bill, please. Brandon already said he wouldn't approve. Please, Bill, dear." She touched his shoulder anxiously.

Alicia had never seen Bill like this. His mouth worked vigorously, yet no sound came out. His eyes were frightened...terrified. The old man looked apoplectic and she was scared for him. She stood up and laid her arm on Bill's shoulder. "We haven't sold it yet, Bill. The property is still yours."

"Six stories!" The old man's eyes filled with tears. "We wouldn't know the place. It would be ruined."

"I told you, dad—" Brandon struggled with his words "—they can't pull it off. I won't let them." He shrugged. "God, I didn't think it would upset you this much."

"I don't see anything upsetting about it at all."

They all turned to see Elaine smiling warmly at Brandon. "I can't imagine why you're all carrying on. This island is pretty dull. I say we *need* some changes around here, a little life in the place. We could use a disco band and a couple of swimming pools. The place is so quiet it's spooky. I'll bet your company has some good ideas, Brandon. Tell us."

Michael looked away, his face hard.

Surprised but grateful, Brandon shot Elaine a quick look, then lapsed back into confusion. "Yeah, maybe they do." It was clear he hadn't expected anyone to defend him.

"You know, Brandon," Elaine went on, oozing charm, "lots of resorts—even Michael's in Hawaii—have tall buildings. I don't see what's so terrible about it, either. Six stories isn't so terribly tall, is it? You all act as if the place was going to blow up or something. Brandon's not bringing in a volcano, just a little development—and God knows you need it. What's so terrible about a few changes, anyway?'' Elaine tossed her head defiantly. ''I've been bored ever since I got here. The beaches are practically deserted—you can never find anyone to talk to. This island is three-quarters dead, if you ask me. It can take plenty of big buildings!''

Nobody looked at her, not even Brandon. She was speaking to a table of averted faces. Embarrassment lay heavy on all of them. For once Alicia felt almost sorry for Elaine. Almost. It would certainly take more than one foolish outburst to make her truly sorry for the lady, Alicia decided.

Even Michael had been smart enough, she thought, not to buck her family head-on. But Elaine was either brainless, insensitive or uncaring—Alicia wasn't sure which.

She looked at the others one by one. Bill's head was in his hands, discouragement evident in every muscle. Lily's hand was on his shoulder. She looked off into space. Michael's face was closed and hard. Even Brandon fidgeted in agitation.

Suddenly Michael stood up, taking a firm grip on Elaine's arm. He looked at his watch. ''Let's go, Elaine. I have a meeting in the morning.'' He nodded at everyone, deftly moving Elaine sideways. As far as Alicia could tell he seemed bent on propelling her all the way to their cottage.

But Elaine had other ideas. She wriggled free of his grasp and declared, "I'm going to the gift shop! It's still open. At least something might be going on in there!" Hips swaying, she marched away in the opposite direction.

Michael shrugged and turned to Bill. Laying a hand on the old man's arm he said, "Please forgive her. She gets carried away."

Bill nodded without lifting his head, his faint acknowledgment of Michael's words merely the requirements of good manners. He was unconsoled.

"Well, good night," said Michael, and walked away by himself.

Alicia watched him go. The scene had overwhelmed them all, but it had given her a chance to see another facet of the many-sided Michael—his concern for a stricken old man.

Bill and Lily rose heavily and walking arm in arm turned toward the road.

Brandon strode away to the gift shop. Now alone, Alicia stood watching him and Elaine through the glass door. Brandon was saying something, his face earnest. Elaine nodded and pinched his cheek. They were still talking when Alicia left to walk down the road by herself.

CHAPTER TEN

ALICIA WOKE UP feeling at odds with the world.
In a rush of memory the previous evening came
back to her. First there had been Michael's gift
and the awkwardness surrounding it. She felt
for the pelican—yes, it was still there. Then
there was the embarrassment of a cornered
Brandon, fending off waves of disapproval
from everyone except Elaine, and Elaine's
opinion didn't count for very much.

She came out to find Bill and Lily gone and
Brandon standing at the kitchen drainboard
eating a piece of toast. If the previous night still
upset him, Alicia couldn't see it. His face had its
usual good-natured expression.

"Hi!" she said. "You look all right this
morning."

"Sure." He indicated his jogging shoes. "I
went running this morning. At dawn. It felt
good. The air's so clean here it makes you feel
alive. It's good to be back on the island, cous',
though I guess I've messed up my cause pretty
good. I suppose I'm finished with mom and
dad." He shrugged. "I sorta expected it."

Ordinarily she would have flared at him and told him he shouldn't be such a defeatist, but she knew this time he'd picked the wrong cause and it was doomed to failure.

She said evenly, "I guess you just hoped Lily and Bill wouldn't find out what was going on."

"No," he said. "I think in a way I hoped they would. Maybe I didn't want responsibility for what would happen—that must be it. I guess I figured if I could persuade them in spite of everything it wouldn't be my doing, it'd be theirs." He smiled. "So it didn't come out a surprise. I'll just have to find another job, that's all."

"Brandon!" She was shocked. "You mean you'll lose your job over it?"

"Sure. I know what's gonna happen when I go back to Dallas now. The last words my boss said were 'Bring us Seahawk Cove or else.'"

"Oh. I'm sorry." Unhappiness for him settled around her like a mantle. Poor Brandon. He was so often in a mess. And it always upset her as much as it did Lily. She loved him, darn it, loved him and his easy, laid-back ways and his obvious vulnerability in a sharp-dealing world. He was her brother, or as close to it as anyone could be, and his pain was hers, felt as deeply as it was possible to feel.

She'd always had a protective feeling for him; every one of his failures bit into her. She studied him now, trying to keep the sorrow out of her eyes. Darn the kid, anyway, why was he always on such a thorny path?

She leaned back against the counter, her head bowed. She ought to know what to say to him, she thought. But she couldn't think of anything.

"Hey, Alicia—" he walked over and touched her shoulder "—you always get too upset. Look, I'm not sure it would have worked out for me anyway. I couldn't really picture myself a vice-president of that big company. And the manager's job sounded like work. You know I've always hated paperwork, and what's a manager besides a guy stuck behind a desk shuffling a lot of paper? I've never been a pencil pusher. I like selling, 'Lish. Paper bores me."

She searched his face. Was he serious, or merely trying to console her? Then she decided he was serious, for Brandon had a way of refusing to stay on the down side of anything. He could *be* down, but he never *felt* down. She smiled. "I'm glad you're taking it this way."

"I am. It's for the best. It'll come out all right."

Brave words, she thought. A neat attempt to buck himself up, but the fact remained: once more Brandon would be looking for a job.

He changed the subject. "Elaine's going to the beach with me today; I'm just waiting for her to get through with her tennis lesson. She said she'd borrow a car and pick me up. I like it that way for a change, the girl fetching the guy. They oughta do it more often." He grinned.

So that's what they'd been discussing in the gift shop last night. Alicia pictured Elaine with a fishing rod bent double, hooking one man after another. But Brandon seemed pleased about it, so she shrugged.

Brandon broke into her thoughts. "She's here!" He started for the door, then stopped, and Alicia saw his face fall. Following his glance through the window she knew why—Elaine wasn't alone. Beside her in the front seat sat David.

"So much for the beach," Brandon shrugged. He started through the door halfheartedly, then slouched against the building eyeing Elaine. When he made no move to come closer she called out impatiently, "Well hurry up! Why are you just standing there?"

"Looks like you've got a full house."

"Oh...David. He wanted to come along, so I said why not?" She smiled at Brandon engagingly. "David thought Alicia was coming."

"He did?" Brandon turned back to Alicia, surprised.

When Alicia only stared, feeling icy toward the ever manipulative Elaine, Brandon said under his breath, "Why don't you come, 'Lish?" Then in whispered tones he snapped, "Maybe you can get that octopus off Elaine."

The word "octopus" was uttered so quietly Alicia barely heard it.

She considered the offer. Why not? There was little else going on today. Her one scuba lesson had been canceled. And Brandon had had a bad twenty-four hours. If she could help—even help his cause with Elaine—she ought to do it. What else were relatives for?

She quickly said, "Okay, Brandon, I'll go," and noticed that both Brandon and David looked pleased.

So Elaine hadn't charmed David completely yet, she thought, running into the house for her swimsuit. She hurriedly put on a yellow bikini, and grabbed her white terry-cloth wrap-around. Thrusting her arms into it, she ran back to the kitchen and left a brief note for Lily.

David moved into the back seat and held out a hand to her. The minute she got in the car she could smell Elaine's perfume. Strong, sweet. She found it amazing that Elaine could have a tennis lesson in this heat and still come out smelling better than after a shower. But then women like Elaine were capable of just about anything. She derided herself, momentarily, for helping Brandon's cause with this male-consuming black widow.

They drove northeast along the island until the road took a sharp upward turn and emerged at a point of land that overlooked water in two directions. David said, "Stop the car, Elaine. Let's get out."

Below them the land narrowed radically, forming a neck that separated two bodies of water. On the right they could see the Atlantic, grayish and opaque, its water rough and choppy. On the left was the Caribbean, so different in character from the neighboring Atlantic that Alicia was amazed. Here the water was a calm brilliant turquoise and transparent enough to reveal clearly the underlying coral formations. One would have expected such vastly different seas to be separated by hundreds of miles, yet here they were, parted only by the narrowest fragment of land. A tempest on one side, a kind of tenderness on the other. Tempest and tenderness, she breathed to herself. She wished Michael were here to share the poignancy of the sight. How well these two bodies of water represented their relationship, she thought. Never ordinary. Never dull. Always in turmoil or bliss. She sighed.

Hearing her sigh, David reached for her hand. "What are you thinking, Alicia?"

"Only that these two oceans are at such odds with each other."

"Like us?" He said it softly so the others couldn't hear.

"Maybe."

He stared at her, trying to read her thoughts, the hunger apparent in his eyes. She stared back, sorry for him, wishing she hadn't left his desire for her unfulfilled as Michael had left hers. But what could she do about it? It seemed to be the way of the world—each person yearning for someone who in turn yearned for someone else. It was only accidental and miraculous if people who wanted each other ever got together.

Alicia's mind worked its way back to the present. She took note of Elaine. Standing at a distance with Brandon, the woman looked utterly seductive in her white flared tennis dress. The daring neckline swooped downward like a roller coaster, and the bottom of the dress only scantily covered her panties. She saw that Brandon kept his eyes fixed on Elaine's face as if deliberately avoiding the embarrassment of being caught peering down her dress. Even from her distant perspective Alicia could see that the dress would afford a rather impressive view of Elaine's breasts.

Soon back in the car they turned off, at the island's narrowest point, onto a mere path. The car bounced along unpredictably on this small rut-scarred dirt road as dust whirled behind them. Abruptly the car plunged down a short grade, crowded and brushed by trees on either side.

At the wheel, Brandon clearly found the going difficult—the ever present ruts grew deeper and more menacing the farther they traveled.

He proceeded slowly, often coming to a near stop as he eased the car carefully down each gully and coaxed it back up the other side. Alicia knew what he was thinking: all they needed right now was a ruptured oil pan!

"Where are we?" asked Elaine, her eyes darting to the window and back to Brandon. "This isn't the road, it's a trail! It's going nowhere."

"Have faith," he laughed. "I know what I'm doing."

"Do you, honey?" she purred. "Well, I hope so...."

In the back David snickered.

The road wandered randomly through the dense overgrowth, stopping at last in a semi-clearing in the junglelike terrain.

Brandon fought his way into a sand wallow, parked the car and ran to the other side, opening the door for Elaine. She patted his arm as she emerged. "Thanks, honey."

Then, as they all reached back into the interior for towels, Elaine announced, "Now you'll all have to go off somewhere. Be a good boy, Brandon, and scat. I have to change into my suit."

Her patronizing tone made Alicia nauseous. How—and why—did Brandon stand it? But he walked off dutifully, without comment. A moment later the three emerged from a sandy path onto a deserted white-sand beach. They spread towels and sat down, staring out to sea from the curve of Savana Bay.

It was a wide spectacular bay, perhaps a mile across, and its protective arms stretched far into the sea. The water was a light emerald green that changed gradually to a purplish blue. Tiny wavelets lapped at the sand.

In a few minutes Elaine came down the path wearing a provocative one-piece purple suit with a tiny belt. Its sides were cut so high Alicia had the distinct impression Elaine was naked. Brandon's bold stare evidentially amused Elaine, for she twirled in front of him and asked sweetly, "You like?"

"Sure," he swallowed. "Yeah. It's a great suit, Elaine. Not too much of it, either."

They all laughed.

David stood abruptly. "For some reason I've never made it to this beach. I hear there's a sandbar out there that goes on and on. I'd like to explore. You want to come with me, Alicia?"

She didn't. She'd just sat down, and the warm sand felt good on her bare legs. "Not now," she demurred. "I'll join you later."

His face fell. "How about you, Elaine?"

"Hey—" Brandon stiffened "—she's *my* date!"

"So." David stared at him. "What do you think we're going to do out there?"

"It doesn't matter. I don't like you asking my date."

"Gentlemen, gentlemen." Elaine laughed. "I

apologize for being only one person. But don't fight over me.''

"Who's fighting?" David looked annoyed. "I just wanta go for a swim. And not alone. I could ask Brandon, I guess.''

Alicia stood up quickly. "Come on, David. Let's go.''

They waded into warm water, just cool enough to be a pleasant contrast with the air. Alicia resolutely refrained from looking back. Let Brandon have his date to himself. His interest in her couldn't last. How long could anyone stay interested in Elaine? Even as the question came to her, so did the disappointing answer: a long time, apparently. Hadn't Michael kept Elaine around now for a year?

Though they waded through what seemed an endless distance, the water was never more than waist high. About a quarter-mile from shore, the bar finally ran out—but only momentarily. Through the clear water they could see a ten-foot drop.

They swam over the deeper area and a moment later were in shallows again, this time over coral.

"Darn," said David, "I *would* forget my fins. Walking on coral's for the birds.''

"Don't walk, then," Alicia grinned. "Swim.''

David plunged below the surface, then popped up again. "There's a certain kind of coral I'm looking for. Fan coral.''

"You shouldn't touch it," she said.

"Sure I should. What's the difference?"

"What if everyone came out here and plundered coral?"

"Nobody is," he laughed. "Do you see anyone else? No, there's just me. Sometimes you're too uptight, Alicia." He swam toward her and put his arm around her waist. "Come on, lovely one, kiss me." His blond head bent toward her, and his lips closed over hers stifling her.

She pulled away. "Don't," she panted. "I can't swim and kiss at the same time." Odd, she thought, how one man's kisses were sweet and irresistible—honey and hunger all mixed together—while the other's were merely suffocating.

"Let's get out, then," he said. "We can concentrate on kissing."

"With *them* here? No, David." She wished he'd go back to his coral hunting.

He frowned at her. "Are you *ever* going to want me to kiss you? 'Cause I sure as hell never see it anymore."

"Please don't be cross," she said, avoiding the issue. "Come on, let's race to shore. One. Two...."

"Forget it," he said sullenly. "Either I'm going to make a little love to you or I'm going back after fan coral. None of this racing stuff. That's for kids."

"Suit yourself," she shrugged. "I think I'll

go in, then. I haven't stretched out on the beach for a long time."

"By God," he said, staring at her, "you're going to have to tell me something soon, Alicia. I can't be kept on a long string forever. This thing between us—it's getting stronger every day. You don't want me but you won't let me go."

"Maybe I ought to let you go," she said softly, regretfully.

She put her feet down seeking a smooth spot on which to stand. "David, I know that what I'm doing isn't fair."

He stood beside her, his hand groping for her waist. "Alicia," he said into her hair. "Oh, Alicia. Why don't you love me? Will you ever be able to love me?"

She shook her head. "I don't...I don't know, David. But it isn't you. There's nothing wrong with you. It's me. But please, David, be my friend."

The water surged and lifted them together, so momentarily they floated, both of them light and drifting inches above the coral. Then the wash of waves set them back again, gently.

"So that's how it is?" he sighed. "Forever?"

"Nothing is forever. But for now...yes." She turned to look at him sadly. "I'm going back. Stay if you like."

"I'll see you after a while," he delivered stonily.

Looking at his handsome face, his generous mouth now set in unhappy lines and his hair wetly plastered to his well-shaped head, she felt a mix of regret and nostalgia. She liked David; she always would. But at that moment, she knew for certain she'd never love him.

With or without Michael, she wouldn't marry David, and it was better that he know, instead of always wonder. She gave him a small wave, which he didn't return, and swam back toward the beach.

The water felt cool but not cool enough to calm the turbulent emotions she felt at having dismissed David once and for all. Saying goodbye to anything was hard; to a person, harder still. Goodbye to the fun and good times they'd once known—they'd be hard to give up. But everything ended in time, didn't it, she mused. What in life, after all, didn't end in goodbye?

Her thoughts pursued her as she hit shore and ambled up the beach in search of her towel.

She looked around. Where was Brandon? And Elaine?

She stretched out across the sand, letting the sun dry up the salt water and warm her body.

The sun—welcomed at first—grew quickly hot. She needed suntan lotion and wondered where she'd get some. Perhaps the car....

Starting down the little path, Alicia thought she heard voices and stopped. The voices filter-

ing through the bushes near her were those of
Elaine and Brandon.

She overheard Elaine saying, "Your dad and
Alicia and Lily...they're all wrong. You've got
to make them see it, honey."

Alicia skulked guiltily toward the bushes. She
felt like a spy, yet she was convinced she ought
to hear what was being said. Through a small
gap in the bushes she could see Brandon leaning
against the car. Elaine was there, too—in his
arms. His hand caressed her hair, his eyes
looked down into hers.

Alicia pulled back out of sight. But she
couldn't make herself leave.

A pause. Then Brandon said, "Be serious."

"I am serious," Elaine pronounced emphati-
cally, then continued. "Your little Seahawk
Cove...who's ever heard of it? You've got to
grab this deal, honey, run with it, or you'll lose
it."

His voice came back defeated. "It won't do
any good. They'll never go along."

"Brandon—" a sharp note touched her words
"—you *must*. It's your once-in-a-lifetime
opportunity. Don't you see? The chance will
never come again. You *must* do it."

"Why do you care so much?"

"Shall I show you?"

Silence followed—Alicia guessed what they
were doing. In whatever way Elaine had set
about showing him, it went on so long Alicia

contemplated leaving. But the bushes rustled and Alicia froze in her tracks, holding her breath.

"There!" Elaine said huskily. Then, "Don't lose what is yours by right, Brandon, please. Don't let your selfish family ruin it—the vice-presidency, the managership. If you wait till everyone's dead you'll lose it another way. Everything!"

"What makes you think so?" For the first time Brandon sounded interested.

"I just know," Elaine declared. "Don't ask me how I know, but believe me, honey, I know some things you don't. I share a bungalow with Michael and—"

"What's he got to do with it?"

She cut him off. "Brandon. . .you *must* fight for it! You must! Do it! Now show me you love me, honey."

The voice conjured up images of a stalking tigress: fierce, stealthy, lethal.

And then there was silence. Elaine was enjoying the kill, no doubt.

Alicia's conscience finally revolted and she crept away. Once out of their line of vision she hurried back to her towel.

Disgusted with her eavesdropping, equally disgusted with them, she sat down. So Elaine had some interest in Brandon's plans.

Alicia had no doubt that the woman's motives had been purely selfish. Elaine never did anything for anyone but herself. But why did she care so much? Why would she bother?

Whatever it was Elaine was trying to accomplish, she'd sought out the only person she dared work on: Brandon. But, Alicia thought wryly, she'd also picked the only person incapable of accomplishing it. Because Brandon would never—*could* never—buck his whole family.

As Alicia pondered Elaine's motives, something Elaine had said came back to her. "I know some things you don't...." Then she had mentioned Michael, and Brandon had interrupted. Suddenly a question came to her: did *Michael* want to buy Seahawk Cove? Was that it? And was Elaine trying to make that impossible?

It all fitted, she decided. It even fitted with certain things Michael had said earlier, sparks of interest he had shown and then quickly extinguished, a pretense of disinterest in the place.

Yes, that had to be it. Michael had already decided to buy Seahawk Cove!

Well, she'd never let it happen. Never. Not with the kind of development Michael had in mind.

Brandon's company wouldn't get it and Michael wouldn't get it, and now she knew she had to stand at the gates like a sentry—a role she'd never wanted but now found thrust upon her.

Well, she'd fight them all: the man she loved like a brother and the man she yearned to make her lover.

How ironic that her life would turn out this way. She was still smiling grimly when the others came back.

A FEW DAYS LATER the season's first winds struck the islands, churning the ocean to mammoth swells, forcing sailboats and cruisers alike to find shelter in the quieter bays. The wind blew the trees around Alicia's house and whistled through the screens, magically turning the big blades on their ceiling fan.

She and Victo canceled their scuba lessons temporarily. The ocean had taken on a murkiness that reflected the dark skies. There was little point in diving into waters so dark only the fish could see.

With time on her hands now, Alicia yearned more than ever for Michael. She'd heard rumors of changes at Pelican Point and assumed he was busy directing them, but she still expected to see him each time a car drove up. She found herself dwelling on his last cruel words: "Sorry it wasn't what you expected." Fingering the pelican around her neck, she ached to cry out to him, "Michael, this pelican is the dearest thing I own."

Lily noticed Alicia's look of despondency and asked if she felt ill. But before Alicia could answer, Lily's sharp eyes offered a different assessment. "Michael loves you," she said. "You don't have to worry about that."

"What makes you think so, Lily? If he loved me—even cared for me he'd be here."

"Honey, I can't answer why that man isn't at your feet every minute of the day. Men are strange. You can't always know how they reason, but I know how he *feels*." She smiled and walked over to lay an arm on Alicia's shoulder. "Alicia, I can see how he feels with every look he gives you."

With strong feelings of doubt, Alicia fingered the pelican at her neck. "I don't know anything, auntie. With him every moment is different. We fight and we never explain. We just find each other again and start over. I think I know him, and each new day I find I don't." She wanted to add, *with each kiss I feel him mine anew, feel him trembling in my arms, but it never lasts.* She didn't. She kept silent.

Her aunt sat down in a rocking chair. "Never mind, child. They say the course of true love is never straight, but you've had it a little more crooked than most. Once you'd loved and lost Michael I never expected you'd find him again." She sighed. "Generally one doesn't; those first loves are just over, once they're done. But you've been lucky, Alicia."

Her aunt picked up one of Bill's shirts and began to sew on a button. "When Michael turned up here I was afraid he'd forgotten you and your heart would be truly broken. The stories all come out that way—one of them shows up later and always someone is already married. I should have thought Michael MacNamee, of all men, would have found another wife. When he hadn't, I guessed his feelings for what they were. Seeing him told me all I needed to know. He does love you, Alicia.''

"I hear you saying it, Lily, but I don't believe it. Oh, I really want to—I just can't.''

Alicia poured herself a glass of water from a jug in the refrigerator. "If it were up to me,'' she went on, crossing the room and settling on the rattan couch, "I'd be with him every minute. I'd hound him. I'd follow him like a shadow. Oh, Lily!'' Immediately she jumped up again. "Don't you have string beans that need cutting? I have to have something to do.''

Aunt Lily watched Alicia trimming tips off beans and breaking them into a bowl. "Whatever it was you fought about last—why don't you just talk it out? Bill and I never harbored grudges when we were young.'' She laughed heartily. "Now we don't talk enough to fight.''

"I think that's what's wrong with us, Lily. We talk too much. We argue because there's so much we don't agree on. Things we'll never agree on.'' She wanted to confide in Lily her fears about Michael's plans for Pelican Point— even for Seahawk Cove. But Lily had such confidence in him. The thought of her aunt's face sagging and the quiet disappointment that would follow made her revelation impossible. Some things she had to keep to herself.

Not only do I have to face this alone, I have to stop him alone, too, she thought dismally.

And there was that other problem. She gazed thoughtfully at her aunt. "You know that Michael's never going to marry again, even without our quarrels. He was burned once and he won't take the chance again. He could have married Elaine, you know, anytime he wanted."

"Pooh!" Her aunt snorted. "He doesn't *love* Elaine. He barely tolerates her. A man like Michael wouldn't marry Elaine, ever. He only keeps her around—" she shrugged "—I'm not sure why, actually, but Elaine must serve some useful purpose. What that might be, you know better than I."

"She acts as his hostess."

"It had to be something like that. Those two are as different as night and day. She's beneath him."

Alicia opened her eyes in surprise. Her aunt rarely criticized anyone, yet she'd just shown contempt for Elaine. "You sure don't like her," Alicia grinned.

Lily frowned. "I'm sorry I said that—it wasn't Christian of me. One shouldn't let personal antagonisms overcome one's ethics. I suppose Elaine has some goodness in her—somewhere." She knotted her thread and laid the shirt down.

"There'll come a day when Michael feels like marriage."

"I don't know...." Alicia drained off the beans and set the bowl on the counter. "All I know is, Lily—I love him!"

Later that day, Alicia was mashing potatoes for dinner, banging away in the metal bowl with all the strength she could muster—as if unloading her frustration on potatoes would bring her relief.

As she whipped them to a fluffy consistency she asked herself why she had to fall for a man like Michael. Why did she seem so intent on pursuing a hopeless situation? If she'd had any sense, she would have fallen in love with someone simple, someone like David. It would have been so easy, so uncomplicated!

Sometimes I don't even love Michael, she said to herself. "I hate him!" she cried aloud as she gave a final smack of the metal masher against the mixing bowl.

"Hate who?" The answering words caught her so much by surprise that she dropped the handle of the potato masher. Her gesture sent the bowl spinning round and round across the counter.

Michael stood in the doorway of her kitchen, laughing.

"Michael!" Alicia stared at him feeling the mad thumping of her heart.

Meanwhile the bowl whirled its way to the

edge of the counter. With one quick lunge Michael crossed the space and stopped its mad rotation before it crashed to the floor.

"The potatoes look well beaten," he said, peering into the bowl. "In fact, I think you've killed them." He put out his hand. "Come with me. I want to talk to you."

When she stood transfixed, he steered her outside and led her across the lawn. Out there the wind had its way with the trees and they bowed majestically.

Some distance from the house he pulled her down beside him on the grass. "I don't like the way we left things the other night."

"It was a strange evening." She forced a smile. "Not too good for Brandon."

"Or you. When I looked back you were alone. I'm sorry. I should have come back."

"It's all right. You're not responsible for me."

She caught him off guard, and he looked past her without answering. He snapped off a blade of tough grass. "Yesterday I went to Puerto Rico to buy horses. This island has endless places to ride. I spotted them when I went out looking for building sites—" he looked at her strangely "—and wrestling with myself, I might add. Things you've said have got under my skin."

Momentarily a bright spark of hope danced its way across her consciousness. It died when he added, "I figured we might as well have horses until the building starts."

A gust of wind whirled through the trees, and Michael brushed flying hair out of his eyes. "The wind will die soon, they say. When will you go riding with me?"

Before she could answer, a voice broke in on them. "Alicia!" She turned to see who was calling with such urgency. It was Victo.

He raced up from the beach, shouting her name once again. His dark brown legs propelled him swiftly, his bare feet running lightly over grass and stone alike. Then he stood in front of them, panting slightly.

"I'm Victo." He held out a hand to Michael and offered an engaging smile. He was wearing cutoff jeans and no shirt. His bare chest was muscled, the legs extremely well proportioned. But what always drew Alicia to Victo was the expression on his face—alert, confident and full of zest. He was quite unlike his grandfather, who was so much more reserved and seemed almost courtly by comparison. But then nearly fifty years separated them, she reflected.

Michael nodded pleasantly. "Victo...I've heard a lot about you! I'm Michael MacNamee. Don't you run the scuba school?"

"With Alicia I do." Victo skipped over Michael's words. His eyes bright with excitement he announced, "The wreck's shifted! The swells moved it, I just heard from someone who came back on a boat! They say it's settling down on its side, so we can get in now. I've gotta take the boat and go out there tomorrow—that is, if the wind dies down. But first I have to go down to the harbor and buy us a new propeller. It's cracked; it must've hit something. I need the car."

"Lily will give you the keys." She nodded toward the house. "I'd like to go with you, Victo—maybe there's treasure in that ship!" She turned to Michael, her eyes shining. "Will you come, Michael? We call it Victo's wreck, because he found it, but none of us could get inside before. There are always fish there—and lots of coral, too. It went down in 1867—in a big hurricane."

"Tomorrow?" Michael frowned. "I don't know, Alicia. I promised Elaine we'd go to Caneel Bay tomorrow."

Alicia felt struck by a blast of arctic air, and she turned away. When she didn't move, Victo said cheerfully, "You can tell me later, Alicia. There's room for him—for Michael—if he wants to come." He ran into her house and a moment later drove away.

As the car disappeared down the road, Alicia started to walk off. "Never mind, Michael, you don't need to come. The two of us will do fine."

She felt his hand suddenly gripping her arm. Angrily he said, "I keep promises to others beside you. She wanted to go, and I said I'd take her. We're going in my cabin cruiser. She's never been in it before.''

"It's okay,'' she said, her voice husky. "Take her. You have to keep your promises.'' She despised the tone of voice that gave her feelings away.

"Come on, Alicia,'' he said urgently, "we'll go to the wreck another day.''

"No, we won't.'' She had control of her wavering voice now. "We won't, Michael, because I won't go with you. Your first duty's to Elaine. Please. . . please. . . let go of my arm. I want you to take care of Elaine, she's your—Michael, let go of me. I'm going in the house!'' She jerked away from him just as he released her voluntarily. She shot off into an ungraceful spin and nearly fell. It was all she needed, she thought bitterly, catching herself on the way to the ground, to make a fool of herself by stumbling at his feet.

Dignity shattered, she went into the house. She didn't look back to see how long he stayed.

An hour later he was gone.

SHE WAS AWAKE MOST of the night, berating herself. *Oh, you fool,* she said over and over. *You silly jealous fool.* Why couldn't she accept Michael's allegiance to Elaine? He'd known Elaine a long time, after all. He owed her something. They were sharing a suite of rooms; no one had denied that!

Another voice demanded, *why does he throw her in my face? Why can we never get rid of her?*

When she finally fell asleep, she kept seeing images of Elaine—Elaine smiling, Elaine laughing, Elaine riding a horse beside Michael.

It was a puffy, distorted face she presented to her mirror when she woke at dawn. Her eyelids felt as heavy as if she'd had no sleep at all and had been crying all night. But she'd been too angry for tears. She splashed cold water on her face, determined to make some attempt to look normal, though she knew it was a useless gesture. Lily's shrewd eyes would notice her state immediately and understand what the trouble was. Though she'd refrain from asking, her silence would somehow make it worse. If only she could restore herself to normal before someone saw her.

Tentatively she opened the door to the living room. No one was around. It was early enough that even Bill was still asleep. Quietly she slipped out of the house, crossed the lawns and made her way to the beach.

The air was calm after three days of wind. Dawn had come gently, easing over the island, now gradually dispelling a faint mist. It was barely warm and she shivered, though more from emotion than temperature.

When she reached the beach she thought she heard a large engine somewhere near the arm of land that separated Seahawk Cove from Pelican Point. She stood waiting to see what it was, and presently a luxury boat rounded the point and came toward their little dock. She had no idea what time it was, but it must have been before seven—the owner of this boat was up early. She stood where she was, watching curiously. The engine stopped and soon a broad-shouldered man jumped lightly over the side and onto their dock, holding a thick rope. It was Michael!

His back was to her, and now she had no recourse but to run. He'd think she'd been waiting here all night just to see him go by on his way to Caneel Bay. Lightly, quietly, she ran, hoping he wouldn't notice, until she came to the nearest cottage. She would duck behind it until he went away. She was only a few feet from security when she sensed, rather than heard, the footsteps coming up behind her.

It was obviously no use trying to outrun him now and no use pretending she hadn't been there, either, so she walked slowly, her back to him. Let him do what he might, think whatever he wished; these past twelve hours she'd outdone herself in clumsy behavior, sharp words and poor timing.

Each step she took she felt him coming closer, and suddenly he had her wrist and was whirling her around. "Alicia!" He stared down at her, his dark eyes unfathomable.

She could think of nothing to say.

He studied her face for an instant, then pulled her to a small bench under a tree. Gripping her tightly he folded his arms around her; it was hopeless to try to get away.

Still she struggled against him as he held her gently but firmly against his chest. He did not kiss her but simply held her in an attempt to quiet her trembling. When she had stopped moving and fallen against him with a sigh, he eased the pressure of his arms. One arm now held her tenderly, the other stroked her hair. Softly and more sweetly than she could ever have imagined possible, he caressed her, and his caress embraced nothing of passion, but rather of love. In his arms she felt like a beloved child.

"Alicia," he murmured against her ear. "My Alicia. Why would you run from me?"

Unable to answer, she merely shook her head. She would spoil the moment if she said anything, so she lay against him, feeling his gentle hand move tenderly across her forehead.

"Don't run from me ever again."

"Why did you come here?" she managed at last. "I wasn't waiting for you." The words were whispered.

"I know." After a while he finished, "I know you better than that. What were you doing up so early?"

She shook her head. She'd never tell him. They sat together in silence, his caress infinitely tender.

As the misty dawn turned into a brighter morning, he said, "I've come to take you to Victo's wreck. We're all going in my boat, I've arranged to make a party of it. Since most of the scuba gear is here, I brought the boat over. I was going to surprise you, Alicia."

"What happened to...to your trip with Elaine?"

He shrugged. "A substitution. I talked her into a scuba trip. I'm sure it was her second choice, but she couldn't pretend she didn't want to get out on a boat." He gave her a soft, wry grin. "She'd already committed herself whole-heartedly to that part of it. Brandon and David are coming. And Victo, too, of course. I arranged it all last night. There's plenty of room, and we need company for Elaine. Lots of it, to replace me—since I'm going to be busy with you."

"You might have asked me," she smiled up at him.

Instead of answering, he leaned closer, and suddenly he was kissing her fully, passionately. The force of him and his eager searching desire made her tremble once again. His mouth explored her face, her lips, with every nuance a man could summon. She imagined herself stretched out beside him, his sensitive hands exploring every inch of her as she yielded herself to him in every way a woman could.

Then the passion turned to peacefulness again

as her daydream faded and he brushed his lips across her nose and her eyelids. Still she trembled, for she found his tenderness as overwhelming as his fiercest kisses, not knowing which moved her more.

"Michael, Michael," she murmured.

"I should have found you sooner," he breathed against her cheek. "The sun is up too much for this."

"I wasn't here sooner."

"I know, I know." Slowly, reluctantly, he pulled her to her feet. "We can't go on this way here—it's indecent. Later, Alicia, later. My God," he groaned, "how much can a man take?" Straightening stiffly, he walked her to her house. She walked alongside him, transported by passion and the joy of being with him.

CHAPTER ELEVEN

MICHAEL'S BOAT, with all of them aboard, pulled away from the dock at eight-thirty. Tucked in the hold were four red-and-white food hampers provided by Pelican Point. One of the hampers contained several bottles of wine.

The cabin cruiser was forty-eight feet long, with six chairs riveted to the deck. Dark blue cushions filled out the molded seats.

Elaine, in a vivid pink string bikini, reigned supreme in the large chair nearest the bow. Behind her, Alicia could see Michael standing erect in the elevated navigation room. Eyes on the horizon and hands on the ship's wheel, he appeared unaware of what was happening on deck. Alicia wanted to join him in the small enclosure but contented herself with quick occasional glances at his strong profile. With Elaine so close by, Alicia felt self-conscious about being with Michael too much.

Even from here on deck, Alicia was filled with a sense of Michael's competency. Just as he'd handled the small boat coming back from

Honeymoon Beach, he now was master of the big one, and her awareness of his strength and forcefulness made her yearn to have him master her. After their dawn on the beach she ached for more than just kisses.

Always, though, another part of her was aware of Elaine. The two women had hardly spoken. Alicia felt she had nothing to say to Elaine, and she hadn't noticed Elaine making overtures to her, either. They'd ended that day on the beach with noticeable coolness. It was almost as if Elaine knew she'd been overheard.

With amusement, Alicia watched Brandon and David hovering over Elaine as if she were a sex ornament. Now that David was sure Alicia would never marry him he apparently felt free to pursue Elaine. Subconsciously Alicia wondered if he hadn't wanted this liberty some time ago. Or was his behavior a pretense? Was he hoping to incite her to jealousy? She didn't know. Nor did she care.

As for the sex queen herself, she favored both suitors equally with warm smiles and light banter. The two men reminded Alicia of kittens taking turns batting a ball of yarn. The yarn itself had little to do except provide itself for their amusement.

Michael had been right: bringing along a couple of eager men for Elaine was the best way to keep her happy.

Steadily the boat made its way into deeper

and deeper swells, heading for Peter Island. At the stern of the boat, Victo sat reading a scuba-diving magazine. Occasionally he looked up to check their heading, but otherwise he left the navigation to Michael.

Alicia, by this time bored watching the triumvirate in the bow, decided to climb the three steps to the navigation room and join Michael at the helm.

"I was wondering when you'd come to see me," he remarked, not turning to look at her. "Sit up here—" he indicated a padded swivel captain's chair "—and tell me where we're going. Is it near that island somewhere?" He inclined his head toward an irregularly shaped mass in the distance. "I don't see any markers pointing out the wreck."

She laughed and gave him an approximate area, still about thirty minutes away. Then she said, "I didn't come up sooner because Elaine was watching me. She makes me nervous." Elaine's harsh warnings in the gift shop still sought refuge in Alicia's mind, but she determinedly pushed them back. Telling Michael what Elaine had said would only sound like the jealous caviling of two immature girls. She settled back into the captain's chair. Why did she have so much trouble talking to this man about the things that mattered, she asked herself. About her. About him. But especially about their future together.

What went wrong between his kisses and his conversation? In his arms she felt totally, belovedly his, the only woman in his life. Yet in their dealings outside of their embraces she was forever falling short. Or he was. Together they stumbled, always misunderstanding, always scraping bottom on hidden, dangerous shoals.

Was she hoping for too much? Was she any closer to having him forever than she'd been two weeks ago? She shrugged to herself. Questions, questions. Would she ever know for certain?

Perhaps, ultimately, she'd have to settle for surrender, pure physical surrender, knowing this was all she was going to get. *But not yet.* She sent warnings to her own insistent yearnings. *Not yet. Today is not the day of surrender, nor tomorrow. After that we will see....*

From the navigation room she could see David and Brandon exchanging harsh words and Elaine looking on benignly. She couldn't hear what they were saying; she only knew by their expressions that both were angry.

But Elaine wasn't upset. If anything, their squaring off, like two angry cocks, merely amused her.

Just then Victo appeared. "Take a sonar fix and see if the wreck isn't nearby. Then you can start cutting her back; we're about there."

Alicia gazed out over the familiar seas. Islands were scattered around them: Salt Island

and Cooper Island northeast, Norman Island due south. They had come down the Sir Francis Drake Channel, which ran like a slot between the islands that divided the Caribbean from the Atlantic. It was peculiar, she thought, how this body of water kept changing names when the oceans were all interconnecting. How did anyone know at what precise spot a ship left one body of water and entered another?

Michael had cut the engines almost to idle. Victo stood beside him, taking readings on the sonar. "Now," he said suddenly. "Shut her off." Dashing to the back of the boat, he hastily lowered the big anchor on its thick chain. All forward momentum stopped. Victo and David began laying out tanks, weight belts and buoyancy compensators.

Michael and Alicia joined the others on deck.

"How many are going down?" Victo asked.

Alicia, Michael and David indicated their intentions with raised fingers.

"That means I'm the fourth," Victo nodded. His dark eyes assessed them thoughtfully. "Alicia," he said, "let Michael be your buddy, and David and I will go together. That leaves two on deck, which is good."

They all fell silent as they began pulling on their gear. Because they were going deep—the wreck was ninety-five feet down—they all wore lightweight neoprene wet suits. Even in this warm sea the temperature dropped markedly at greater depths, and the seawater would sap their body heat with astonishing speed. Alicia thought of the ragged, knifelike coral that had built up on the old wreck and shivered involuntarily. Her thin wet suit was not protection enough against deep gashes.

Once into her suit, Alicia buckled her weight belt around her waist, then pulled a buoyancy-control vest over her head. With difficulty she strapped a diver's knife in its sheath to her left ankle. It occurred to her that she hadn't tested the knife in ages, so she pulled it free and gently felt the edge with her thumb. She frowned; the knife was dull. She knew she'd been careless. In her years of diving she'd never used the knife for its intended purpose, which was to cut herself free of impediments in an emergency. She knew it was foolish to go down with a dull knife, but now it was too late to do anything about it. She resolved to sharpen it as soon as she got home.

Moments later Michael was helping her into her tank's backpack. She smiled at him. "Stay with me, Michael, and we'll really explore—you won't believe how they built ships in those days! And if we can go inside...." Her voice trailed off as she thought of what they might find inside the old carcass, the remains of an old, seagoing era. "In other wrecks they've found rum bottles still full of rum! And old locks and

chains and bells and—'' she smiled ''—sometimes necklaces and rings!''

With an edge of sarcasm he answered, ''I
knew you had to be going down ninety-five feet
for something!'' He turned his back on her, letting Victo help him with his own tank.

Alicia felt rebuffed and stopped smiling.
Michael's sarcasm, meant as a joke, had cut her
almost like the coral she'd trodden on in the
past. She now wished that he wasn't going to be
her ''buddy.'' She suddenly felt icy cold—as if
struck with a premonition of harm. She considered, momentarily, abandoning today's dive.
She sat on the rail of the ship, thinking. Michael's sharp comment had somehow changed
everything—it had certainly taken away her
mood of gaiety, and it boded ill for the dive.
Perhaps today was the day to stay home.
Though she wasn't normally superstitious, she
felt strangely uncomfortable. But at last she
shrugged it off, knowing if she gave up today
Michael would have to abandon the dive, too.
Divers always went in pairs. She'd just have to
ignore his wisecracks and hope he didn't mean
them.

Victo had finished helping David with his
tank and in turn was getting assistance. Alicia
and Michael leaned against the rail, waiting.

Michael touched Alicia's hand. The touch
was gentle. She looked into his eyes: they stared
back at her, owllike behind his diver's mask.

Then she saw the corners crease and knew he was smiling. It reassured her. He nodded toward the edge, motioning her to go first. Clumsily she eased herself over the side of the boat and dropped backward into the water, rolling. Finning away from the spot, she waited for Michael to follow. There was a splash, and then he was beside her treading water.

Alicia pointed her head downward and left the surface, using her fins to give her maximum propulsion. Knowing her arms would only slow her descent, she kept them at her sides while her feet continued to push her at an angle ever deeper into the water.

Remembering that she must breathe constantly during descent, she kept her mouth tightly on the mouthpiece, unconsciously listening to the sound of escaping bubbles.

Around her, schools of almost transparent fish the size of minnows shied to one side. Larger fish, swimming singly, lurked in darkness away from her immediate path.

Water seeped into her suit imperceptibly as her body quickly warmed it to her own skin temperature. The bright visibility of the top waters changed slowly to dimmer arenas as she traveled deeper in the ocean. Yet the sun continued to give light, even at this depth.

She glanced at the depth gauge on her wrist. Almost twenty feet. Feeling the uncomfortable buildup of pressure in her ears, Alicia swallowed once, then twice, as she'd done earlier. But this time the pressure merely increased and the swallowing didn't help. She stopped swimming and squeezed her nose through the mask, blowing gently. On her second try her ears popped. In a few minutes she'd have to do it again.

Turning her head slightly she saw Michael clearing his ears, too, and waited. After a moment he made a circle with his fingers, the sign for "okay" and the two resumed their progress downward.

As Alicia propelled her body ever deeper into the ocean, she was conscious again of the sense of freedom she always felt under the surface. No longer confined by gravity, she could twist, turn and move her body in any dimension without bowing to the limitations imposed on shore. She understood, here, what it must be like to be a fish or a bird, without confinement, without bounds. She exulted in the freedom and sensed her rising excitement. Her freedom, her weightlessness made her feel strangely omnipotent. These feelings were what brought her back, over and over again, to scuba diving.

Today Alicia could only dimly recall the feelings of discomfort she'd experienced on her first dive. She'd felt hindered then by her wet suit and the gear she carried, uneasy in the knowledge that the mouthpiece was her only link with breath. She accepted it easily now and nearly forgot it, no longer conscious of the fine line between lungs filled with air and lungs filled with water! As an experienced diver, breathing through the regulator was as natural to her as breathing in her sleep. Her mind focused elsewhere.

A few minutes later Alicia could see the dim outline of the wreck poised on the ocean floor. It was lying on a sloped shelf partway down the incline. Alicia could see the dark outline of forged-metal strips ringing its starboard side. But distortion changed and disfigured the old ship. Coral, clinging to its wooden parts, sent plantlike tendrils off the hull, as though the ship had become a fossilized foundation for an exotic garden.

Oblivious to the divers, schools of fish ducked in and out of the formations as they went on with their business of feeding. Crabs crept stealthily out of cavelike shelters, exposing themselves momentarily before scurrying for cover.

Alicia looked up to see Michael at a distance from her, hovering just above one of the hull's portholes. He gestured for her to follow but she held up a hand, indicating he had to wait. Now that they were at the bottom of the ocean the water pressure had compressed her neoprene suit, reducing its buoyancy and forcing her to exert too much effort to continue floating easily above the wreck. She knew she needed air in her vest. Quickly removing her mouthpiece, Alicia held her breath and blew a lungful of air into her vest, inflating it slightly. But at that moment the mouthpiece floated away from her. Reaching behind her, she tried to retrieve it quickly but couldn't. She held her breath calmly as she reached out again for the mouthpiece. It was attached by the hose to the tank, she told herself, so it couldn't have gone far. She felt for it again, her arms restricted by the wet suit.

Again she came up empty. Her mind split into two demanding voices, one warning that she didn't have much time, the other demanding that she stay calm. Her lungs began to ache with the need to breathe. Seconds seemed like hours as she searched again for the mouthpiece. Running her fingers carefully along the hose, she found the elusive mouthpiece at last, dangling loose along the right side of her tank.

Quickly Alicia brought the end to her mouth. She pressed the regulator-purge button to clear the water, then inhaled cautiously. When she found that no seawater came through with the air, she indulged herself, taking in several long, slow breaths as relief flooded through her.

It was only then that she was conscious that for a split second she'd been afraid. Fear, a precursor of panic, was the cardinal sin of scuba divers. But she'd been able to control her fear and it had made her feel stronger. Elated and proud of herself, she swam toward Michael.

He was exploring the entrance to the hull, directing a beam of light across ghostly timbers.

As they pointed themselves downward again, preparing to swim into the interior of the ship, they saw David and Victo coming toward them. One by one, the four swam cautiously into the dark interior.

In here, the sun's light didn't penetrate. Victo and Michael, bearing underwater lights, flashed their way into what Alicia supposed was an old engine room. It was full of enormous wheels, overturned metal tables and an assortment of pipes leading in all directions. The machinery, each piece illuminated by a single beam from one of the two underwater flashlights, appeared in good enough condition to have been in use just last week. Corrosion had covered and pro-tected the iron pipes so that each remained af-fixed in its original position. Alicia was awed by the sight. She knew that living men had once stood in this engine room trying to fight off the disastrous effects of the hurricane, defending their ship against the force of fate until the mo-ment when the seas overcame them. She shiv-ered, feeling strangely sad, as if they were all somehow intruding on other men's graves. These sailors had a right to rest undisturbed, she thought, without the curious living coming down to pry.

Probing deeper, the four found the ship's bunk room and scanned the sleeping slots, set close together like so many shelves, when Victo flashed his light against his wrist and indicated it was time to go. It had been eighteen minutes since they'd entered the water, and though they still had some time, Victo always left margins. He wanted to avoid a graduated decompression ascent.

Victo and David swam out through the entrance first, and together they disappeared off to the right. Alicia and Michael swam away in the opposite direction and had nearly cleared the area of the wreck when Alicia saw two enormous nylon nets ahead of them. They were fishermen's nets left to seine the water for small fish. An opening between the two nets allowed Michael to swim through easily. With one kick of his fins he was through it and gone, his regulator leaving a small following of bubbles before he disappeared.

Carefully Alicia edged between the nets, noticing that the opening shifted slightly to the left as the current moved. Her neck and shoulders were through when suddenly she realized she was no longer moving forward. Something, some part of her equipment, had caught in the net, and now she was trapped as surely as if the fisherman were seining for her! Angrily she wriggled from one side to another, trying to break free.

After a moment of useless flailing she realized that the T-shaped handle to her regulator valve was snared by one of the nylon loops. Alicia reached behind her, trying to find the handle with her fingers, only to have the wet suit pull her up short. Its bulk hampered her movements severely: she could reach back just so far and no farther, her fingers stopping somewhat short of the valve.

For several minutes she labored at the net, twisting it, jerking it, hoping that it might be induced to come off. But nothing worked. Instead she sensed that she had made matters worse— the net seemed to be more taut than before. In dismay, Alicia realized there was no longer any slack, that her body was drawn tightly against the nylon. It was as though she were on a hook and every attempt to escape caused the barb to sink in deeper.

And then she thought of the knife!

Instinctively she tried to bend from the waist to reach her ankle but the net kept her from doing so. She was forced instead to draw her leg to her chest, where she awkwardly unsheathed the blade.

With clumsy fingers Alicia cut at the strands of nylon holding her prisoner. For several minutes she sawed, realizing with dawning hopelessness she was getting nowhere. The nylon was too tough, the knife blade too dull. Tears of frustration came to her eyes as she mentally cursed the useless knife.

Then she glanced at her watch, did a quick

calculation and realized she had only seven minutes' worth of air left in her tank. How long, Alicia asked herself, before Michael would realize she wasn't with him and would come back for her? Unless she escaped soon... the implications sent a wave of fear hurtling along her limbs and into her stomach. She felt weak and sick. Stark terror made her momentarily irrational, to the point where she considered throwing off all her equipment and trying to surface without it.

But the wave passed and was followed by an icy calm, a calm so profound that Alicia saw her whole situation with almost detached clarity. The idea of shucking her equipment was nonsense—she was sure she couldn't reach top without it. Further, she could not count on Michael's return; there was too little time left. No, hope lay in saving herself.

She turned her head to study the net at her back. Then she looked around for anything in the vicinity that might have a sharp edge... something on her person, perhaps. There was nothing.

At last Alicia decided her only recourse was to remove her pack and face the regulator valve head-on to see what she was doing.

Steeling herself to prevent a second wave of panic, she made one last attempt to cut the loops with her knife. Reaching behind her, she sawed away at the net.

It was then that it happened—the depth gauge on her wrist tangled in the nylon loops, holding her arm up so she could no longer unhook her pack. Struggling now to free her wrist, she realized if she didn't get loose within the next few minutes she would die here on the ocean floor. Her body would join the company of those luckless sailors. She would no longer be an interloper, but one of their own.

And that was when she saw Michael's light flickering in the distance!

Alicia knew what he was doing—he was using his light to show her he was coming. *Oh, God,* she thought, *hurry, Michael. Hurry!*

Floating helplessly with one arm over her head she watched his easy swimming, saw him coming closer.

Then he was beside her, understanding her plight instantly. Positioning himself behind her, he began to work at the entanglements.

She expected it would happen immediately, that he'd free her and they'd be gone. But though he released her wrist at once, the seconds went by and she remained a prisoner.

She could feel him back there, tugging and pulling at her back, but nothing happened. And that was when she knew it was much worse than she thought—*both* of them might die here on the ocean floor.

She became aware that he was reaching around in front of her now, pulling her toward him and tight against the net, and she understood what he was trying to do—that he was bringing her in as close as possible to release tension on the nylon loops.

The passing seconds brought their distortions, a sense of hours rushing by, then a fresh kaleidoscope of fear within her brain.

Again Michael grasped her urgently and she could sense the expertise he brought to the task as he worked near her neck. Momentarily the net tightened, then became loose again.

It wasn't over yet. The seconds were becoming minutes. One, two, three.... Waves of desperation washed over her, fear that Michael would never be able to free her and would die needlessly himself. She wanted to talk to him, to scream that he must leave now and abandon this hopeless task. It was enough that one of them was trapped.

She tried to gesture and point upward, but her arms were pinioned, her body caught in his grasp. And then it happened, a sudden splitting sound and she was free!

It was over!

She swung to face him, but he gestured wildly, pointing to his watch.

She understood, and even as she began to swim upward, she felt him helping her.

She swam on, as calmly as she could. Though she no longer felt his hand on her body, she never looked back, knowing he was following.

Up, up, up she went, the seconds of her life trailing away as surely as her supply of air. Yet she knew she must never hold her breath.

Breathe, Alicia, she told herself. *Breathe.* The litany formed in her brain. Then a new thought. *Oh, Lord,* she prayed, *let the supply of breaths last.*

The light strengthened, streaming down toward her stronger and stronger, the murkiness changing to clarity.

She swam on, reaching for the sunlight.

At last she saw she was nearly there, and stroking hard she broke through the surface.

Spitting out her mouthpiece, she gulped air, her tension increasing her need. Next to her, Michael panted without speaking. His face was grim, its expression bespeaking a sense of horror. She knew by looking at him that he'd thought them both dead. She also knew he would have died needlessly before he left her there alone.

They rested on the surface, letting the ocean lift them up gently and set them back again. Finally he said, "It was closer than you'll ever know, Alicia."

"I do know." Seawater lapped into her face.

"You were tangled . . . my God, how you were bound up in that net. It was hopeless! I don't know how you got so tangled. You'd managed to get four separate pieces over your regulator handle. But I couldn't see them very well, and they weren't on in any logical order.'' He paused, breathing hard. ''I had to work them off one by one, trying to figure out which was on top of which...but you kept drifting away. Then they'd all tighten up again. The second-to-last strand....'' His eyes went heavenward. ''I thought we were goners, Alicia—it wouldn't come free. Oh, God, dear one, I thought we would die there together. I was sure of it.''

It was the first time he'd ever used a word of endearment with her. She took note of it, the word burning in her consciousness.

''Your trap was hopeless, Alicia; I don't know yet how it came apart.''

It didn't come apart, she thought. *You made it come apart.*

''You saved my life,'' she said softly.

''I did.'' He smiled. ''And now I'm forever responsible for you.''

''What do you mean?''

''It's a Chinese proverb: when you save someone's life you have a duty to them forever.''

''I won't hold you to that,'' she smiled back.

Water lapped between them and licked at his face. He brushed at his eyes and looked at her tenderly. ''How precious something becomes when you almost lose it.''

Here in the ocean, with tremors of fear only recently gone from her limbs, she felt a new emotion, a surge of hope stronger than she'd ever felt before. Wasn't he telling her that he loved her? That she was precious to him? She swam closer.

"Well, let's get up on the boat," he said, reaching for her. "You're shivering." His arm went around her waist, a touch she could scarcely feel through the layers of equipment. As he pushed her toward the rocking boat he said, "Boy, it's good to be alive! Thank your lucky stars, Alicia! We're among the living!"

Yes, she thought. *I'm overjoyed. But my joy goes far beyond that....*

Victo and David were at the rail, watching. In another few minutes Alicia and Michael were being helped over the side.

The four of them pulled off their wet suits and sat in the warm sun letting the heat penetrate their cold bodies. Alicia, especially, felt the need for warmth now that the emergency was past. A delayed reaction overtook her and she shook uncontrollably. Michael wrapped a sunwarmed towel around her, his arm remaining around her shoulders even under the gaze of Elaine. But he didn't seem to care.

"Hey, everyone," Elaine said, "we're hungry!"

Angrily she stared at Michael, but he sat on a chair next to Alicia and kept his arm around her. "Alicia's had a shock," he said evenly. "She's going to warm up first."

Elaine saw the look on his face and fell silent.

Brandon asked, "What is it, Alicia? Are you sick?"

Alicia pulled the towel closer around her shoulders. "Tell them, Michael. I'm getting warmer now."

In a matter-of-fact voice Michael began telling the others how Alicia had become hooked on the fisherman's net. As he told the story, the horror of it registered on the faces of his listeners. Elaine drew back, almost in revulsion.

Victo's bright expression became a scowl. His mouth hardened and his eyes flashed anger at Alicia. "Why did you dive with a dull knife?" he demanded.

"You know we've never had to use our knives before, Victo!" she countered. "I'll bet yours is dull, too."

"It isn't! I sharpen it often! How can you tell our students to do what you don't do yourself?" He was so genuinely angry she felt cowed, then defensive.

"Don't worry, Victo, the lesson sunk in. I'm sorry I'm not as perfect as you are." When he turned his head without answering she felt quick shame. "I didn't mean that."

"It almost cost you your life." Victo faced her again. "Stupid accidents always makes me angry." He stood up. "I'm going to get the lunch."

Michael helped him bring down the four hampers, and in a few minutes the men were spreading ham, cheese and turkey sandwiches on a towel. Little containers of coleslaw, pickles and creamy fruit salad were laid around the edges of the towel. On a second towel they arranged the carrot cake and cookies. It was another of the Pelican Point feasts.

Alicia stared at the food, wondering at this world of normalcy—of luxury, really. Half an hour earlier she'd thought herself dead. It all seemed so incongruous.

David sat down intimately close to Elaine, and Alicia caught her cousin throwing him a faintly hostile glance.

With a wine bottle in his hand, Michael proposed a toast. "Let's drink to the gods. They were good to us today." He poured wine into their plastic cups.

The wine warmed Alicia and eased her tension. At first she felt unable to eat, but gradually wine and sun had their effects and she grew hungry and ate first one sandwich, then a second. David, she noticed, was starting on a third. Everyone seemed starved.

They sat quietly on the rocking boat, the food wholly occupying them.

Abruptly, the sandwiches were gone. Brandon looked around, searching among discarded papers, and seeing nothing he looked up to find David devouring a fourth and final ham. "Hey," he said, "that ham sandwich was supposed to be mine! You've had four!"

"Yeah?" David gave him a cocky smile. "Come and get it then!" He held out the last half and as Brandon reached for it popped the whole thing in his mouth. Lazily he chewed, his eyes fixed insolently on the other's face.

With uncharacteristic ardor Brandon shouted at him, his eyes moving from Elaine to David, "Do you think you get *everything* around here?"

"I get everything that's offered to me, old buddy. And lots of things have just come my way!" His grin dared Brandon to catch his meaning. He picked up three pieces of carrot cake and waved them around. "These just came my way, too!"

As he slowly began unwrapping one piece of cellophane, then another, Brandon lunged at him, grappling for the cake. Inadvertently he knocked David backward, and David, angered, gave his assailant a vicious push. David's palm caught the thinner, taller man off guard, sending him sprawling.

The others leaped out of their way, abandoning the desserts.

Quickly David jumped to his feet, fists ready. Brandon, moving awkwardly, took a swing at David, a weak blow to the chest. His second punch, thrown hastily, smacked against David's shoulder, obviously infuriating him.

Alicia screamed, "Stop it, Brandon!" But he was deaf to her cry.

The two worked their way toward the ship's railing, scuffling clumsily, then exchanging a flurry of blows.

Turning to appeal to the others, Alicia found herself staring at Elaine in amazement: the woman was smiling!

"Do something, Michael!" she begged, but she was too late. Just as Michael stepped forward to intervene, David gave Brandon a last angry push. Alicia watched as her cousin toppled overboard, fully clothed in shorts, shirt and tennis shoes.

"Oh!" she shrieked.

The others ran to the edge.

Elaine leaned so far over the railing that Alicia wondered briefly if she intended to dive in.

At that moment Alicia's eye fell on one of the ship's life preservers. Worried that her cousin might bog down in all his clothes, she snatched it off its hook and prepared to throw it to him.

She drew her arm back, took in a deep breath and gave a mighty heave—just as Elaine chose to straighten up from the railing.

Alicia's aim was perfect. The heavy life preserver, on its way to the ocean, struck Elaine first and carried her with it. Together they flew overboard, marked for splashdown.

Alicia's hand went to her mouth, muffling her horrified exclamation.

Treading water, Brandon stared in amazement as the two objects cleared the rail and splashed into the ocean in perfect unison a few feet away. Eyes wide, he watched as the life preserver bobbed to the surface about the same time as Elaine.

She surfaced angrily, her nose spouting water.

Grinning, Brandon asked, "Which one is supposed to rescue me?"

Elaine threw him a furious look, its effect diminished by the stringy hair plastered across her face and her eye makeup running down her cheeks. Rocking gently in the swells, she emitted a shrill, "Ooooogh!"

Up on deck, Michael exploded into uncontrollable laughter, bending over and slapping his knees. "My God!" he exclaimed. "How did Alicia ever do it?"

With visible effort, Victo stifled a grin and removed himself to another part of the boat.

David was still at the rail. Galvanized into action at last, he climbed down the ladder to help Elaine, and with Brandon pushing manfully from below, the two men extracted the sputtering woman from the sea.

"Anyone else need this?" Brandon asked, holding up the life preserver. When no one answered, he heaved it back on deck and began a lazy climb up the ladder, accepting David's help for the last few feet.

David grinned at him. "Sorry about the scuffle," he said, extending his hand.

"It's okay," Brandon said, shaking hands with him. "I don't know what got into me." His puzzled glance took in the disheveled Elaine.

Michael disappeared up top, and now Alicia felt she ought to apologize to Elaine. She approached as Elaine was getting out a comb, but before she could say anything, Elaine's expression warned her away. Hatred burned in her dark eyes.

Stunned, Alicia gaped at her, then turned on her heel and left. For the first time, Alicia had noticed gratefully, Elaine didn't look so good. Wet, she had all the appeal of a drenched poodle. She needed that full coiffure for her thin sharp features.

Alicia went to stand by herself in the stern. The events of the day had shaken her.

Presently Brandon joined her. "She didn't come off looking too good."

Alicia grinned wickedly.

Her cousin smiled. "Did you see it? Her eyelashes aren't real."

"I saw."

"My gosh. That day we all went out she looked like a queen." He shook his head, confused. "Man, Alicia, she's changed. I can't believe it. I never noticed she was so plain before."

Alicia nodded.

He leaned on his forearms, gazing out to sea.

"I never thought so much stuff could wash off." Smiling ruefully, he made a pronouncement Alicia would always remember. "Before I ever get married, Alicia, I'm gonna see the woman when she's wet."

When Alicia went back to join the others, David was sitting with his arm around Elaine. Brandon had gone to the navigation room to join Michael, and Victo was gathering the scuba equipment.

A short time later they were underway. The sea was rising, the swells now twice what they'd been on the way out. The boat dipped and fell, sliding halfway down one valley before it caught an incoming mountain of water and jerked precariously back up again.

The motion was irregular, and Alicia felt she would never quite adjust to it. Her body would nearly adapt to one rhythm, only to have the motion abruptly terminated and a new one begun. Though she felt all right, she could understand how people got queasy.

Nobody spoke going home.

Up in the bow, Elaine clung desperately to a bucket. Elaine was seasick.

It was dusk when they docked the boat at Pelican Point.

Elaine stumbled awkwardly off the boat with David at her side. Her thin drawn face was devoid of color. Her string bikini, stretched by its unexpected encounter with water, hung like a sagging fishnet around her body. A towel draped over her shoulders only partially concealed the ill-fitting suit. In spite of David's protective arm around her, Elaine shivered as she waited for the others by the dock.

Michael and Victo carried off the empty food hampers, and Alicia lugged scuba gear. The group stood momentarily on the dock, each of them unable to think of appropriate words to cap their crazy day. Just then Lily and Bill, out for an evening walk, strolled onto the dock.

"You all look tired," Lily observed. Her sharp eyes assessed the various strange and sullen expressions, but Alicia knew Lily would be too discreet to comment.

"We *are* tired, Lily," Alicia said, hugging her warmly.

Michael cleared his throat and looked around uncomfortably. He seemed unable to think of anything to say. Then he brightened, "Why don't you all come to Caneel Bay with me tomorrow for dinner?"

If he'd expected a joyous response, Alicia thought, he must have been disappointed. Victo was back at the boat tying up and didn't hear the invitation. Brandon declined, explaining that he was expecting a call from his company and would have to hang around the house.

Elaine pouted noticeably. "I can't possibly go on that boat again, Michael," she whined. "I've never been so sick in my life. Can't we fly? Please?''

"There's no landing strip on the island,'' Michael said flatly.

Before David could say anything, Elaine quickly took his arm and in honeyed tones inquired, "Don't we have a tennis lesson tomorrow, David?''

David said he guessed they did.

"That leaves Bill and Lily and Alicia,'' Michael said cheerfully. "and I won't take no for an answer. You're all going!''

"Bill and I would love to see Caneel again,'' Lily smiled, patting her husband's arm. "It's been a long time...." Bill nodded his assent.

Pleased, Michael picked up the gear and walked across the beach.

Alicia was silent. She'd see about that idea tomorrow.

CHAPTER TWELVE

AT BREAKFAST THE NEXT MORNING Alicia, Lily, Bill and Brandon ate together. It was a rare event. Brandon often slept late, believing it his vacationer's right, while her uncle usually left at an ungodly hour to putter among the cottages. Alicia took a second cup of coffee, enjoying these companionable moments with the family.

The telephone rang and Brandon answered. After a few cryptic responses, he hung up and turned to Bill. "Can you come to town with me, dad? There's something we need to do." When Bill hesitated, Brandon said hastily, "It's important." His father nodded, and moments later the two left.

Alicia went down to the dock to meet her scuba class. Moments later she was demonstrating equipment, but her mind kept drifting away from her work. Yesterday Michael had spoken to her with rare tenderness, declaring he had a duty to her forever. But did he still feel that way today? Was she really more precious to him now than before? Or were those merely the euphoric words of someone who'd nearly died and found himself still alive?

Absently, she watched one of her male students struggling with the regulator, her concentration dissipated by thoughts of Michael. Finally, Victo's sharp reminder, "Help him, Alicia!" brought her back and she went to aid the student. Still her thoughts intruded. If Michael truly loved her, what would he do about it? Would he, even now, shy away from a commitment? They'd been so close, and yet. . . .

With nimble fingers she adjusted the man's gear, helping him until he was fully equipped and hidden behind his face mask. In some odd way the man represented Michael. . . except Michael was hiding behind Elaine!

Once the scuba lessons were completed she walked back up the beach, a feeling of mild anticipation stirring her. It would soon be time to dress for Caneel Bay.

She found Lily hanging up laundry outside the house. Her aunt was humming, as though full of some inner pleasure.

"Lily," Alicia said, "come and have lunch with me. I'll make us toasted cheese sandwiches." She looked at her aunt curiously. "You look awfully happy about something."

Her aunt put down her laundry bag and gestured toward the house. "I'll make the lunch, honey. Get in there and press your loveliest dress. You know what an elegant place Caneel Bay is." Almost as an afterthought she added, "You and Michael will be going alone."

"Why?" Alicia asked, surprised. "What's happened with you and Bill?"

Her aunt picked up the laundry again and put two clothespins in her mouth.

Alicia waited.

Finally Lily said offhandedly, "We have to discuss Seahawk Cove with Brandon—there's so little time left."

Alicia leaned against a tree. "What is there to talk about, Lily? You know you're not going to do it!"

Her aunt swung to face her. "My dear, I don't know any such thing. Come on now, get in there, make yourself lovely."

Minutes later, Alicia was on the phone to Michael. It was only fair, she decided, to tell him Bill and Lily weren't coming. She had to give him his out.

To her surprise, Michael laughed at her. "That conscience of yours, Alicia. It works overtime. Give it the night off, huh? I knew they weren't coming."

Good, she smiled, tingling with anticipation. How wonderful to be alone with Michael!

Suddenly he seemed impatient. "I have to get off now and placate Elaine. She's been suspicious all day that this was going to end up you and me. She may choose to be seasick rather than let us go unchaperoned." He laughed ironically. "I've got to convince her the boat will be rocking like hell! See you in a little while,

Alicia.'' The phone clicked and he was gone.

Alicia dressed carefully. She slipped on a shapely aqua dress of soft crepe. Bare at her shoulders, it had a pretty ruffle at her breasts and swung elegantly away from her hips. To complement her sophisticated look she brushed her hair into the fluffy upsweep Michael liked so much, then fastened it with two bone combs. The combs' delicate pattern traced with veins of aqua picked up the lovely shade of her dress. As she stepped into silver pumps, she wondered if her efforts would have any effect on Michael.

She studied her face in the mirror and decided to apply a thin dark line of eyeliner to her lids. She touched up her lips with a light-colored lipstick.

Finished at last, she stared at her reflection. Thanks to the eyeliner, her eyes appeared round and soulful in contrast to her light skin. Well, she'd done all she could.

A thrill of anticipation went through her when Michael appeared at her door. His dark hair, his dark eyes. . . his dark presence seemed to fill the doorway. She had never seen him look handsomer. *Oh, Michael,* she wanted to cry out, *take me with you and let's not come back.*

He was wearing a cream-colored dinner jacket and dark brown slacks. His matching cream-colored ruffled shirt was outlined in brown. Another man might have seemed a dandy in the ruffled shirt, but not Michael.

He held out his hand to her, his eyes traveling up and down her body. His appraising look produced in her a shiver of excitement. In dark and vibrant tones he said, "You look stunning, Alicia!"

Unable to meet his intense gaze any longer, she murmured, "Let me get my purse."

They said goodbye to her aunt and uncle, who stood smiling in the doorway.

"They look exceptionally happy today," Alicia remarked as he opened the car door for her. "I wonder why."

Michael offered no explanation. He only started the engine and guided the car toward the dock.

The cabin cruiser rocked gently at its mooring. Up in the navigation room Michael started the engine, while Alicia sat on the familiar captain's chair gazing out the window.

For two hours he guided the boat among the islands toward St. John island, home of Caneel Bay. He knew exactly where to go, she thought, as he always seemed to know his way in this world.

Looking out the window she noted almost impersonally the brilliant blue green Caribbean. The rich beauty of the sea could usually captivate her for hours but today her thoughts were on this man sitting beside her.

From time to time she stole a look at Michael's strong profile, determined and unyielding. The familiar aloofness weighed heavily on her and she wondered when he would ever say the words she wanted to hear.

As they approached the dock at Caneel Bay, a brilliant red sun hovered over the top of St. Thomas island to the west. Michael jumped off the boat and tied it to the dock.

"Hurry!" He turned to her, pointing. "Let's try to see the sunset from the Sugar Mill." Taking her hand he helped her off the boat and propelled her the length of the wooden dock.

At the main dining room, one of three at Caneel Bay, they paused. Waiters were preparing the tables, setting out napkins and candles. For just an instant she took in the spacious dining room with its two levels. "How beautiful," she breathed. "Just the way I remember."

"We'll see it later," he said urgently. "Come on." He was almost running again, skirting the edge of the dining room and leading her along a stone walkway toward an ancient building that guarded the entrance to Caneel Bay resort. She could see it ahead, backed into a hill.

Though they were rushing, Alicia noticed the resort's grounds. Endless lawns dotted with spreading trees and separated by curving roads were spread out lavishly. She noted a brightly lighted wooden building with a thatched roof. It was new to her and she guessed it was a gift shop.

Ahead of them the old gray ruin, festooned with vines, wore a mantle of antiquity and decay. "The old sugar mill," she murmured to herself.

Along one side precipitous stone steps rose up the hill, and now Michael climbed them rapidly, almost pulling her off her feet.

"Slow down, Michael," she panted.

"Sorry. I'm racing for a sunset." He gripped her elbow and she felt herself propelled, weightless, up the remaining stairs.

They arrived on a small wooden platform.

To their left, the Sugar Mill dining room formed a great round deck, its sides open to the air. The pagodalike roof gave it the look of a large gazebo.

At the mention of Michael's name the headwaiter abandoned his guest list and said, "Of course, Mr. MacNamee," and led them to a table next to the curved rail. Out here there was no man-made roof. Michael and Alicia looked up to an endless ceiling of sky.

Alicia propped her elbows on the table and gazed west across an expanse of water to the outline of St. Thomas island. Above its mountains the sun, like a fiery orange globe, dominated the sky. Alicia and Michael found themselves staring in fascination at a redness that suggested a world consumed by fire.

As the blazing orb shrank and withdrew, hovering clouds absorbed the remaining colors—salmons, pinks, oranges, violets, grays and blacks. The color-tinted clouds filled the horizon, arranging themselves in random artistry as if against a luminous pink canvas.

Finally the sun became a sliver of light and disappeared.

Yet the drama wasn't over. Even as nature's fiery colors faded, man's own lights began dotting the distant island until, in full darkness, the mountains of St. Thomas looked back at them with a thousand yellow eyes.

Through it all, Michael held Alicia's hand without speaking, and Alicia remained silent, sensing that conversation would ruin the mood.

Quietly the waiter set down tall glasses of the planter's punch Michael had ordered.

As the lights winked across the water Alicia remarked, "St. Thomas looks so close. I've never seen the view from here at night. I feel I could swim over."

In the distance they heard the sound of an airplane growing louder, then settling into silence somewhere in the vicinity of the dock. Alicia turned to Michael. "You said they have no airstrip here."

"They don't. That's a seaplane." He squeezed her hand lightly and smiled. "Elaine would have given up her inheritance to come over here tonight. When I left she was in a real snit, pouting like hell, cursing her seasickness. But she couldn't blame me—I invited her to come." His smile grew wider. "Somehow I forgot to mention seaplanes."

The waiter brought them menus, but Michael

shook his head, motioning him off. "I called in our order this morning."

"Thank you, sir. Then the headwaiter must have it." Tucking the menus under his arm, he left.

"You called it in?" Alicia asked, her eyes widening in pleasure. She smiled. So this was a preplanned party. Their date *had* significance. Then surely he would say something about *them*—about their future.

Michael leaned across the table and took her hand. "It's our first real date since—" he stopped, considering "—since San Diego, I think."

"Yes," Alicia whispered, noting his silhouetted form against the light from the single candle. The inward curves of his face—his eyes and the area around his lower jaw—were deeply shadowed. The dark areas gave him a brooding quality and enhanced his appeal. "The rest have just been...encounters," she explained reluctantly.

"More than encounters, Alicia." Just as he seemed ready to say something else the waiter was by their side. "Cold fruit soup," he informed them, placing bowls in front of them.

Michael withdrew his hand and picked up his spoon, looking at her intently. His dark eyes were so intense, so questioning, they seemed to bore into her very soul. They were almost more than she could stand. But she continued to gaze back at him, waiting.

"Have you ever had cold fruit soup, Alicia?" he asked innocently.

"Oh, Michael!" she gasped, bursting into laughter. She picked up her spoon but couldn't eat.

Across the table he gazed at her, waiting patiently for an explanation.

"I thought you were going to ask me something important," she smiled, amused. "Somehow I expected the most earthshaking question. Instead you ask if I've ever had cold fruit soup."

"Well," he grinned, "have you?" He shook his head, the corners of his eyes crinkled with pleasure. "One needs to know these things."

"No," she said. "As a matter of fact, no."

"Let the soup be a sign between them," he intoned, and began to eat.

How pleasant, she thought, sitting here like this with him. It was good just being with him, hearing him laugh, loving him. Surely he'd speak his piece soon....

Soup was followed by hearts-of-palm salad and then freshly caught lobster with creole rice and fresh asparagus. She noticed that Michael ate slowly, thoughtfully, as if his mind were on something else. And she kept expecting him to bring up the subject of *them* . . . but though she waited expectantly and had the feeling it was on his mind, he never seemed to find an opportune time to say anything.

After the meal was finished, the table was

cleared and Michael leaned back in his chair,
once more lapsing into thoughtful silence. At last
he said, "This is a beautiful resort, isn't it?"

"It's the lawns," she said. "The acres of
lawns."

"You like that."

"Oh, yes. Don't you?"

He shook his head. "Lawns aren't practical.
They take too much water."

She flared up and demanded, "Does everything have to be practical, Michael? Can't some
things be done for the sake of beauty?"

He merely looked at her.

She felt like challenging him. She was frustrated with him and she knew why. He hadn't yet
spoken about *them*, though she waited for that to
happen. And he was proposing again to destroy
the island. She felt angry. "You're still going to
put up those ten-story buildings, aren't you?"

"I haven't decided. I'm thinking about it."

"But you still think Virgin Gorda would be
better off crowded?"

For a moment he didn't answer; instead he
twirled his wineglass slowly round and round.
"How did we get on this subject again?" When
he faced her, his expression had turned grim.

"I don't know...how did we?" She stared
back at him, knowing her defiance showed in a
narrowing of her green eyes. Suddenly all her
hopes, all her expectations for the evening were
dashed. They were arguing again, back to square

one, and she knew that out of tonight had come merely a flaring of old resentments and no forward progress at all. For whatever reasons, Michael was afraid or unwilling to get to the subject of *them*. Disillusioned and angry, she stood up suddenly. "Let's go home, Michael."

"Is that what you want?"

"We're not doing any good here, are we?"

"No." He sounded remote. "I suppose we aren't."

He thrust his hand into his pocket for money, paid the bill and walked ahead of her toward the stairs.

And though he helped her down the stone steps with his hand under her elbow, everything had changed.

The spark between them was gone.

Michael and Alicia crossed Caneel Bay Plantation on the narrow stone path and found themselves once more on the dock. She felt tense, anxious and frustrated—now they were going home after an evening that had turned out empty and flat. She couldn't believe they'd topped it off by quarreling.

Once on board the boat, depressed, she went below into the single small bedroom, and sat down on the bed. Let him take the boat home; she'd nurse her unhappiness down here.

But it wasn't to happen that way. Moments later he followed her down, entirely filling the small doorway. She noticed he'd removed his coat. To her surprise she also saw that he looked, if anything, more upset than she. "You plan to stay down here, Alicia?"

"Yes. And let me be, Michael. We're hopeless, you and I. Please. Just leave me alone."

She tried to turn away from him, but he wouldn't let her. He sat down beside her on the bed and took her by the shoulders. "Don't turn from me, Alicia. Look at me, please."

When she struggled to bring her eyes to his, she found him staring down at her and saw in his expression the haunting depths of torment.

Tears crept into her throat, but she wouldn't give them vent. Resolutely she swallowed, and he took her chin in his hand.

"Oh, my Alicia," he said. "Why are you as tortured as I? What is this thing we keep creating between us? Building, mortaring, adding to bit by bit so we can never quite come together? Why do we do it, Alicia? Have we no sense?"

She shook her head numbly. She didn't know. Yet it happened. Over and over.

"We're prideful people, you and I. It's our salvation...and our damnation. Look at me, Alicia." He stroked her hair. "Let our wall crumble. Let it go."

It moved her more than anything he could have said, and she eased closer to him. He took her in his arms, pulling her close...so close she felt crushed. Yet his drawing her in seemed right, and she nestled against him. He said, "Alicia...my Alicia."

For long moments he held her close, not moving, so that she was conscious only of the small things that made him human: his heart thumping near hers, his breath on her neck, the warmth of his skin.

But there was so much more, she thought, for these small processes could be anyone, yet they were not. It was that intangible part that moved her beyond words, that essence that could not be defined in heart, skin or breath. It was his own unique being, the soul of him—yes, his soul—that was what she grappled to understand and, having glimpsed, had come to love.

She sank against him, utterly yielding, wanting to melt into him and be part of him, now and forever.

He knew it. His hands found her dress and gently slipped it down, off her shoulders and down over her breasts, so that the aqua material gathered at her waist.

"It's time, Alicia," he whispered. "Come to me, darling!"

Even those few words added to her pent-up emotions, throwing them into a crazy tilt, so that what had been yearning only moments before changed and became wild uncontrollable hunger. She knew what was happening yet she felt utterly, hopelessly, unable to resist.

And glad, too. Surely this rising sense of longing couldn't be wrong.

Deftly he slid the dress down over her hips and let it fall to the floor.

She felt his hands on her bare back, felt him move her gently onto the bed so he could stretch out beside her.

Eagerly she clung to him and felt his skin beneath her hands—warm, firm. She shivered.

He rose above her on an elbow, first looking into her eyes, then at the rest of her body, exposed. "You're beautiful, Alicia. So beautiful."

She smiled back at him.

A moment later he was speaking tenderly against the curve of her throat, sending new shivers coursing through her body. "I'm good with my hands, Alicia. You'll see."

And then she found he was. Every part of her body felt his touch, tender, caressing, slowly moving her toward sensations she'd only guessed at before. With fingers that seemed both to seek and to assess, he softly stroked her smooth inner thighs, his fingertips light as a butterfly's touch. She'd never known a man's hands could be at once so tender and so knowing. Little by little his hands moved up the curve of her hips and explored her tiny waist. She gasped instinctively as his palms gently covered her breasts and his lips found her lips. She felt pleasure begin to sear her like a brilliant light—a strangely focused light that gradually changed and encompassed her whole body.

"Alicia!" he said softly against her ear, and she dissolved against the pillows, unable to move.

"Alicia...you're beautiful, my one. Oh, God, Alicia!"

Though she felt she no longer had a muscle in her body, he lifted her for a moment, pulling her off the bed to a sitting position, so his arms could enfold her—all of her. "You don't know how much I've needed you. How long I've wanted you. It's been like a flame within me, a flame that never went out. Day in and day out the flame burned, consuming me. How could I have let it eat away at me so long?"

"Michael," she gasped, "oh, Michael!"

Alicia stroked his face, his neck, his back with her fingertips, feeling the strength of him, his strong chin, the powerful muscles in his shoulders, the smoothness of his back. *I've always loved your shoulders,* she thought, *the strength of them looming over me.* Now she felt them forcing her once more against the pillow, and her excitement grew as his body—his warm, sensuous flesh—covered hers. He was as powerful as Alicia imagined he'd be, as strong and insistent.

Yet he was more tender by far. His lips moved over her breasts and focused there, warm and titillating, then moved upward again, tracing the soft curves of her throat. She shivered as she felt the tickle of his warm breath and the moist kisses that aroused her. The sweetness of his touch, running the length of her body, made her quiver and brought sensations she'd never imagined possible.

She felt she could revel in his caresses forever. She'd never thought that his touch would incite her so gently, that his fingers and his lips would treat her so wondrously and yet so maddeningly. *Oh, Lord, Michael,* she thought. *You are opening new worlds in me—hunger and satiety, thirst and quenching, desire and fulfillment all at one time. And you do have wonderful hands. Wonderful!*

Startled that lovemaking would involve every nerve, every inch of her body, Alicia was even more surprised when his passion brought hers to near pain—a pain and pleasure that grew and grew, taking her breath away. She felt a flush of intense heat just before her sensual climb burst into ultimate, almost unbearable pleasure.

Instantly, feeling so much his, so one with him, she cried, "Michael! Michael!" and seizing his back with her fingers, clutched him to her tightly as though to keep him there forever.

Slowly her exultation faded, but her pleasure remained, and she smiled at him, loving him in a way she would never have believed she could love any man.

"Happy, Alicia?" he whispered.

"Oh, yes," she sighed.

"Me, too."

She lay in the crook of his arm, feeling his warm skin with pleasure and deep contentment, and moments later drifted off to sleep.

When she woke a short time later, she knew it

hadn't been long, yet she was pleasantly surprised to find his body still next to hers. She was amazed that she could turn to him and induce him to repeat the experience she'd just been through. She'd imagined herself reaching these heights perhaps once in a lifetime, but never twice in the same evening.

After a while he simply stroked her hair, brushing it back into its natural waves, staring into her eyes and smiling. "Have I said it before? You're beautiful." Whatever she'd believed about him earlier, she was sure now that he loved her. He didn't need to spell it out.

Without speaking they lay together for a long time. Finally he sat up. Leaning on an elbow he looked down at her earnestly. "Alicia, there's something I want to ask you...."

The tone of his voice made her heart quicken.

Just as she started to answer, "Yes, Michael?" the sound of footsteps carried down to them and startled them into instant attention. They realized someone was on the boat.

Alicia grabbed her clothes from the floor and began to dress, her efforts desperate and clumsy. Michael, too, hastily buttoned his shirt. The fact that someone had joined them now changed everything. The magic of their private moment was gone.

"Michael, are you there?"

It was Elaine. Her high heels clicked on the deck, and now Alicia was sure that she was coming down. Another, slower step followed Elaine's. . .whose, Alicia couldn't tell.

She scrambled for her dress. She had to get it over her head. Before she asked, Michael reached above her and helped her into the soft material. He was fully dressed himself now except for his shoes, though his clothes had a rumpled look.

Suddenly he reached toward her and pushed her back against the bulkhead, to make her look as though she'd been sitting on the bed for some time. He positioned himself at a little distance from her and placed his feet in her lap comfortably, giving the impression that they'd been in this casual position all evening.

Moments later, when Elaine appeared at the head of the stairs, Michael and Alicia looked up, feigning surprise. But Michael made no move to remove his feet from Alicia's lap.

"What are you doing here, Elaine?" Michael stared up at her.

Instead of answering, she started down, her slinky black dress hobbling her so severely she could hardly negotiate the steps. Exasperated, she finally hiked the skirt above her knees and irritably plunked down one foot after the other.

Behind her they could see David impatiently waiting. He started down. His light blue suit set off his blond hair and blue eyes admirably.

"What are *you* doing?" Elaine snapped.

"What does it look like?" Michael's voice

was smooth, cool. "Actually, we've been making mad love," he said. "She rubs my feet and I go into spasms of ecstasy."

"Oh, don't be stupid." Elaine looked around the room sourly. Searching for clues, Alicia guessed. "How long have you been here?" Elaine asked. "We've been looking for you everywhere."

"*You've* been looking," David corrected her. "*I* came to eat dinner." He looked at Michael and Alicia. "She kept us running from restaurant to restaurant. And those darn places are a long way apart. Frankly, when we didn't find you at Turtle Bay I said, 'Let's not try to join them—let's just eat here by ourselves. The prime rib looks great.' Do you think she'd let me have any prime rib?" He laughed, evidently an attempt to disguise his irritation. "She didn't. She was bound and determined we were going to eat with *you*. So I've seen the menu at three different restaurants. But I haven't had a bite. I'm damned hungry." He looked at his watch. "They jolly well better not close."

"We came to join them, and that's what I intended to do." The indomitable Elaine spoke in a strident tone of voice.

"Well. I'm sorry." Michael reached for his shoes. "You must have gone to the Sugar Mill last. Unfortunately, we've eaten. At sunset."

"Son of a gun!" David exploded. "I *knew* it.

Now I suppose the prime-rib bit is over. Son of a gun!''

"They serve at the main dining room till ten, I think." Michael stood up, yawning casually. "We'll go and have a second dessert and sit with you."

"Thanks, honey!" Elaine put her hand on his arm, but her voice was just short of nasty. "Now that we've found you—thanks for nothing."

"Do you want us to come with you or not?" Michael's curt tone carried a faint warning. When she didn't answer, he asked, "How did you get here, by the way?"

"Seaplane. David told me you could hire them."

Michael and Alicia turned to exchange a quick, meaningful look. Just as quickly, both turned away.

So it *was* her, Alicia thought—Elaine pursuing them like a repossessor. She suppressed a smile.

But Michael could not contain his amusement. Laughing, he said, "I don't believe it—a seaplane!" For a moment he looked toward the ceiling, thinking, then in a droning voice he recited, "'Neither seasickness nor distance nor dark of night shall keep them from their appointed rounds....'"

"What's that supposed to mean?" Elaine asked shrilly.

"Nothing, my dear Elaine. Nothing at all."

But he was still smiling as he helped her up the stairs.

The four of them went back together in the seaplane after David and Elaine had eaten. They left the boat behind to be picked up. It was very late, as dinner in the main dining room had taken almost an hour and a half. Throughout the meal Alicia sat suffused in a warm glow, thinking back on her exquisite moments with Michael. She heard very little that the others said, and even Michael was less than his usual conversational self. If Elaine noticed she didn't mention it. And David, wholeheartedly engrossed in his food at last, could only comment on the belated pleasures of dinner.

As they were climbing into the seaplane Alicia sighed and said, "It's been a wonderful evening, Michael."

Elaine whirled around before he could answer. "Has it?" she asked, and Alicia, noting Elaine's hard, unhappy expression, wondered how much she'd guessed—then decided she really didn't care.

CHAPTER THIRTEEN

THE SEAPLANE LANDED near the Pelican Point dock and the four jumped out. Michael took Alicia's arm, saying pointedly to Elaine, "I'll walk her home. See you two later."

With that, David slipped a possessive arm around Elaine's waist. "I'm taking her to see my tennis trophies." He smiled suggestively but his voice had a curiously happy quality. Alicia sensed that David really cared for Elaine. "Lucky for us, honey," he said to Elaine, "we've plenty of night left," and he began to lead her away.

But they'd only gone a step or two when Elaine stopped, staring at David distractedly. "I can't." She shucked off his arm. "I have something to tell Brandon. I'm going with them." And without a backward glance, fell into step with Michael.

It's just an excuse, Alicia thought.

Now all four of them stopped, confused. David's look of surprise quickly turned into a frown.

"For Pete's sake, Elaine!" said Michael.

"It's late! They'll all be in bed." He looked at his watch. "It's twelve-fifteen!"

"Brandon will want to hear this," Elaine purred. "He won't mind my waking him."

Quietly Michael said, "I don't believe you should come with us, Elaine."

"Oh, let her," David muttered. "She'll end up doing what she wants. I was under the impression I had a date, but it seems I don't. The lady's forgotten who brought her." Angry, he turned toward his cottage.

As he walked away Elaine ran back to him and caught his arm. She stood on tiptoe and brushed his cheek with her lips. "You don't mind, do you, David, honey? I'll come to your place tomorrow. Honestly. There's my sweetie, I knew you'd be a good sport." She gave his arm a quick squeeze.

Under her breath Alicia muttered, "Ugh!"

"What's that, Alicia?" Michael trumpeted. "I couldn't hear you!"

She threw him a quick warning look. *Do that to me again and I'll kill you!*

Elaine was tripping beside them again, and in complete silence they walked the short distance to Seahawk Cove.

To Alicia's surprise, her aunt and uncle and Brandon were still up. The lights were all on, and Lily quickly put down her embroidery and gave them her biggest smile. Bill, half-asleep in his chair, sat up with a grin. Brandon stood up.

"What's all this?" Alicia asked, confused.

Lily said, "We know, honey. Michael told us. This morning he talked to Bill." Her aunt rushed over and threw her arms around Alicia. Alicia returned the hug perfunctorily, still baffled.

Bill beamed and said, "Congratulations."

"Yeah, congratulations!" echoed Brandon.

"For what?" In total confusion Alicia turned back to Michael, whose face revealed nothing. "For what?" She felt her heart pounding strangely.

"On your engagement, honey. You don't have to pretend. We know!" Lily's happiness bubbled out of her uncontrollably.

"Oh," said Alicia, dumbfounded. Instead of the joy evidenced by everyone else, she felt only bewilderment. What engagement?

"It's all going to work out so nicely," her aunt went on, her face creased in pleasure. "We've been talking to Brandon, and he admits it was never going to be feasible, his company buying this place and having such different goals from ours. With Michael developing it, it's all going to be done right! He's the kind of man we wanted to sell to all along!"

Shocked, Alicia felt her mouth drop open. She turned to look at Elaine. The woman was white with fury and suppressed rage. "Damn you, Michael!" Elaine shouted.

Before anyone could react, Elaine opened the screen door and stormed out. Her sudden outburst sobered Bill and Lily momentarily. They looked questioningly from Alicia to Michael. Michael merely shrugged.

But everything was clear to Alicia now. Her aunt had just revealed the missing links and nobody had to tell her more. Inside she trembled, her bewilderment changing to fury. She could see the whole picture, everything that had transpired—and Michael too, as she'd never seen him before. She'd never known such a schemer. He had used people and taken advantage of their tenderest emotions.

Yet her aunt's and uncle's happiness was so profound she hesitated to say anything. For them, not knowing the kind of development Michael had in mind, giving him control of the resort appeared to be the answer to their dreams.

"We've had a wonderful time this evening discussing it." Lily went on, "You know it's what we've always wanted—having Seahawk Cove in the family, with someone like Michael! We're so happy he'll be our nephew-in-law!"

Alicia glanced at Michael and saw his attempt to hide his strained expression. She still stood mute, forcing a smile.

Bill spoke up. "I been thinking about your Arizona offer, Michael. Decided sure, why not stay on your ranch there till we get settled? Sounds fine. Mighty fine." His thin body straightened in a gesture of hopefulness. "I hope this time next year I'm gonna be standing a bit straighter.''

To herself, Alicia thought, *this can't be true: Michael has decided to marry me...as a business deal!*

Brandon, usually unperceptive, asked unexpectedly, "What's the matter, 'Lish?"

"Nothing." She tried to smile but failed. Her fury was at a bursting point.

She glanced at Michael again. He caught her eye and smiled sheepishly. Satisfied, Brandon went on, "I finally realized everyone was right, 'Lish—my company was just using me. I'm fairly sure they would have dumped me right after they'd got the deal. Yesterday they even threatened me over the phone. But Michael talked to me about going back to college, and I know that's what I oughta do. He said if I took some public-relations courses I'd have a job with his company for sure. At least I know I can trust Michael.''

"Well, I can't!" Alicia burst out, unable to contain herself any longer. She was almost in tears.

"Alicia!" Her aunt was shocked. The reaction was electric. Her aunt's hands flew to her face and her uncle rose from his chair. Eyes blazing, Alicia faced them all. Her uncle, her aunt, Brandon all gaped at her horrified.

It was Michael who spoke first. Quietly he explained. "I never had a chance to talk to Alicia.

I haven't asked her to marry me yet. I started to, but... well, I just never got a chance. I should talk to her alone. We should talk right now."

"Of course," said Lily and Bill together.

"There's nothing to talk about," Alicia replied. "Go back to Pelican Point, Michael."

"I'm not going to do that, Alicia. Not till I've had a chance to explain." Firmly he took her arm, not allowing her any chance to resist, and led her through the door and out to the road behind the house, far enough away so nobody back home could hear.

She was trembling, shaking in rage as all the implications of what she'd just heard came to her in fuller and fuller measure... and all the ironies, too. Here was the marriage proposal she'd been hoping for—hers at last. But without any expression of love... with her whole family knowing before she did!

It had come as part of a business package, part of Michael's scheme to gain control of Seahawk Cove, because, Alicia thought grimly... this was the only way he could get it!

Seahawk Cove would be his at last when he married into it! That he'd so brazenly deceived her aunt and uncle in the process made her realize he would deceive anyone... and use everyone!

It was obvious to her now why Michael hadn't mentioned marriage to her earlier—had never hinted at commitment. He had first to get Bill's agreement to sell his precious bay!

Michael stood on the road eyeing her, his face set in a curious expression. He looked as if he were midway between laughter and tears... wanting to kid her, wanting to sympathize with her. It was an odd expression. "Please, Alicia...listen," he said.

White-hot, she retorted, "There is nothing you can say to me, Michael MacNamee. Nothing. I understand it all, and the answer is no. I wouldn't marry you as a business deal even for Lily and Bill. But they've been used, too. How did you manage to hide your intentions from them? Or did you really sell them on high rises?" Her tone was as sarcastic as she knew how to make it.

"Alicia, let me tell you one thing: whatever I planned to do at Pelican Point, Seahawk Cove would stay as your uncle desired it."

She thought she saw hurt on his face but she was too angry to care. "Oh, really," she spit out. "So you're a big conservationist all of a sudden. Well, I don't believe you. You've never talked seriously about anything but desecration, as far as I'm concerned. Oh, sure, you gave lip service to the loveliness of Caneel Bay, but show me you've really changed, Michael. Show me!" She stared at him defiantly.

"I have," he said, putting his hands on her shoulders. "You've made me change." He dropped his hands and shrugged hopelessly. "And about our marriage...you have that all wrong, Alicia. I meant to ask you this evening to marry me. I thought we had plenty of time; all along, I thought I had the whole evening, that I'd save that part of it for last. I never expected what happened on the boat."

"You *didn't*?" she blazed at him.

He winced and went on, patient but determined. "Afterward, Alicia, it seemed the right time to ask you. I even began—but how was I to know Elaine...?" He shrugged, a rare moment of futility and speechlessness.

"Don't try to explain it, Michael. There *is* no explanation. I've been seduced and used. Oh, I can see how it all was, even the seduction a part of the deal...the 'softening up,' is that what you call it? The 'warming her to the proposal'? You knew I'd be vulnerable. You knew."

When he didn't answer and his face turned stony, she felt herself crumbling. "Oh, Michael, I wouldn't have believed it of you! Never! Never!"

Turning away from him she sought control, fought the tears that threatened to come. She tried to hold it all in, but a sob escaped her.

"You have it all wrong," he said helplessly. For the first time since she'd known him, Michael was unequal to the situation. He stood next to her without touching her, and now he seemed unwilling to try to convince her further. His very silence proved to her she was right. She looked up and found his dark eyes unreadable. She felt he was waiting her out.

After a moment anger overcame her again

and her mind burst into new understanding. "How smoothly you must have talked to Lily and Bill this morning, convincing them I'd marry you. How happy you must have made them. . . their only daughter—well, I am like a daughter—finally blessed with the man of her choice. Oh, it was all so wonderful. . . a husband for their child, a buyer for their resort. Oh, what a morning you must have given them, Michael! No wonder they came home from town glowing. I saw Lily after my scuba lesson—she could hardly stop smiling, and I couldn't figure out why! And all along she never knew we were all being used!"

Alicia clenched her fists and stared at him hard. "Well, I've already given enough, Michael MacNamee. You're not going to use me anymore for your pet projects. I'll tell you this one last thing. You'll never get Seahawk Cove—I'll see to that, whatever else I have to do. I'll make sure you never—"

Angry speech came back to him then. "And you'll see Bill destroyed first, is that right? You know he can't keep on this way—it's impossible. And the place will go to ruin, too, because he doesn't have the money. But you don't care about any of that, do you, as long as you can keep it from me? God, you are selfish, Alicia. I'd always believed you cared about others. . . . "

His eyes flashed steely anger, an expression so cold she understood at last that she'd stripped him down and found the naked man. She'd found him, at bottom, to be scheming, hard, cold. Why hadn't she seen it sooner? How had he managed to keep it from her?

Just then she had a thought—it boiled up from her subconscious. She added icily, "Don't you worry about Seahawk Cove. Nobody needs you to take care of the place. I'm going away for a while, and when I come back I'll take it over myself. You aren't the only person in this world who can run a resort, and neither is Bill. So don't flatter yourself that you're all he's got! I'll run it myself, and I'll do it as well as you!" She laughed bitterly. "Better, if you're lying to me about keeping the place the same!"

A last vicious thought came to her. "Whatever money you intended to make from the place, *I'll* make—me, Alicia. I'll have money at last, and I'll spend it as wildly as I please!"

He shook his head, staring at her as though fully understanding her at last. His penetrating gaze bored into her only a few seconds, long enough to make her realize that he, too, felt as if he were seeing the true Alicia.

"Yes," he said slowly, "I believe you will."

With that Michael walked away slowly toward Pelican Point.

Alicia stood on the road alone. Which way should she go? She wouldn't go after him— never, not in a million years—and she couldn't go back home.

Glancing down, she realized she had her purse

in her hands. There wasn't much money in it, but she had credit cards. She still wore her high heels and her long dress, and they were both unsuitable for going anywhere except back to her own house. Yet she was as incapable now of facing Lily and Bill and Brandon as she was of pursuing Michael.

Finding it impossible to think clearly, she began walking. The road led in one direction back to the narrow, desolate part of the island; in the other it veered around a sharp point toward the small shopping center and ultimately ended at the airport. It made more sense to walk toward civilization than away from it.

In her high heels she stumbled down the road, past the Pelican Point turnoff, then out to that straight stretch that led to the yacht harbor.

It wasn't entirely dark out here. A half-moon lighted the pavement in places where the jungle growth kept a respectful distance back from the road. There were stretches, though, where deep shadows obscured her way and she approached these with dread, running through them till the road seemed less menacing. These spots tested her nerve and impelled her to turn back. But she wouldn't. There was no one she wished to face tonight. No one.

Determinedly Alicia pressed on, trying to make out the place where the blacktop split, half going toward the airport, the other toward the most distant Pelican Point cottages, high on a hill.

A few minutes later she realized she'd gone down the wrong road—a minor problem immediately aggravated by a bigger one when her right foot stumbled into one of the pavement's many holes. She regained her balance but came up minus the heel of her shoe. At first, when she put her foot down again and felt the heel flatten she assumed she'd merely dropped into another hole. Then the realization came to her: she would have to walk awkwardly the rest of the way to the airport with one heel high and the other low.

She picked up the useless heel and smiled in spite of herself. If Michael hadn't been right about anything else, he'd certainly been right about these roads!

She retraced her steps, an awkward heel-toe, heel-toe, until she was back on the main road. Without a usable shoe it seemed ridiculous to continue. Yet stubbornly she did.

She walked on, impelled by some strange irrationality, and eventually asked herself why and how she had gone from the happiest moment of her life this very evening to a pointless trek along a desolate road at three in the morning?

After a while, tired of suffering with her awkward gait, she took off both shoes and carried them in her hand. Then, realizing her stockings would be instantly ruined, she took them off, too, and stuffed them in her purse.

She had been walking perhaps twenty-five minutes when she heard a distant engine, then saw a light coming up behind her. Had she been in one of the dark areas she would have cowered deep in shrubbery until the vehicle passed. But here in this open stretch there was no place to hide. Fully exposed to whoever was in the vehicle, Alicia clutched at bravery and marched determinedly on, head held high. At least they would know she was not afraid.

To her horror, the vehicle—it was a truck— began to slow and gradually came to a stop beside her. For just a second she considered running barefoot... and then she heard a soft puzzled voice ask, "Miss Barron?"

She turned to see Anselmo!

Without asking questions, Anselmo drove Alicia to the airport. If he noticed her bare feet and her damaged shoe, he gave no sign. He treated her with his usual quiet courtesy, and for all anyone knew, he was accustomed to picking her up on the road at three-thirty in the morning.

A few casual questions on Alicia's part revealed that Anselmo's wife had a bad toothache and he was on his way to the yacht harbor to try to rouse the local druggist.

When they arrived at the small deserted terminal, Anselmo paused before opening her door. "You going to be all right here, Miss Barron?"

"Yes."

"I don't know." He shook his head. "Don't like leavin' you...."

"It's not long till dawn, Anselmo," she smiled. "I'll be okay."

Finally, cocking his head at her hesitantly, he left.

But it *was* long till dawn. It seemed hours to Alicia, sitting on the wooden bench outside the building, her back against the rough stucco.

Huddled there, she asked herself what she intended to do next, and the answer was uncertain—she didn't know.

She'd call her aunt and uncle at first light and then take the earliest plane to St. Thomas. Beyond that she had no plans.

THE TINY PLANE curved slowly over the island of St. Thomas. Below her, Alicia could see the red sheet-metal roofs of Charlotte Amalie, the island's capital, scattered randomly among the lush hillsides, as though an artist had accidentally spattered red paint from his brush.

She glanced down at her long aqua dress, soiled around the bottom, and viewed herself with distaste. Last evening's finery, soiled by her predawn trek, left her looking more like a down-and-out prostitute than the despairing lover of her mind's eye. Though her rumpled evening dress and heelless shoe had attracted brief attention among the travelers who arrived for the earliest plane, once aloft she felt protected by a kind of anonymity created by the roaring engines. For a short while she and all the other passengers took on a comforting sameness.

The little prop plane at last dropped over the

runway like a bird of prey and came to a quick stop near the terminal building. From her tiny porthole Alicia could see tractors biting into the hills on either side of the landing strip. A few years earlier a jet had failed to stop in time on the short runway and, screaming uncontrollably off its end, had torn through a gas station and small eatery, killing nearly half its passengers. Soon afterward St. Thomas had begun building a new landing strip.

Alicia took a taxi to the center of Charlotte Amalie. The busy narrow street ran alongside the harbor, where fishing boats, private yachts and a multidecked ocean liner from Norway lay at anchor.

The taxi had no air conditioning, and Alicia, feeling unusually hot and tired, opened the window. When the driver stopped for traffic the sticky heat crawled inside her long dress and almost stifled her.

She got out in the heart of the town. Famous as one of the world's exotic free ports, the place had a bustling international flavor that suggested Hong Kong, London and San Juan, Puerto Rico, all in one. Most of the shops were concentrated on this one long narrow street, and here among the cosmopolitan shoppers of the world Alicia's strange costume attracted scant attention.

Passing the endless jewelry, perfume, gift and liquor stores, Alicia found a boutique and bought a simple cotton shift. The white embroidered dress hung loosely on her small body, its freshness a marked contrast to her face. Though her auburn hair fell in its usual easy waves, her eyes were rimmed with dark circles. Feelings of uncertainty were reflected in her drooping mouth. She willed the image to smile back at her, but the result was not much of an improvement.

Misery showed on her, she thought. Losing Michael had marked her. Anyone would look at her and say she was unhappy. Well, she was, darn it, she was. She stood staring at herself. Solving the dress problem had occupied only the first hour of her first day. What if this were to be the first hour of a hundred empty days... a thousand? What then? How would she spend her time, she wondered sadly.

This morning she'd told Lily she needed a few days to think. It seemed the truth then, but perhaps it would not be the truth after all. Perhaps the time would go on and on. Alicia was so tired she could not bring herself to dwell on it further. Having paid for the dress she drifted out of the store and went in search of shoes.

Presently she was wearing flat white sandals and had left her broken-heeled shoe to be fixed in a tiny slot of a cobbler's shop. By eleven o'clock Alicia realized she was hungry. But the hunger spoke only from her body. Between her empty stomach and her brain a gap existed. She knew she needed food, but she didn't actually want it.

Eventually she bought some milk and a hamburger. It was tasteless, but she ate it anyway. Then she went out on the street again, seeking a hotel.

In this heat the pavement began to blur, the people swimming by her in sickening waves. She looked around desperately, seeking someone to ask about a hotel.

At last Alicia found a policeman, who told her there was a very nice hotel, small and not too expensive, at the top of the hill.

A taxi took her to the Ocean View Inn at the end of a long winding road. She asked for an inexpensive room and was led to a small cubicle at the front, its single window overlooked Charlotte Amalie's expansive bay. For a moment she stood at the window, aching for a breeze, but there was none.

She felt dizzy and her head was beginning to hurt. Searching for a switch she turned on the overhead ceiling fan and collapsed onto the bed. She fell instantly asleep.

CHAPTER FOURTEEN

WHEN ALICIA AWOKE it was dark. She knew somehow that she'd slept a very long time, but she didn't know how long a time it was. She looked at her watch—or, rather, she tried to look at it but realized she couldn't see it. Not only was the room dark, but something seemed to be wrong with her eyes.

Instinctively she cried out, "Michael!" and was horrified to hear her voice emerge as a faint croak. It was only then that she realized she was sick.

Shakily she reached for a light switch on the lamp next to her bed and found her fingers too weak to turn the knob. How long had she been here like this, she wondered. What had happened in these past hours?

She lay back, unable to make any further effort.

Slowly, slowly, impressions came to her. Sleep—not restful but feverish with nightmares. Horrible images—people looming over her, screaming at her, retreating into thinness then fading away just as she reached for them. She saw herself lying on a mattress—a mattress that shrank in size until it became but the thinnest of threads, and her balance began to fail and she knew she was falling off.

Nightmares.

She closed her eyes and opened them again. Her vision had cleared somewhat.

Her body felt hot, but she knew it had recently been hotter. Much hotter. She guessed her fever must have been high; that would account for the fact that she couldn't truly recall any of the previous hours.

How long had it been? One day? Two?

She had no way of knowing.

Her mouth was desperately dry. She wanted water. Oh, how she longed for it. She would have done anything for a small drink but was unable to make even the slightest effort.

Then she fell asleep again.

She awoke a second time to daylight. Dazzling yet cool light came in her window, and she recognized its coolness as being partly her escape from fever. She had been hot so long the ordinary temperature of the day seemed refreshing.

She sat up. She felt light-headed, a little dizzy, though her head didn't hurt. But back in her nightmarish state she knew it had hurt like crazy. Before she could do more than sit up, she needed to think. For a moment she wondered where she was.

As she leaned against the propped-up pillow

her awareness of her physical illness—pain and fever—receded, and memories of what had motivated her journey filtered into her consciousness. First, she remembered the precious hour spent with Michael on his boat...the way he'd possessed her, the heat of love she'd felt for him, even the quiet assurance within her that he loved her, too. Next, as if looking over still frames from a filmstrip, she saw the two of them angrily confronting each other. The outrage she had felt at realizing that Michael had been using her all along swept over her again. Her fury heightened still at this betrayal of trust.

The cruelest blow of all was the realization that Michael had never really loved her. Lying there weak against her pillow, Alicia saw the whole picture at last. What Michael wanted most out of life was to create an empire on Virgin Gorda, melding Pelican Point and Seahawk Cove into one vast playground with himself, Michael MacNamee, at its head!

Oh, he could do it, she thought. For him this project would be the culmination of everything he'd started in his years of developing resorts. But she, Alicia Barron, was the key to his master plan. Using her, he could buy what he needed. Without her, he could grow in only one direction, and Seahawk Cove would merely stand in his way—or worse, fall into the hands of a company like Brandon's.

How interesting, she thought, that Elaine had

been privy to all his plans from the beginning. No wonder Elaine had been working so deviously behind Michael's back—trying to get Seahawk Cove sold before Michael could finesse his way into the Barron family.

At last Alicia understood what Elaine had long known better than any of them: everything Michael wanted was tied to Alicia Barron, and if Elaine could get rid of the land, she'd likely be rid of Alicia, as well.

She sat up a little straighter in bed. Her health was coming back to her. Slowly she put her feet down, testing their strength. Uncertainly she rose and at that moment knew she would still have to fight to regain her energy. The sun was fully up, and she guessed it must be about noon. Her watch had stopped—how many days ago she had no idea.

Before making her way out of the room, she washed her face and combed her full auburn hair. With some pink lipstick on her lips, she felt revived. The mirror revealed a wan white face with dark hollows under the eyes, but a bit of attention did wonders—she overcame some of the effects of her illness.

Downstairs in the hotel restaurant she ordered tea, whole-wheat toast and a poached egg. Her starched waiter raised an eyebrow, asking, "For lunch?" She assured him that yes, this was to be her lunch.

A wall clock told her it was twelve-forty-five,

and when she saw the date on her credit-card receipt she found she hadn't been sick as long as she'd thought: it was just forty-eight hours ago that she'd fallen onto the bed.

She ate slowly, letting her eyes roam over the dining room. Only a few tables were occupied, she guessed because most of the guests were probably either shopping or swimming. She sipped her hot tea, savoring its flavor.

Afterward she sat at the table for a while, looking out over the bay, waiting to regain her energy.

"Anything else, ma'am?" the waiter asked, and Alicia shook her head.

When she stood up later to leave, she contemplated taking a taxi back down the hill. But for what? She realized she had no plan—nowhere to go. Uncertainly she made her way back up the stairs.

She spent the rest of the day in her room, working out the next months of her life.

MORNING BROUGHT another fresh day and a sense that she'd been in the backwater too long. It was time to let Lily know what was happening, and in spite of her somewhat shaky limbs, Alicia pushed on with her dressing, determined to start moving her life forward.

As soon as she got down the hill she phoned Lily.

Though she tried to minimize her illness, her

aunt sounded alarmed. "Why didn't you call us immediately when you got sick?"

"I couldn't, Lily." She hesitated, searching for the words to couch what really happened. "I was. . . sort of unconscious."

"Unconscious! Oh, my dear, no! Michael's been so worried about you. . . we all knew you ran off with no extra clothes and very little money. But you didn't sound fit even to discuss it the last time we talked. We've all been thinking about you. . . are you sure you're well now? Is your strength back?"

"Yes, yes," she lied. But the weakness *was* gradually abating. "You needn't worry about me." Alicia forced her voice to sound cheerful. "I've decided what I'm going to do, auntie. You know I've always been fascinated with marine life. . . ."

"Yes."

"I'd like to go back to Scripps in San Diego— and become a marine-life expert. I know I can do it."

"Yes." Lily's response was careful. Flat. Alicia knew her aunt was trying to mask her disappointment.

"I think I can have a real career. With what I already know about scuba diving. . . ."

"You can do it, Alicia. If that's what you really want to do." There was a pause. "Is it, Alicia?"

It was Alicia's turn to hesitate, and she knew

her aunt caught the moment's uncertainty. But she said quietly, "It's what I want to do, Lily. And I'm sorry...you'll have to understand... but I can't come home first. I just can't. I love you more than you'll ever know—you and Bill— but I'm going to fly to San Diego straight from here. I have to do it this way. If I don't—" Tears came to her eyes. She held her breath, willing them away. In a second she had regained control.

"Lily, when I get there, will you send me my clothes?"

"Of course."

"And will you send me a check...here... about seven hundred dollars to see me over until I get some kind of job in San Diego?"

"Where shall I send it, Alicia?"

She thought for a moment. She didn't want them coming over, trying to find her. "Just send it to the Charlotte Amalie post office, in my name. Please do it soon. I want to leave the day after tomorrow."

"Oh, Alicia." Her aunt's voice broke. To Alicia's great dismay, she knew Lily was crying.

A silence followed, during which Alicia waited miserably.

"Honey—" her aunt's voice came on again, its attempt at control breaking Alicia's heart "—don't do anything foolish, my girl. Please." There was another pause. "We love you, Alicia. If that's all, I'll say goodbye."

"Goodbye, Aunt Lily."

Alicia hung up the phone. She couldn't remember a time when she'd ever been more unhappy.

She took a taxi to the airport and used her credit card to buy a one-way ticket to San Diego. For the rest of the day she sat in her hotel room, reading. It was the only way she could escape the pain of what she was doing. She could either read or agonize, and reading was easier. Reading didn't allow her to think, to consider what she was doing to her aunt and uncle—to Brandon. Perhaps...yes, perhaps even to Michael. But what rights did he have, she asked herself fiercely. Even thinking about Michael, about all he'd done to her, made her harden her resolve. She owed him nothing.

A small voice inside her whispered, *not even for your life?*

No, not even for her life. He did that because he...because he...she could think of no satisfactory explanation for why he'd stayed under the surface of the sea so long to save her. Nothing came to her about that except a sense of his courage, his competence, his stubborn heroism in the face of personal danger. She couldn't fault him on that one, she told herself angrily. He saved her life either because he was noble or because he loved her. But neither explanation suited her purposes.

She remembered that he had never said he loved her. She had to keep reminding herself about that. *Fly to San Diego and forget him. Consider him an incident in your life—a boyfriend you'll laugh about when you're old and married. When you're married....*

Oh, no. She twisted away from the thought. She couldn't be married. Not to anyone except Michael.

She badly needed sleep, but that night she slept fitfully again. Dawn found her still wrestling with regret, pain and longing for the people she was hurting. That was what bothered her most—hurting those she loved. With daylight creeping into her room, she dropped off to sleep at last.

In the afternoon she returned to town. At the post office she found her check. With it was one sentence from Lily. "God bless you and keep you, Alicia. Lily." No condemnation, no sign of hurt.

But, oh, the little note hurt her. Hurt her more than a long letter full of tears and blame. She had destroyed all of Lily's and Bill's dearest dreams, but they could only bless her in return.

With a few hours to kill before suppertime, she wandered down the little street. Its smells and sounds conjured up images of old cosmopolitan cities: the scents of leather and perfume, the sight of an electric populace ambling or hurrying by, bustling shops protected by wrought-iron grillwork over the windows and the street impossibly clogged with vehicles. She paused to watch a brown-skinned woman collect a trinket from the gutter and drop it into a shopping bag.

Absorbed, she failed to notice the familiar face until she heard a voice cry out, "Alicia!"

She whirled around to see David standing there grinning at her.

"David!" she exclaimed, smiling up at him as she extended her hand.

He took it, holding it warmly. "Well, at least I've found you," he said. "I thought it might be a possibility."

"Why? Were you looking for me?"

"Not really. But I knew you were here. Everyone knows. Hey...you look thin. You've lost weight."

"Have I?" Involuntarily her hand went to her cheeks.

"Got a few minutes?" he asked. "I was looking for someplace to get a drink. Man, it's hot. Not much air on this street."

"Sure, I was just killing time. Where shall we go?"

He shrugged. "Must be a place around here somewhere."

Together they searched for a restaurant and found one on the second story of a building that faced the harbor. Noticing that Alicia slowed on the stairs, David gallantly took her elbow and propelled her up. They found a booth with a view and settled on either side of the table.

"You've got Seahawk Cove—and Pelican Point, too—in an uproar," he began, looking at her searchingly. "You sure know how to run off dramatically."

"It wasn't intentional."

"Yeah, but it happened."

She changed the subject. "What are you doing here, David?"

He grinned and his voice was casual. "Looking for something for Elaine."

"Elaine? Why?" She knew her voice betrayed her but she couldn't help it. The coldness that always crept into her voice at the mention of that woman was there again.

David turned his blue eyes on her and something about his expression looked firmer than she could ever remember. "Elaine needs cheering up, Alicia. She's had a bad few days."

Alicia waited. She was curious but didn't want to show it.

"I don't suppose you care, though."

With a shrug she opened the menu. "What's wrong with her?"

"I'd like to make you understand, Alicia—just because we're friends." He frowned. "But maybe it's more than I can expect—the way she's treated you and all."

A waitress sauntered over and in a laconic manner took orders for iced tea. When she left, David took a deep breath and plunged on. "I found her on the beach. That's when I found out what had been going on around there. She was crying, Alicia. You wouldn't believe how she was crying. I figured something terrible must have happened, because she was all doubled over, kind of, and sobbing out loud. She tried to quit when I came up, but she couldn't. I kept asking her what was wrong, and I guess it took her fifteen minutes to calm down enough to say anything.''

Alicia tried to imagine Elaine crying. Somehow she couldn't. It seemed that Elaine was always on the attack, but crying. . . she shook her head, uncomprehending. The tea came and she sipped it. Over her glass she asked, ''Did she tell you what it was about, David?''

''Finally she did.'' He studied her, his eyes perceptive. ''Do you really care, Alicia?''

''I guess I do.'' At least she was trying to care.

He drank some of his tea, then said, ''It's Michael. He's been so rotten to her these past few days you'd never believe it. He's shut her out completely. For the last three days he's hardly spoken to her, just walked past her, she said, and looked the other way. And he wouldn't eat with her or answer her questions. He just ordered room service and stayed in his room. I guess she finally got furious at his coldness and—well, you know Elaine. She must have taunted him about you a little. That was when he took her by the shoulders and shoved her out the door and locked it on her. She tripped over a patio table on the way out.'' He finished his tea. ''But it wasn't the fall that made her so angry. It was that locked door. Even when she pounded he wouldn't let her in—just listened to her pound and yell and wouldn't unlock it. She said she had nowhere to go after that but the beach."

Alicia stared at him. It was a scene she couldn't imagine. She shuddered.

"Last night he finally unlocked the door, but she told me later he yelled at her, told her to keep the hell out of his sight. She'd never seen him like that—so out of control. He promised he'd make her life miserable if she even squeaked. So now she's afraid to speak to him."

"I'm sorry," Alicia murmured, affected. "It must be...rough." It was the first time she could remember empathizing with Elaine.

"Yes." David looked at her and nodded. "She's needed me, I can tell you. I think right now I'm the only friend she's got." Again his eyes seemed to appraise her. "You know why he's acting like this, don't you?"

Did she? She watched his face and waited.

"It's all on account of you."

Something inside her snapped then. "I'm afraid Michael is just frustrated," she said coldly. "Like a baby having a tantrum. He had a big scheme to take over our place and I scotched it for him. Well, I can't feel sorry for him. Michael will have to solve his own problems. It's too bad about Elaine, but Michael can go jump."

With that, David stood up quickly and looked down at her. "I've known you a year, Alicia, and

I've never seen you like this. I swear, you're almost as bitter as Elaine. It doesn't suit you, Alicia, it doesn't fit you at all. Man...." He shook his head. "Trouble on both islands. I'll pay the bill." He fished in his pocket for change.

Contrition struck her immediately. She stood up, too. In a tired voice she said, "I've been sick. But I guess that's no excuse."

"No," he said. "It isn't."

"I'm mixed up, too," she said, and tears came to her eyes, unwanted, hateful tears. Before he could notice she turned sideways and brushed them away.

"Well, Alicia...." He smiled at her as he put change on the table. Even as she saw the smile she knew David had changed these last few weeks. She saw a new maturity about him and heard insights he'd never expressed before. "You can't stay bitter," he said, "that's for sure. It'll wreck you. And it won't affect *him*."

"I know."

They went down the stairs together. At the front door he said, "I've gotta do my shopping, quick, and get back on the last plane. So take care, huh?"

"Sure."

"Anything you want me to tell the others?"

"No. I'll be talking to them myself."

"Okay. Well, again, take care."

She watched him walk away with a sense of purpose she'd thought would never be part of

David's makeup. As he rounded a corner she realized with a sense of wonder how much David had changed for the better. She felt a tinge of regret—his transformation had come too late for her.

Alicia found herself back in the shopping area with time to spare. She wandered down the narrow street idly looking into store windows. In the past she'd found these shops fascinating—or at least they'd always been so in happier days.

Now they were only a way of spending time. Fourteen hours left on St. Thomas: at this hour tomorrow she'd be on a plane to San Diego.

How ironic her situation was, Alicia thought to herself. She once flew away from Michael to Virgin Gorda, and now she was about to fly away from him again, albeit in the opposite direction. Would she spend her life forever airborne, running away from that man? In spite of her unhappiness, she felt the beginnings of a small, silly laugh. It *was* ridiculous.

She wandered into a jewelry shop. As always, she was fascinated by the gold charms. This shop had more of them than anyplace she'd ever seen.

And there amid hundreds of odd and unusual shapes was the gold coral piece of Seahawk Cove!

She would say later it was the coral that did it.

She stared at the tiny charm she'd designed, and something inside her changed. She would never know exactly what or why it happened then, but at that moment she decided she would return to Virgin Gorda after all.

Her decision had nothing to do with Michael. She would go back knowing Michael didn't love her, that he'd been trying to marry her for all the wrong reasons, and accepting that fact she'd learn to live with it.

No, when she returned it would be because of Lily and Bill and Brandon, her family who cared for her right or wrong and who had taught her the meaning of unconditional love. Her allegiance was to them and to Seahawk Cove, and now she was about to give them the first truly unselfish gift of her life. She would marry Michael, if that was the way it was to be, but she would do it because of the others.

As she turned in her ticket to San Diego for a ticket to Virgin Gorda a small hope flared briefly in her heart, then flickered out. Perhaps Michael would one day learn to love her after all.

CHAPTER FIFTEEN

ALICIA TOLD NO ONE she was coming.

When she landed on Virgin Gorda the next day, carrying her handled plastic bag with her few purchases, she wondered briefly how she was going to get back to Seahawk Cove. Resolutely she resisted the idea of calling Lily and having someone pick her up. She preferred to surprise them by simply walking into the house.

She looked around her, trying to decide what to do, noting that her fellow passengers were still in customs.

Then the Pelican Point van drove up.

Quickly she scanned it to make sure Michael wasn't aboard. There was no sign of him.

She spoke to the driver, who agreed immediately to let her hitch a ride as far as the big resort. "Miss Alicia," he laughed, "you don't need to ask such a thing. Of course you can ride. You belong here." It made her feel good.

Suddenly she knew she'd made the right decision. She had no idea what would come of it, whether Michael would even see her again, much less marry her. Perhaps, she thought in an instant's panic, he'd already left the island.

At that moment Alicia had the insane urge to tell the driver to hurry. The van was lumbering up the last hill, its lazy speed quite out of keeping with Alicia's impatience. It was as if she suddenly had to get there, to stop whatever it was Michael was on the point of doing. *Wait for me, Michael,* she felt herself crying inside. *Wait for me....*

Then the van came to a halt. She thanked the driver and awkwardly climbed out of the high seat with her little bag of possessions and her purse and began the short walk back to Seahawk Cove.

She opened the screen door and found Lily standing at the sink, her back to Alicia.

"Hi, Lily," she said softly.

Her aunt whirled around, startled. For a moment she stared, disbelieving, then she dropped her paring knife and rushed to Alicia, opening her arms wide, enfolding the girl to her full bosom as though she'd been away years.

"My, Alicia! Oh, my!" was all she seemed able to say.

"I'm back," said Alicia, smiling.

Her aunt held her at arm's length momentarily, then gave her another quick hug.

"I've decided to stay."

Her aunt nodded, beaming, and walked toward the living room. "Come and sit down." She wiped her hands on her apron and dropped heavily into a chair. "Oh, Alicia. I hadn't realized I was missing you already." A tear ran down her cheek, and she hastily wiped it away with the corner of her apron. "Let me look at you." After a moment's scrutiny she remarked, "I can tell you've been sick. You've lost weight, haven't you?"

"I don't know. I didn't have a scale." Alicia pinched her waist.

"Never mind, it's not important."

Hesitantly Alicia began, "I should explain—"

"Honey, you don't have to explain. Unless you really want to. We never wanted anything for you except what you wanted. Of course, Bill and I...." Another tear was dabbed hastily. "It seems so silly to miss someone who's only been gone a few days...less than a week. Bill and I are getting old, I guess. I tried not to think of the coming years...." Her voice trailed off. Gathering her energy again, she said, "Bill was in bed when you called. He'd been there two days, but he didn't want you to know. His arthritis flared, worse than I've ever seen it. He just couldn't get up."

Alicia said, "I didn't know. But I'm back because of you."

To her surprise, her aunt looked shocked. "My dear, that's the wrong reason. You can't be here because of us! We're old, Alicia—you can't live for us. I thought you were back because of Michael!''

"No."

"Alicia, he was waiting for you. Those first four days he came by every day. And he'd changed, honey...he was grim, like I've never seen him. When I finally told him—of course I had to tell him—that you were going to San Diego, I've never seen such a look on a man's face. Terrible. I thought he was going to fly into a rage. But he didn't say anything, he just excused himself quickly and left. It frightened me, Alicia. I don't know what he's been doing these last two days, we haven't heard from him. But when I saw you, I assumed—" Stricken, she stopped. "Oh, my, Alicia, you better call him. I'm rather afraid—"

As her aunt talked, something inside Alicia drew back and her previous sense of urgency subsided, replaced by an even, almost icy calm. She crossed her legs and sat thoughtfully, hands clasped around one knee. "No," she interrupted her aunt, shaking her head. "I'm not going to chase him, Lily. If he wants me, he'll find out I'm here."

"Alicia, I wouldn't wait." Her aunt's face acquired a look of foreboding. "I somehow know you shouldn't—"

Alicia turned away from her aunt's pleading face. Resistance settled over her like a fog. Let him call her!

But her aunt was still talking. "You *must* call him—he has to know. I told you he loved you, and he does. Go, now, call him." She gestured toward the phone. "He has the right—"

Wearily, Alicia stood up. "All right, Lily. But I'm only doing it to please you." She dialed the number.

"Mr. MacNamee?" The voice on the other end sounded courteous but hesitant. Alicia guessed it was Michael's secretary. "He's very busy. He's settling some last-minute business. Can it wait?"

Alicia almost said yes. Of course her business could wait. She had no business with him, and that was the truth. But she knew from the other's words that waiting now might mean waiting forever. Michael MacNamee seemed to be leaving.

Summoning her will she said, "This is Alicia Barron. I'm afraid it can't wait. He'll want. . . I know he'll want to speak to me."

The other woman said, "Of course," and asked her to hold a moment.

But would he want to speak to her, she wondered. Would he even come to the phone? She'd taken a terrible chance, laying herself open for rejection like this. It would be likely now that he'd never speak to her again.

When someone finally came to the phone, Alicia found to her horror it wasn't Michael but Elaine.

Without preamble Elaine said coolly, "I can't find Michael just now. He's getting ready to leave, and he's off somewhere. I'll have him call you later, if you like. That is, if there's time. It's not important, is it?"

In a moment of fury Alicia thought to herself, *the same old Elaine. Nothing's changed.*

"Yes, it's important," she said, her ire showing. "Tell him it's very important." See if Elaine would carry that message.

"Michael doesn't jump every time he's called," she replied smoothly. "We're leaving on tonight's plane and he's short of time. He does have other resorts to run, you know. If he wants to, he'll call you. Goodbye."

The phone clicked and Alicia stood with the receiver in her hand feeling impotent rage. Oh, that woman! That infuriating woman! Once again Alicia wondered how Michael put up with Elaine even for a day.

She returned to find her aunt waiting expectantly.

"I couldn't reach him," she said.

"Oh, no!" Her aunt's hand flew to her face. "He left! Just as I expected!"

"Not yet. But he's getting ready to leave. Nobody seemed to know where he was, but I left a message."

"Oh, well, then...." Her aunt looked instantly relieved. "He'll call you. I know he will. You don't have to worry—I know Michael a lot better than you think." She laughed. "Sometimes I think I know him better than you do. You two people have such a lot of foolish pride. I've seen it get in the way these past two weeks, over and over. But those silly acts of yours don't fool me."

Alicia wanted to tell her aunt that Michael might not call, that he surely wouldn't if Elaine never gave him the message. But her aunt would only be alarmed all over again. And besides, Elaine would *have* to give him the message. She wouldn't dare not....

For the rest of the day Alicia stayed in the house near the phone, unable to do otherwise. Her emotions, she thought ruefully, were as inconsistent as the wind, blowing first in one direction, then in another. One minute she was glad to be rid of Michael, the next she was yearning for his call.

Was the path of love always this tortuous?

Alicia helped her aunt with the laundry, dusted the furniture, peeled potatoes for dinner. As the hours went by her sense of apprehension grew. She knew the last plane left Virgin Gorda around five-thirty, and after that he'd be gone.

Five-thirty. The time imprinted itself like a brand on her consciousness. Once he'd left, she knew his pride would never allow him to return. Michael was that kind of man. You could fool with him only so long, batter his pride with so many blows. After that, he'd be through.

At five-fifteen she stared at the clock. He'd be at the airport now. If he intended to call, he'd have done it.

Her aunt looked up from her crocheting, frowning. "He must not have got the message." Her old face sagged, the wrinkles lying in deep folds around her outer cheeks.

When five-thirty came, Lily stood up. "Brandon wants me. . . I was supposed to go down to the beach and tell him when it was five o'clock. He has a lot of packing to do. He's leaving tomorrow—though nothing's been decided. I can see I'm late." Her thick shoulders drooping, she walked through the screen door, letting it bang after her. From behind, Alicia saw her lift the corner of her apron and wipe her eyes.

It's over, thought Alicia, *as surely as if he were dead. My love—my brief, sad love—is over.*

Yet she couldn't comprehend it. Once back on Virgin Gorda it was impossible not to believe Michael was still just next door at Pelican Point.

Her heart ached and her mind fought the truth. *It's over. He's gone. You must accept it. But I can't. Everyone thinks he loves me. Aunt Lily said he loved me; it has to be true. He's gone. Gone. Tomorrow and tomorrow and tomorrow. Then you will know for certain.*

The pain was too deep for tears. It was as though she no longer had the capacity to feel. This wasn't Alicia walking around the room, washing lettuce for a salad, setting the table. It was a shadow, a shell of a person. The shadow cooked, the shadow talked, the shadow even smiled. But inside there was nothing. The shadow could only move, not feel.

Throughout dinner with Lily and Bill and Brandon she heard their talk but didn't absorb anything. After a while her ghostly self got up to clear the table.

It was still early. Alicia looked out at a brilliant sunset and, feeling no sense of its beauty, went to her room to read.

She heard the phone but paid no attention. She'd taken off her dress and was pulling her nightie on over her head when Lily appeared in the room, flustered and excited. "Alicia! It's Michael!"

His voice, his dear voice, deep, warm and vibrant, brought her to life as nothing on earth could. Alicia heard him say her name and trembled excitedly. Instantly she felt wonderful. Alive. Happiness flooded her so completely she was dazzled by it. "Michael!" she said.

"I just got your message, Alicia. This moment. We're over at St. Thomas, between planes." So he *had* left. "Elaine said she forgot to tell me until now. I'm not sure she's...." He started to say more but changed his mind. "She said you called from Seahawk Cove."

"Yes, Michael. Yes, I did. I came home today

about noon. I...I called you right away. They said you were busy."

"Not that busy," he growled. "Why didn't you tell us you were coming back, Alicia? We thought you were off to San Diego. Your aunt was almost sick—"

"I know. I wanted to surprise her—to surprise all of you."

"It *is* a surprise. A great surprise. Are you planning to stay?"

"Yes, oh, yes. This is where I belong."

His end of the phone went silent for a moment. Whatever he was thinking in those long moments, Alicia could only guess. Finally he said, "I'm turning around, Alicia. I'm coming back. You and I have a lot to talk about."

"We do." Her heart pounded, her head spun madly. She would see him again, soon. Whatever was between them, it could be worked out. Somehow it would come out all right.

He wasn't finished. "You'll probably be glad to know I'm sending Elaine on home. It's hard to operate with her in the vicinity. It'll take some doing, separating all our luggage, but we just have time to accomplish it. I'm not sure when I'll see you—tonight, if there's a plane, or possibly tomorrow. Sleep tight, Alicia."

She said goodbye and pirouetted away from the phone. She wanted to dance, to sing, to clap her hands. Her happiness knew no bounds. She wanted him, she loved him, she yearned only to clasp him to her forever. She wanted to go outside and shout to the world about him.

Michael—her Michael—was coming back!

MICHAEL HIRED a small plane to bring him back to Virgin Gorda that night.

To Alicia, his coming so quickly had great significance. Perhaps, after all, he cared as much as she.

Yet when she saw him she knew something was different.

It wasn't the same Michael who kissed her almost with detachment, then suggested they go for a walk.

Together they strolled in the soft air. She'd been prepared to surrender to him completely, to agree to anything, but when she glanced at the silent man walking beside her she wondered if surrender might ever be necessary. For the first time in their relationship he seemed to want nothing from her. As they talked Alicia felt a wariness in him she'd never seen before.

Holding her hand perfunctorily, Michael talked to her in a voice without passion—almost without interest. "Why did you come back, Alicia?" he asked after a while.

"For Lily and Bill. Because I couldn't desert them. I couldn't do the things I planned and hurt them any further. They needed me. Someone has to run this place."

"It had nothing to do with me?"

She paused, trying to decide what to say. His coldness had unnerved her. Could she tell him how she felt—what had brought her back? No, she couldn't. "No, Michael, it didn't." She studied her shoes.

He was silent. Could he be hurt, as well?

After a time he said, "I'm glad you told me the truth. I would have guessed, anyway."

"Yes, I know."

They followed the road until it started up a small hill. He turned to her. "You can't really do much to help them without me, you know. Lily told me Bill's getting worse. He won't be able to work much longer. If you hadn't come home, he'd have been forced to sell...to Brandon's company or to me. But even if you've really decided to run the resort, you're going to need me—my expertise, my money. Without me this place will flounder, I'm sure you know that. It's on the brink of collapse already."

"Oh, really?" He was starting to rankle her, though she knew he spoke the truth. "I figured we could manage. We're not stupid."

"You have no money, Alicia. Your aunt and uncle don't have the resources, either. Seahawk Cove is just supporting you, and that's all. You don't have the capital to fix it up. Soon the buildings are going to rot away. What will you do then?"

She was silent. They began walking again. "We'll figure it out," she said finally. "I still have six thousand dollars of the money my parents left me.''

He laughed, a deep, hearty laugh. "Six thousand dollars? Do you know how far that will take you? That will repair two buildings, maybe only one. What will you do for the rest of them?''

When she made no reply he gripped her arm. ''You need me, Alicia—all of you need me. I propose we get married, just as we—'' he corrected himself ''—just as I planned. I'd like to have your aunt's and uncle's trust. It will be the best thing for all of us.''

''A business deal, Michael?''

''If you want to call it that.'' His voice was strange, unreadable. ''Sure, call it a business deal, Alicia. This seems to be where we're at.''

She didn't know what possessed her then. She'd been prepared for this—no, resigned to it. She'd changed her whole life around, predicated on her acceptance of a cold-blooded marriage to Michael. So why, when it was offered, did the idea seem so repugnant? Why was she suddenly holding out for something more? Yet she found herself shaking her head. ''No, Michael, I don't think so. I won't do it. I'm not going to marry you this way.''

Coldly he said, ''It's the best offer you're going to get.''

When she gazed past him without answering,

he added, "I could probably buy Seahawk Cove without you. I might even offer Brandon a vice-presidency." His smile was wintry. "But you'd be a better bedfellow."

She jerked out of his grasp. "Oh, you're infuriating!"

Instead of getting angry he merely watched her. His detachment was so complete she knew if she thwarted him now he would never offer again. They had come to the end of the line, she and Michael. Either they would get married this way, under his terms, or it would never happen at all.

And there was something else, she thought grimly. By marrying him she had some hope of controlling the destiny of Seahawk Cove. She was strong—and Brandon wasn't. As Michael's wife she'd be stronger still.

Deep inside her a small voice said, *take what you can get, Alicia. Take it now, in good grace. Or you'll end up with nothing.*

Clearly, as though a beacon had finally pointed a bright pathway for her, illuminating her passage through the future years, she realized that having nothing of him would be unbearable. Without Michael she'd never truly "live" again.

"All right, Michael, I'll marry you," she said quietly.

"Good," he said. But he didn't kiss her; he merely led her back to her own home.

MICHAEL WAS EFFICIENT. Oh, he was terribly efficient, Alicia thought grimly. Their wedding would be in three weeks, a ridiculously short time to arrange a marriage, but quite enough for him, it seemed.

They would be married in the Pelican Point dining room at noon. The guests staying at Pelican Point would be shifted that day to the Spring Bay resort for lunch.

Michael ordered his chef to create their wedding cake and brought a seamstress from Puerto Rico to design and sew Alicia's wedding dress. Flowers would be shipped from St. Thomas and Puerto Rico, and a photographer brought over from San Juan. He arranged to have Lily, Bill, Brandon and even Anselmo and Victo taken to St. Thomas by plane to buy clothes. A minister was being brought from a small Presbyterian church on St. Thomas. The day before the wedding, his father would arrive with Helen. Elaine, he noted, had other plans.

In the midst of this, Alicia had almost nothing to do. One day she asked Michael irritably, "What have you planned for our honeymoon, since we already live in honeymoon heaven?"

His reply was distant, ignoring her waspishness. "You'll see. But that's arranged, too."

"I thought so," she said.

Michael had even sorted out Brandon's affairs. He'd put in a call to Brandon's company, arranging for an extended leave plus two more months' employment before Brandon left for college. For reasons Alicia never understood, the Dallas company was eager to please Michael and gave him everything he asked for. When she quizzed Michael about his uncanny influence with them he just smiled and said, "They know me pretty well. They've owed me a favor for a long time."

For all her irritability at Michael's officiousness, deep inside Alicia felt a core of something akin to happiness. If Michael was never to love her, at least he was willing to live with her, and that was something. It would never be enough, she knew that, but she had come to accept this as the most she would ever get.

During those weeks Michael never kissed her, never took her away alone. It was as if this job he was doing consumed him entirely, making him forget who it was he was doing it all for.

Even Lily saw something amiss and asked Alicia one day, "Are you happy, honey?" Her expression held a moment's concern.

"Yes, Lily, I'm happy." To reassure her aunt, Alicia gave her a quick squeeze.

In those moments of closeness Alicia was tempted to confide in her aunt, to tell her about the tentative nature of the marriage, to reveal her doubts about what Michael would really do with Seahawk Cove once he had it. But somehow it seemed wrong to upset Lily any further.

Her aunt was worried enough about Bill, who spent more and more time in bed.

Still, she often found Lily watching her, turning her head away when Alicia noticed. There was no fooling her aunt completely, Alicia knew. Yet she also knew that even happiness was a relative thing. She wasn't unhappy. It was just that this marriage was going to have a crazy tilt to it—with her doing all the loving. How long could a lopsided marriage last?

Looking back on that strange time before her wedding, Alicia realized it was David who brought home to her how much she was missing.

He showed up at her house and explained he wouldn't be coming to her ceremony. Once again she was aware that he looked older, more mature. His blond hair still had its faintly tousled look, his lean shape its boyishness, but something about his face had changed. There was a different quality to it, a new seriousness and something else she couldn't define.

"Why can't you come?" She searched his face. "We're still friends."

"It isn't that, Alicia. I'm flying to San Diego day after tomorrow, and I just came to say goodbye. We *are* friends." He smiled. "You're an exceptional woman—I've always known it. If Michael hadn't come along...." He shrugged. "But that's how it worked out. And anyway, I'm happy. I'm going to San Diego to marry Elaine—if she'll have me."

"You are?" She hoped the extent of her surprise didn't show.

He nodded. "I suppose it looks odd to you. I hope it doesn't, but you've never got to know her, so it must. She's pretty much kept her good side from you. She never liked you. I'm sure that's no surprise; you must have known she was being eaten up with jealousy over Michael. She's a bad enemy, I could see that. But the part you've never seen, Alicia...well, she's a pretty good friend, too. Loyal. If you ever get her on your side, you've really got something. She'll stick with you through thick and thin."

Alicia smiled ruefully. "I'd make sure she's definitely in the friendly camp."

"She is...now. It took some doing, figuring her out. But I did after a while. I got past all that exterior stuff, the act she was always putting on. She finally let down with me. That day I found her on the beach I learned a lot about her—things I didn't tell you in the restaurant. In spite of all her obvious sophistication, she's vulnerable. She's not such a secure person, Alicia. Not nearly as secure as you. She needs me. And she does have some special qualities."

"That's good." Alicia was still unconvinced. "I hope you'll be happy, David."

He smiled. "I'll be happy, Alicia. I love her.

Now I've just gotta figure out how to make her happy.''

"She's lucky," Alicia said. "Really lucky. How did she ever find anyone like you?"

He laughed. "A good question. I keep asking her how she lucked out finding someone like me! Well, have a good wedding, Alicia." He gave her a quick peck on the cheek and left.

Watching him go, seeing his confident step, thinking of the love she'd seen in his eyes, Alicia thought that in some ways Elaine had it better than she did!

CHAPTER SIXTEEN

FOUR DAYS BEFORE THE WEDDING, Alicia called Pelican Point to speak to Michael and was surprised to learn he wasn't there. He wasn't on the island at all, his secretary said, but he'd left a message for her in case she called: "I'll be back tomorrow. I'll explain fully when I return. Don't do anything foolish."

The minute she hung up, she exploded. What was she, a child? Who was he to tell her—through his secretary—not to do anything foolish? These past weeks, as restless as she was, had she done anything unreasonable? What foolish deed was available to her, anyway—besides leaving? They both knew now that she'd never do that!

Alicia went to bed that night feeling vaguely ill at ease, though not about Michael. Outside the wind was blowing and she'd heard talk of a spawning hurricane. The wind shook the trees beyond her windows, moaning softly through the house. She sensed a feeling of alarm among the people on the island.

But she should have been used to such feel-

ings, she thought. Every time the wind blew
much in the late summer season, people talked
of a hurricane. Every year at this time hurricanes formed in distant seas, and almost every
year they bypassed the British Virgins, huffing
and puffing and never blowing anyone's house
down. When she considered how seldom the
hurricanes came here it seemed foolish to worry.
Yet she found herself fighting a nagging apprehension and went to sleep with difficulty.

When she awoke the next morning to hear
rain tapping on the roof and wind blowing
through their house, she instantly sensed that
something was wrong. She sat bolt upright in
bed.

It wasn't the force of the wind that brought a
sense of alarm to her. It had more to do with the
look of the sky and something else. . . something
indefinable. The wind was blowing only slightly
harder than when she had gone to bed, and the
rain still came and went. Still, the sky looked
almost black, ominous, and there was a feeling
in the air she didn't like—a kind of electricity
that made her ill at ease. It was nothing she
could pinpoint exactly. Rather she sensed it all
over her skin, a foreboding that made her shiver
uncomfortably. The humidity was high and her
nightie was quite damp.

Alicia got out of bed and went to the kitchen.
Bill was drinking coffee and Lily was buttering
toast. Somehow, this morning, she wanted them

all there. She wondered where Michael was, but instead of voicing it she asked, "Where's Brandon?"

"He went down to the boat harbor." Bill set down his cup. "A man came by and asked him to help secure his boat. Victo went with him. They say it's going to blow pretty good."

"I don't like this," Lily grimaced. "The air feels all wrong."

"You noticed it, too, Lily?"

"In the middle of the night I felt jumpy." Lily poured herself coffee. "You want some, Alicia?"

"Yes. I think I will."

"I woke up with this odd feeling," her aunt went on. "I began worrying about your wedding. . . for no good reason. I didn't sleep much after that. Bill says he felt it, too."

"Seems like we're waiting for something," Bill muttered. "Don't know what." He sat hunched over his coffee cup looking old and frail.

They remained at the kitchen table saying little. The wind hummed and purred and carried, inexplicably, a menacing sound. They'd all felt stronger winds without this sense of foreboding. But today it was different.

Lily asked, "Did you put the sailboats away, Bill?"

He looked up. "Thought I did." A puzzled expression came to his face. "You know, Lily, come to think of it, when I came in last night they were still out. I remember thinking I oughta secure 'em...." He stood up, scratching his chin. "I know what happened—a lady asked me about our scuba classes, and afterward I just came in without doing it. I'll go now. I should get 'em clear up on the beach out of harm's—"

"I'll help you, Bill." Alicia rose abruptly, glad to have something to do. "They'll be hard to manage in the wind."

She felt the rustle of air coming through the screen; it was stronger now, and the sky was blacker. "Ooooh...what a day." She shivered, glad the rain had stopped again. Together she and Bill crossed the lawns and walked down to the beach.

The ocean was beginning to change. Its usual glassy appearance had vanished, and in its place the surface undulated, as though something unseen were lifting and lowering it.

They found the boats tied loosely near the dock. Their furled sails flapped around the edges. Alicia realized there were only three sailboats here. The fourth was missing.

Puzzled, she looked around. "Where do you suppose it is?"

Bill shrugged. "I don't know. I'm sure they were all here last night." He peered anxiously around him. "You don't suppose...?" Then he shook his head. "Those young boys in number seven...they were using them all day yesterday.

But nobody would be fool enough to sail today.''

"Then where is it, do you think?" Alicia stared out into the bay. Way, way out, she thought she saw something, perhaps a boat, but it was too small, too indistinct to identify. No, the boat had to be.... She looked around carefully once more. It had to be here. But it wasn't!

Bill was on his way to cabin number seven. After a brief wait, a woman answered his knock, two heads appearing behind her. Alicia hurried over.

"Do you know where your boys are?" Bill asked.

"Sure," the woman smiled and looked down. "Two are here and one's swimming."

"Swimming? Are you positive?" asked Alicia.

"Well, I—"

A thin, high voice came from behind his mother. "Duke's not swimming, mom, he's sailing!" The freckled face grinned out at them. "He said this wind's really neat!"

"He's *sailing*!" His mother looked down at the boy, fear widening her eyes. "He told me he was going to take a little swim and he'd be right back."

The informant cocked a mischievous head. "Well, he took one of the boats, that's all I know. He said you wouldn't care."

"My Lord, where is he, then?"

Alicia stared at the woman, transfixed for a moment. Then she began to run.

She dashed to the house for the key to their speedboat, then ran back to the dock. On the way she passed Bill. "I'm going to get that kid," she yelled without breaking stride. "If he gets out beyond the reef. . . ."

Bill knew what she meant. "Be careful, Alicia," her uncle shouted hoarsely, "and take the extra can of gas. You may need it out there."

Alicia nodded. Hurriedly she searched through the boat, looking for the gas can. But it wasn't there. Victo must have taken it with him to fill. She studied the boat's fuel indicator. Three-quarters full. That should be more than enough to take her out and back. Anyway, there wasn't time to try to get gas anyplace else. That kid—if the speck she saw was him—was already in plenty of danger.

She quickly started the engine and to her relief it turned over immediately. Unwinding the rope from the post on the dock, she tossed it into the boat and turned her craft toward the bay.

She was dressed in tennis shoes, red shorts and a white sleeveless blouse. She thought about her clothes and wished instead she were wearing a bathing suit in case she needed to swim. But for that, too, there was no time.

Expertly Alicia guided the boat, realizing as she pointed it toward the middle of the bay that today she would need all her seaman's skills. Even in this protected area the billowing water was slowly rising, falling and heaving up again. She was having a hard time directing the nose of the boat, as each swell seemed to want to turn it away from her heading.

She glanced up at the forbidding sky. How low it felt, hovering over her like a heavy blanket. And the wind! She could swear it was blowing harder now. Her hair, which normally lay close to her head, was whipping about madly.

Holding the boat as steady as she could, Alicia searched the distant opening to the bay, looking for the sailboat. She couldn't see it. Carefully she searched all sides of her, too, studying the entire bay. But there was nothing.

Focusing again on the far distance, she saw the whitecaps that foamed along the ocean's surface. She dreaded going out there; beyond the protecting arms of land, the sea would be rougher by far. If she had to go much beyond the bay it would be a dangerous mission. Yet she could not turn back, for the sailboat and the boy were both missing, and there was no place they could be except out there.

Water slapped against the bow, then rose up and cascaded back over her body. Alicia shook her head, throwing off the residual droplets. Her clothes were quite wet. In the heavy wind she began to feel chilled.

She looked back from where she'd come.

Trees on the island bowed low to the wind, and debris eddied in little funnels here and there. If this storm grew much worse it could do real damage to the cabins. She shuddered. Then she turned seaward again, her eyes searching the buckling horizon.

At last she thought she saw it! The red-and-white sail she was looking for was wavering some distance beyond the reef. The little boat was out there bobbing up and down, clearly finding its own direction, unaided. Alicia felt a moment's anguish, knowing how unequipped the young occupant must have been for this kind of weather. She hoped he would stay upright long enough for her to rescue him. If not. . . she closed her eyes momentarily, unwilling to think about it.

Reluctantly she increased the boat's speed. It would use gas at a faster rate, but having seen the sailboat at last, she knew every second counted. She had to get to that kid before he foundered.

Keep sailing, kid, she prayed silently. *Keep underway, but spill the air. Don't try to come about. Just ride with it until I can reach you. Please. Please.*

She pushed the engine harder until its whine rose and she could hear its straining even above the screaming wind. Then she cut back a little. She could burn out the motor this way and she would do the child no good with a dead engine.

Alicia watched the arms of land slowly recede as the boat made its way to the mouth of the bay. Yet out ahead, the red-and-white sail she was watching seemed to get no closer. She must be gaining on him, she thought, but with this wind he, too, was traveling at a great speed.

On, on she went. The seas rose higher and the swells that had been large for the protected bay became monstrous. Great mountains of water lifted her little boat, let it fall, pulled it sideways and sent it sliding down precipitously into yawning valleys.

It was all Alicia could do to control her boat. It tried to spin around and move sideways. It bucked and sometimes refused to move forward at all. She spent all her boat's energy climbing and rolling down the mountainous swells rather than moving forward. Her entire attention was riveted on gripping the steering wheel and gauging each swell as it raged toward her seemingly bent on her destruction.

In a brief tranquil moment she turned her head to one side and saw that she'd already gone far beyond the bay.

She was out at sea!

Well, the boy was out at sea, too, and it was a race between her and the elements to see who would claim him in the end. She was beginning to despair that she would ever reach him in time.

She looked for the sailboat again but she couldn't see it now. Around her in every direction the surface of the water boiled white, the froth building and sometimes exploding in fans of spray.

Wind tore at her clothes and threw the ocean's foam in her face. It was difficult to see. Alicia shielded her eyes, searching the horizon. For a brief second she thought she saw the sailboat... but no, the image flickered and was gone.

Where was it, she asked herself repeatedly.

She increased her power again, heading in the direction she'd last seen the little boat. Perhaps it had dropped into one of the troughs, momentarily out of her vision.

She, too, was in a valley now, then rising, rising. Up she came, her speedboat like a cork on the vast sea, the mountain beneath her lifting her higher than all the other mountains for a brief clear view.

That was when she saw it, midway between her and the nearest island, the little sailboat lying on its side. For only an instant it was visible, then she herself tumbled back into a trough where she could see nothing.

But at least now Alicia knew where she was headed.

She felt herself crying out, "Hang on, child, I'm coming... hang on to the boat...." *Hang on... hang on....* The litany formed in her brain.

I must think only of the boy, she told herself. *I mustn't think about where I am or what is happening to me. Without him, without my purpose, I'll be afraid. What if I panic, fighting this ocean,* she wondered. *What if it takes me in the end, the way it took my mother and father? Oh, mom and dad,* she cried to herself, *I'm sorry you suffered, I'm sorry for your fear and the way you had to die. It must have been like this. . . .*

Then, with deliberate effort she repeated to herself, *hang on, little boy, hang on. I'm coming.*

Alicia had no idea how long she'd been repeating the words, how long she'd been trying to drive out fear when her engine stopped. It had already seemed like hours, this pressing on in one direction.

Then nothing. No engine sounds, only her acute awareness of the howling wind. She stared at the gas gauge. It read empty. Her chase was over.

She huddled in the boat, hung on to the seat knowing she was defenseless. The wind screamed around her—hurricane weather—she thought.

Sadly, she knew she could do nothing for the boy now; she could only try to survive herself.

As Alicia clung to her little craft, her clothes soaked, the sea trying to force itself down her throat, she understood the meaning of futility. . . and then surrender. Complete, abject surrender.

The sea would have its way and she could do nothing. If the sea chose to take her, it would. If by some miracle it looked on her kindly, she would live.

Now that she was powerless, she stopped feeling afraid. *Fear is for fighting,* she thought. *There is no fighting here. The struggle is over. The ocean will do with me what it will.*

A calm settled around her. With a sense of wonder, she realized that even her awareness of danger had disappeared. Having accepted death, she knew it was the worst thing that could happen and she need not dread anything beyond that.

With her hands gripping the seat, Alicia sat in her boat and rode the waves as they rose up and then receded. Each time the waves rose higher, until the moment when the boat swooped down into a trough still surrounded by mountainous waters.

"Death, where is thy sting?" She smiled defiantly.

CHAPTER SEVENTEEN

THAT WAS HOW Michael found her—smiling.

She looked up and saw his boat closing in on her—the great white cabin cruiser only yards away. Down in a trough, she hadn't heard it coming.

Strangely, she felt no relief, only surprise. *So I'm not going to die after all,* she told herself, but it had no meaning. The thought of death had already soaked up and sponged away her fear. Now, knowing she was to live after all, she felt no relief.

Michael was screaming at her, but she couldn't hear him. The cabin cruiser went out ahead of her. Michael yelled back at her through the open portion of his navigation room but words were swept away by howling wind.

Seeing that she didn't comprehend, he aimed his cruiser into the waves and ran to the back of the boat.

She saw him dully, hardly caring.

He shouted, demanding that she understand. Picking up a coiled rope he bellowed, "Tie it to your boat," and with a perfectly aimed throw sent the rope snaking through the air. "Tie it!" he shouted, pointing to where it draped over her boat's stern.

When she made no move, only staring at the thing, he gestured wildly with his arms. "Tie the rope, Alicia, for God's sake!"

At his words she moved toward the rope, her apathy fading at last. Suddenly she wanted to live. She picked up the end and threaded it through the brass ring at the bow.

With fingers numb from too much time in the wet, she tried to tie the soggy rope, but her knot was poor and quickly came apart. A swell of ocean picked up her boat, and with dismay she saw the rope slipping away. She seized it and held on, feeling it slip between her fingers, burning and stinging. Her grip tightened.

When she looked up, Michael was gone. He was back in the navigation room turning his boat into the waves.

Amazingly, the sea cooperated, the two vessels closed and the tension on the rope eased. Quickly she knotted the wet hemp once more, this time giving it an additional twist in the opposite direction. To her relief she saw that it held.

Once again Michael appeared at the back of his boat. Another rope was in his hands, this one thinner than the first. With practiced aim he sent the second coiled rope hurtling toward her, and looking up she made out the words, ''Under your arms!'' Gestures accompanied the words, then once more he ran off.

Quickly Alicia wrapped the rope above her breasts, tying a bowline knot.

Michael ran back and stood above her, staring down, his eyes fierce with intended mastery of the sea and herself, his hair blowing like tossed hay.

She looked up, waiting to hear her next move. But he put up a hand, indicating she was to wait. Then she saw why. The two boats had separated to the ends of their tether, the sea roiling and frothing between them.

Momentarily the gap narrowed, and Michael, standing poised like a man intent on a starting gun, suddenly shouted, ''Jump!''

She knew what she had to do. His boat's ladder loomed in front of her; her objective was to clear the sea and reach the ladder. She got to the edge of her gunwales, stood uncertainly. Then with every ounce of strength in her legs, she sprang forward.

It was not enough. She fell short. Her boat pulled away once more, and the sea took her.

She went down, struggling.

Down, down, until she thought she would sink forever, until she thought she could hold her breath no longer, for the ocean seemed to have risen even as she fell into it.

Suddenly she felt a tug around her armpits. A pull. Strong, insistent.

She struggled to reach the top, paddling and kicking.

At last she was above it all; she could breathe again. Choking, she gulped in air, though her body still wallowed in seawater.

For a moment the rope went slack. She cleared the ocean from her eyes and saw the ladder only a few yards away. And then she saw a new danger. Balanced precariously on a swell, her motorboat was hurtling toward her. She would be crushed against Michael's boat.

With a desperate thrust of feet and hands she thrashed toward the ladder, grabbed it and climbed up. Just then the motorboat smashed against the lowest rungs.

Up she went, up, with all the energy left to her. When she arrived on top, Michael quickly enfolded her in his arms.

Fear receded in a great soothing rush. They stood on the heaving deck, Michael holding on to a metal pipe for balance.

Though she supposed it was less than a minute, it seemed an eternity that they stood there, she gasping, feeling the boat surge and fall under her feet. The wind howled, but she was only dimly aware of it.

The rain started again; it came down fast and hard, driving against their bodies. Then the boat began to slide sideways, and Michael dashed to the navigation room and grabbed the wheel. Slowly they pointed back into the waves. ''Cut the boat loose before you come up,'' he shouted down at her.

Her small boat set adrift, she climbed the two steps that led to the top. Untying her rope she reached back and slammed the door.

It seemed she had shut the storm out. She sat down on one of the chairs. The hush seemed profound. She drank in the near silence, knowing it wasn't a silence at all but merely a muffling of the screaming wind.

Michael was shouting at her and she had to strain to hear. ''We're not big enough to ride out a real hurricane! A hurricane may be coming! We've got to make it to that island, Alicia!'' He pointed and she saw the land ahead of them, a small low island.

He revved up the engine and the yacht drove ahead, hampered by seas that rolled under them, surging and threatening. To Alicia this larger boat seemed nearly as vulnerable as her smaller one, the difference being that here she had Michael. Intensely grateful, she turned to look at his strong profile.

Outside the wind blew unrelentingly.

He gestured and shouted at her. ''You know these islands, Alicia...is there a beach on this one? It's our only chance—beaching it!''

''Yes...on the far side.''

''West?''

''West!'' she shouted back.

He nodded, and now his concentration was

solely on his task and not on her. He pushed toward the island, though sometimes the boat seemed to be thrown back as much as forward. Nearly there, he circled the island's north end, the ocean fighting him all the way. He found the small beach with its narrow strip of yellowish sand.

"Hold on, Alicia!" he shouted. "This is going to wreck the boat!"

Michael turned the craft's engines up full. His mouth set in a thin line, he steered the boat hard and full onto the beach, not easing back on the machinery until the bottom scraped sand with an agonizing crunch.

He wheeled on her, gesturing her out of the navigation room. As he left, he wrenched the ship's radio out of its mooring.

Once on deck, Alicia saw that they would have to jump into churning water, its depth uncertain. "I'll go first," he shouted. He put one foot on the ladder, then jumped into the foam, holding the radio above his head.

The water was up to his chest. Alicia jumped and immediately felt his free hand on her shoulder. Together they struggled out of the ocean toward higher land.

In a grove of trees set back from the beach they halted in their flight from death; they knew they'd won. They saw the boat trying to free itself from the sand. It struggled, its stern bobbing and twisting, its bow caught firm.

"I really rammed it," Michael grinned. "It's going to be here a long time." Then he turned to Alicia. "What's on this island? Do you have any idea?"

"I heard, once, there was an old sugar mill. But I've never been here—I don't know for sure."

"Let's look," he said. "It ought to be here, on the beach side."

Their heads bowed against the gale, they made their way back among bending trees. Just beyond the first screen they found it—an old stone structure with half its roof missing. They walked inside. Trees and vines had grown over the missing area, and inside they felt somewhat protected, almost beyond reach of the screaming winds.

As their eyes grew accustomed to the dim light, Michael broke into a great laugh. "How convenient," he said, setting the radio down. "Someone's been here before us!"

Along one wall were a wooden table and two rickety chairs, and on the floor an old mattress. Tin cooking pans sat on a small ledge near the charcoal remains of a fire.

Michael dropped onto the mattress, gesturing for her to join him.

"I wouldn't sit on that!" she said.

"It's better than the floor," he grinned, and she soon saw he was right. The floor was dirt, and as she looked a lizard ran across one corner.

Gingerly she sat down beside him, wishing she didn't have to feel the old mattress against her bare legs. There was no telling what was in it. She pulled her knees up.

Reading her mind, he smiled. "If there are any bugs in here, they'll get up and move."

He turned on the radio. It crackled and coughed. He fiddled with dials and found Pelican Point's call signal. In a distinct voice he informed them that he and Alicia Barron were on the small island directly west of Virgin Gorda.

"Acknowledged," a static-ridden voice came back to them. "But we can't come to get you now. The storm's been upgraded to a hurricane."

"Okay. Just don't forget us," Michael said.

The answer came back, "Right."

He switched it off.

They sat in silence for a minute, then for the first time he turned to look her full in the face. "You scared me, Alicia. You really scared me. I searched those swells a long time before I found you."

"How did you know I was out there?" She clasped her hands around her knees, wanting to touch him now that she was no longer afraid. All at once she grew aware of his compelling nearness.

"I heard on the radio. I was listening to storm warnings, coming back. Your aunt and uncle must have called Pelican Point. All ships were alerted to watch out for you—but damn few of us were out in that weather.''

Small rivulets of water ran down her face from her hair and she brushed them away. ''I know. I was chasing a little kid in a sailboat. But I lost him.'' She said it sadly. ''When I last saw his boat—''

''He's all right,'' Michael broke in. ''Another boat picked him up.''

She seized his arm. ''Michael!'' Happiness flooded over her. ''Oh, Michael, I'm so glad! His boat was on its side and I thought....''

''They picked him up right after it went over. I heard it all on the radio—even heard him crying.''

She smiled. ''I felt as if I'd lost him, and then I was going to lose my life, too, and it was all so futile.''

She stopped, interrupted by a ferocious gust of wind. ''It's strange what happened to me after the engine died. I was frightened for a few minutes, but it didn't last long. You come to a point, Michael, when danger goes on so long that you realize you're going to die and you don't care.'' She looked at him searchingly. ''I've never faced death like that before—had it hovering over me for such a long time—and I wouldn't have believed it...that I could stop caring. By the time you showed up I no longer minded the idea of dying, so your being there to save me—somehow that didn't matter much, either. I had no emotions left. Can you understand what I'm saying?''

"It explains your apathy...." The tone was reflective. "I thought you were never going to secure your boat."

"Yes. I don't know what made me do it, finally." She thought a moment, then smiled to herself. "Yes, I do remember. It was your will—your awful will."

They stopped talking as the wind broke into renewed howling, rattling the treetops above them.

"I'm glad you knew about this building," he said. "I wouldn't want us out there."

She didn't answer. At the moment she felt she needed no building; she needed only him. Just being here, next to him, she felt suffused with warmth, uncommonly happy. She wondered when he would ever feel as she did. After a while she touched his cheek. "You've saved my life three times now."

He took her hand, pressing it to his lips fiercely. "Don't do it to me again, Alicia. I can't have everything I...everything I care about at risk again."

"What did you say?" She turned to him, eyes wide, her heart suddenly pounding. Outside the world quieted.

"I can't risk losing you. You're the only thing that matters."

"You've never said anything like that to me before." She trembled and stared at him.

He put his arm around her, brushing her cheek with his fingertips. "No. I've never said it before. I've never said it to anyone. I thought I never would." His eyes, looking into hers, conveyed feelings she'd never expected to find there.

He murmured, "I love you, Alicia. Oh, how I love you!"

"Michael...." Her voice faltered and she couldn't say any more. She felt her trembling increase.

He kissed her then, his lips boring into hers so passionately he almost hurt her. His sudden fierce emotion took her breath away.

She found herself pulling back, though, not ready for this, wanting to understand him better.

"Why did you never say you loved me, Michael?" she whispered.

He shrugged. "Sometimes a man's brain is slow to admit what his heart knows. I fought it, Alicia. I didn't want to love you, not like this. I fought my own caring, knowing I'd have to make a commitment. I used Elaine as a shield. One doesn't love and then do nothing. And I wasn't ready for...for a lifetime of being there for one person. I'd done that once and every fiber of my being told me never again. But you, Alicia...." He smiled at her fully. "It's you who changed me, who turned me to you so completely I could never pull away."

"But it didn't happen today," she said. "When?"

He thought back, his eyes unfathomable.

"On the boat?" she persisted. "When we made love?"

"No. No. Before that, I loved you long before." He smiled. "I know when it was, Alicia. The day I rescued you from the fisherman's net. That was the day I had to admit it. I was yours then, having come so close to losing you. But still I couldn't quite say it. My lips were stubborn; they had a way of refusing. Finally I was about to tell you, after we made love. I had just started to ask you to marry me when our intruders arrived." He laughed. "Elaine's timing—it's magnificent. She has the instincts of a cobra."

Together they laughed.

He turned serious again. "It was right, you know—our lovemaking. I felt it and so did you."

"Yes," she murmured. "It was only afterward that I doubted."

"You had no cause to doubt."

"Oh, yes, Michael," she said gravely. "I did. When I found out later everything had been planned. Everything."

"Not everything." He tipped her chin up, looking at her earnestly. "When I made love to you that night, Alicia, it was only because I couldn't help it. I could no more have stopped myself from doing what I did than I could have stopped breathing. Oh, my love, why didn't you see that? And the proposal...what was so wrong about asking Bill first for your hand? What was the matter with its being a surprise?"

"I misunderstood."

"Yes, Alicia, you did. And one last thing, my darling. When have you ever said you loved me?"

He turned away from her, listening to something. "Well, I do...I do love you," she whispered.

At her words he looked at her longingly, lovingly, and pressed his lips softly to hers. She snuggled against his warm body. Together they felt the awe of nature's unexpected silence.

She stroked his hair, her happiness running along her body in feelings sweeter than life itself.

After a while Michael went on, "It's odd, Alicia. I was sure you knew how I felt long ago. I never dreamed you'd leave San Diego. I needed time, you see, a few weeks to get over my shock—that you'd go on a spending spree as wild as any of Dixie's. I needed hours of thinking, getting it through my thick head that you weren't Dixie and never would be." He smiled ruefully. "I've always wanted to ask you...why did you do it?"

"It was Helen MacNamee." She kissed his nose. "She called me to your house while you were away on a trip and told me I was...well, to be blunt, Michael, that I was nothing." She laughed at his surprise. "Oh, yes, Helen as much as said that. That I was all wrong because you needed a socially prominent woman for all your important business entertaining. . . that you'd never remarry after Dixie. . . that I was going to end up as your mistress. I didn't believe it, of course, not half of it, but she made me mad. I went a little crazy, I guess; that shopping was a kind of revenge." She shook her head. "Some revenge. The only victim was my bank account. And me."

At first he made no comment. His head was cocked, and she wondered whether he was listening to her or the rising wind.

Then she looked and saw the tightness in his jaw, the smoldering anger in his eyes. "Helen did *that*?" He laughed, but there was no mirth there. "Even Delilah didn't cause more trouble than Helen."

Outside the wind shrieked malevolently, then stopped.

Michael sat grimly silent. At last he said, "After you left we had bitter words, plenty of them. Frankly, I never wanted to deal with Helen again. But I was forced to. She lived there."

He stopped and seemed to be struggling with himself. When he began again his voice had lost its harshness. "Elaine never filled the emptiness you left behind. Not a tenth of it."

"I'm glad," she said. She gave him a sideways look. "It's funny, though—we had our misunderstandings, even later. . . ."

He took her hand. "We always will. We can't be carbon copies of each other, Alicia. We'll always be our own people, you and I. We can only try to work out each difference as it arises. And I'm already trying." He smiled at her. "I've been drawing up a paper. It gives you final say-so on how I develop Seahawk Cove. And Pelican Point, too. You might say I've made you an environmental impact committee—of one."

She laughed. "You didn't have to do that."

"But I did." He grinned back. "How else would I make you believe I've changed my mind? You were right about the Virgin Islands, Alicia. They aren't Hawaii. What worked there wouldn't have worked here. I think I began to see it almost immediately, but—" he shook his head "—I'm a stubborn man. I don't run around broadcasting that I'm wrong. But this seems to be our hour of confession."

Her hand found his cheek, and she stroked it softly.

He gazed at her, love and tenderness in his eyes. "I'm also a sentimentalist, Alicia. Guess what I've got you now?"

"A ring?" she asked excitedly.

"Not a ring. We're getting married, love, remember? I have something else." He reached in his pocket and drew out a small box.

"Another ring box," she laughed. "Without a ring."

"Open it," he commanded.

As she pulled the top off the small box and lifted the bit of cotton she wished there were more light in the old building. Still she could see enough. Down inside was another small gold charm. But this time it was a pelican diving toward coral, the same delicate coral she'd designed for Seahawk Cove.

"Oh, Michael! It's beautiful!" she breathed.

He smiled and put his hand on her knee. "There I was, over on St. Thomas having this made, and you were out being heroic in a speedboat. When they told me over the radio you were out in this storm I was aghast, then terrified. It was too much, thinking after all this I might still lose you. When will we stop working at cross purposes?"

"Now," she said.

She took off her chain and hung the new charm in place of the old one. Then she slowly removed her damp shirt and her bra and put the chain back on. In the fading light, the gold's soft luster set off her delicate breasts. Facing him she said softly, "We'll stop working at cross purposes right now."

The wind increased its howling and the tree above the old building rattled in reply. The storm grew as the afternoon waned, wind and rain combining in a cacophony of excitement that tore across the island.

Michael and Alicia heard it but they didn't notice.

"I love you, Alicia," he whispered over and over.

For answer she pulled him closer, unwilling to ever let him go. The wind became an accompaniment to their passion, its moaning following the rising intensity of their bodies, until Alicia wasn't sure if the sounds she heard came from without or within.

As he pulled her to him, she gasped in happiness, her feelings of love for Michael and her oneness with him closing the last door on fear and doubt. For the first time in her life Alicia felt utterly, wonderfully complete.

About them the storm raged but they truly didn't hear it.

Eventually the wind abated and so did their passion. They drew apart, staring wondrously at each other, she mirroring the softness in his eyes.

Then his gaze wandered. Looking down at her, he grinned and gently lifted the glinting charm. "The pelican's smiling," he said.